M000299635

LADY OF EVE

LADY OF EVE

A Medieval Romance

A "clean read" rewrite of *Virgin Bride*, published by Bantam Books, 1994

TAMARA LEIGH
USA Today Best-Selling Author

ISBN: 1942326122
ISBN 13: 9781942326120

TAMARA LEIGH NOVELS

CLEAN READ HISTORICAL ROMANCE
The Feud: A Medieval Romance Series
Baron Of Godsmere: **Book One** 02/15
Baron Of Emberly: **Book Two** 12/15
Baron of Blackwood: **Book Three** 2016

Medieval Romance Series
Lady At Arms: **Book One** 01/14 (1994 Bantam Books
bestseller *Warrior Bride* clean read rewrite)
Lady Of Eve: **Book Two** 06/14 (1994 Bantam Books
bestseller *Virgin Bride* clean read rewrite)

Stand-Alone Medieval Romance Novels
Lady Of Fire 11/14 (1995 Bantam Books best-
seller *Pagan Bride* clean read rewrite)
Lady Of Conquest 06/15 (1996 Bantam Books best-
seller *Saxon Bride* clean read rewrite)
Lady Undaunted Late Winter 2016 (1996 HarperCollins
bestseller *Misbegotten* clean read rewrite)
Dreamspell: **A Medieval Time Travel Romance** 03/12

INSPIRATIONAL HISTORICAL ROMANCE
Age of Faith: A Medieval Romance Series
The Unveiling: **Book One** 08/12
The Yielding: **Book Two** 12/12
The Redeeming: **Book Three** 05/13
The Kindling: **Book Four** 11/13
The Longing: **Book Five** 05/14

INSPIRATIONAL CONTEMPORARY ROMANCE
Head Over Heels: Stand-Alone Romance Novels

Stealing Adda 05/12; 2006 (print): NavPress

Perfecting Kate 03/15 (ebook); 2007
(print): RandomHouse/Multnomah

Splitting Harriet 06/15 (ebook); 2007
(print): RandomHouse/Multnomah

Faking Grace 2015 (ebook); 2008 (print edition): RandomHouse/Multnomah

Southern Discomfort: A Contemporary Romance Series

Leaving Carolina: **Book One** 11/15 (ebook);
2009 (print): RandomHouse/Multnomah

Nowhere, Carolina: **Book Two** 12/15 (ebook);
2010 (print): RandomHouse/Multnomah

Restless in Carolina: **Book Three** Mid-Winter 2016
(ebook); 2011 (print): RandomHouse/Multnomah

OUT-OF-PRINT GENERAL MARKET TITLES

Warrior Bride 1994: Bantam Books

*Virgin Bride 1994: Bantam Books

Pagan Bride 1995: Bantam Books

Saxon Bride 1995: Bantam Books

Misbegotten 1996: HarperCollins

Unforgotten 1997: HarperCollins

Blackheart 2001: Dorchester Leisure

*Virgin Bride is the sequel to *Warrior Bride*
Pagan Pride and *Saxon Bride* are stand-alone novels

www.tamaraleigh.com

1

Arlecy Abbey, England
Early Autumn, 1156

O F WHAT BENEFIT was it to be a vision in virginal white if one's groom was not of one's choosing?

Hoping to calm her racing heart, Lady Graeye Charwyck lifted a hand and pressed it to her chest. She loved the Lord, but she did not believe He was any more pleased to have her as His bride than she was to have Him as her groom. If what she had been taught was true, He knew her heart. He knew she did not want this. He knew there was no worth—nothing precious—in vows grudgingly given.

"Dear Lord," she breathed and lowered her chin to stare at the toes of her shoes peeking from beneath the skirts of her bridal habit.

"Be still!" the novice mistress snapped, jolting her charge's slender frame.

Graeye lifted her head, stiffened her spine with well-learned obedience, and sighed—a lack of deference for which she immediately repented. Though not of late, she had more than once felt the sting of Mistress Hermana's strap, for that part of her spirit which had not been broken picked the most inopportune times to declare that this life was not of her choosing. Of the three vows she was about to take, obedience would be the most difficult to keep.

Digging her short nails into her palms, she slid her gaze up the black-clad woman. She need not have gone farther than that square, unmoving chin to know of the novice mistress's displeasure, but she did.

With a snort of disapproval, Hermana reached forward and tugged on the wimple where it passed beneath Graeye's chin up to the stiffened band around her forehead.

Heart sinking further, Graeye lowered her eyes. Over the years, she had become painfully accustomed to such ministrations—a vain attempt to conceal the faint stain marring the left side of her face. Starting just shy of her eyebrow, the mark faded back into the hairline at her temple. Though it was not very large or conspicuous, it might as well have covered her entire face.

The mark of the devil, Hermana called it. Always, the devil in Graeye was responsible for the trouble she got herself into. What would otherwise have been viewed as simple, childish pranks or the foolishness of youth, the superstitious woman attributed to evil. When other novices skipped matins or devised tricks against one another, their punishment was a verbal reprimand and prayers of repentance. For Graeye, it was that and more—a strap across the back, hours on her knees scrubbing floors and pulling weeds, humiliation before her peers.

Though she did not believe the devil was responsible for her penchant for trouble, she knew well the curse her physical flaw afforded her. It was, after all, the shape of her destiny thus far.

Her father, unable to bear the sight of her, had dedicated her to the Church when she was seven, only days following her mother's death. The handsome dowry he had provided the convent at Arlecy had ensured her acceptance no matter what mark she bore. And no matter her own feelings. Now she was to wed—not to a mortal as she might have wished, but to the Church.

On this, the day of her Clothing, she would become a nun, her profession made, blond hair sheared, a black habit her only garment. It burdened her, but still there was a blessing in it, for her passage into sisterhood would finally free her from Hermana's dominance. Though the woman was not a nun, for she had once been wed and her chastity forever lost, she had held the esteemed position of novice mistress for as long as Graeye could remember.

Now Graeye would have a kinder master to serve—the Lord.

If only I could rejoice in that and be content, she whispered into herself.

When the strains of music sounded from the chapel, indicating the commencement of the ceremony, Hermana said, "Eyes forward!"

Graeye began a mental recitation of her prayers—not those devised for a novice preparing to take the veil, but her own pleading that she be freed from this obligation.

Minutes later, the large oaken doors to the chapel groaned inward.

Graeye squared her shoulders and pressed her bouquet to her abdomen, gripping it so tightly her fingers crushed the delicate stems and leaves. But though she commanded her legs to take that first, fateful step forward, they would not.

As always, Hermana knew what to do—in this instance, a sharp elbow to the arm that would likely leave a bruise.

"Halt!" a gruff voice sliced the cool morning air.

As if joined, Graeye and the woman beside her turned to search out the man in their midst.

Though the half-dozen knights who emerged from between two of the outlying buildings came disarmed, as was the only permissible entrance to this holy place, a small group of clergy were vainly trying to halt their advance.

"You dare enter consecrated ground without permission?" Hermana demanded as she hurried forward into the intruders' path.

"Forgive us," a tall, thin knight said, though he sounded anything but repentant. He withdrew a rolled parchment from his belt and handed it to the novice mistress. "An urgent message from Baron Edward Charwyck."

Graeye sucked in a breath. Had her letter of appeal to her father brought about a change of heart? Biting her inner lip so hard she tasted blood, she watched as Hermana turned to put the sun at her back to better read the missive.

The woman's thick eyebrows drew closer, ever closer. Then she lifted her eyes and stared at her charge over the top of the parchment.

Suppressing the desire to wrap her arms around herself, Graeye shifted her gaze to the right. There, a young, fair-headed knight stood beside the messenger, eyes intent upon her. Self-consciously, she lifted a hand to the wimple to ensure the mark remained covered.

The crackle of parchment broke the silence, then Hermana traversed the stone walkway and ascended the steps to the chapel. The abbess stood at the top, having come outside to discover the cause for the delay.

The exchange between the two women was hushed. While the abbess, whom Graeye regarded with affection, mostly listened, Hermana grew increasingly agitated and began to gesticulate. The abbess raised a hand to quiet her, took the parchment, and examined it. Shortly, more words passed between the two, then the novice mistress descended the steps.

Venturing a look past the stern-faced woman approaching her, Graeye was startled by the abbess's serene countenance. Though she could not be certain, she thought the woman's mouth curved toward a smile.

Hermana halted before Graeye. "'Tis your brother, Philip," she began, her voice strained as if with great emotion. "He is deceased." As the words passed her thin, colorless lips, she crossed herself.

Graeye stared. Then, remembering herself, she also made the sign of the cross.

Philip dead.

She felt a flutter in her chest, but little else. Contrite that she could not be said to be grieved, she offered up a silent explanation for her un-Christian reaction. She had hardly known her half sibling, for he had been much older than she, and her few remembrances of him were seeped in pain.

As a child, she had seen little of Philip while he had been in training, first as a page, then a squire, at a neighboring barony. However, she had seen enough to dislike the loud, foul-mouthed boy with whom she shared a father. He had taunted her about her "devil's mark" and played cruel pranks on her when he caught her out from behind her mother's skirts.

God forgive her, but she could not mourn one whose memory dredged up old hurts, and whom she had not seen for nigh on eleven years. He was a stranger, and now would forever remain one. Still, she would pray for his soul.

"Your father has requested you attend him so that your brother may be given a proper burial," Hermana went on, voice choked, eyes moist.

Graeye wondered at the woman's peculiar behavior. She had never known the novice mistress to be capable of any deep emotion other than anger and displeasure.

"And as you are his only hope for a male heir," she continued, "'tis not likely you will return to us."

Leave Arlecy? Forever? Graeye's heart swelled as she stared into that wizened face, her hand reflexively opening to release the ravaged bouquet to the stone-laid ground.

My prayers have been answered, she silently acknowledged. *I am freed.*

In the next instant, she suppressed the smile that tried to bend her mouth into a shape with which it was mostly unaccustomed. Why had God waited until the last moment to grant her desires? Had He been testing her? Had He—?

"You are to depart immediately," Hermana said. "I will have your possessions packed and sent on later."

"I must change," Graeye whispered.

"Nay, you are to leave now so you might complete the journey ere nightfall."

Graeye would not argue it. Atremble with excitement, she lifted the skirts of her bridal habit clear of her feet and walked quickly to the knight who had delivered the message.

He was much older than he had appeared from a distance. In fact, he looked well past two score years, every groove in his hard face stark against his chalky complexion.

"Lady Graeye," he said, "I am Sir William Rotwyld, Lord of Sulle, vassal to Baron Edward Charwyck." His eyes shone with a coldness she feared to fathom.

She inclined her head and clasped her hands before her. "Sir William."

"Come." He grasped her elbow. "Your father awaits you at Medland."

Stealing a look behind, Graeye cast her gaze from Hermana to the abbess. This time, there was no doubt it was a smile that graced the latter's face.

2

Medland, England
Mid-Autumn, 1156

A BROOM IN one hand, a dirty rag in the other, Graeye took a rest from her labors to cast a critical eye over the hall. Through her efforts this past month, the castle had seen many changes inside and out, but none were as obvious as those found here.

Gone was the sparse, putrid straw that had covered the floor and upon which she had slipped on her first day at Medland. In its place were fresh rushes that smelled of sweet herbs. Immense networks of cobwebs and thick layers of dust had been swept away. Tattered window coverings had been replaced with oiled linen that held back the night's icy draught and let day's light spill beams throughout. Trestle tables and benches that had threatened to collapse beneath a man's weight had been repaired, though they did not look much better for all the effort. Even the threadbare tapestries had been salvaged by days of cleaning and needlework.

Still, no matter how hard she toiled, the donjon would never be grand, Graeye conceded with a wistful sigh. But at least it was more habitable than before. And she had the castle folk to thank for that. Despite her determination to set Medland right, she would have accomplished little without their aid.

It had taken persistence and a considerable show of interest in the reasons behind the sorry state of the demesne before the people had set aside their superstitions over the mark she bore and revealed what had transpired these past years.

Four years earlier, her father had relinquished the responsibility of overseeing Medland to Philip, and it had been a poor decision. Unconcerned for the welfare of his people, the young lord had squandered time and money.

By the second year, his neglect had led to diminished stores of food for the castle inhabitants. Hence, he had appropriated livestock and grain from the villagers to meet the demand within the walled fortress. That had weakened the once prosperous people and resulted in winter famine.

Philip had also been a cruel master, doling out harsh punishment for minor offenses and using his authority to gain the beds of serving wenches and village women. There were even whispered rumors that his cruelty had extended to the taking of lives when he was displeased—that his late wife had met her end by such means.

Graeye had chosen not to delve too deeply into that last matter. Instead, she set to righting the wrongs, and it was that which brought the castle folk and villagers to her side. It had taken courage she had not known she possessed, but she had opened the stores of grain her father hoarded and distributed a goodly portion among the people. Though Baron Charwyck and his men had grumbled over her actions, none had directly opposed her.

When she had toured the villages and fields, she was relieved to find that the peasants' crops had fared better than their lord's. This she kept this to herself for fear her father would lay claim to that which the people needed to see them through the long winter portended by cool, brisk autumn winds. Through her efforts, the harvesting of the lord's sparse fields and the sowing of winter crops were set in motion, and she had faith that the state of the demesne would look less grim a year hence. Unfortunately, though the changes she had wrought were significant, there was yet much to do before season's end.

With that reminder, Graeye drew the back of a hand over her warm, moist face. She was tempted to remove the stifling wimple but squelched the impulse. As much as she longed to discard it altogether, the one time she had eschewed it in her father's presence, he had made it humiliatingly clear that its absence would not be tolerated. Thus, she removed it only when certain he would not happen upon her.

"Lady Graeye," a man called.

She propped the broom against the wall and turned to face the one who crossed the hall toward her. It was the young knight who had caught her notice at the abbey—Sir Michael Trevier. During her first days at Medland, he had been instrumental in helping her gain acceptance among the people and implementing changes. But though he had been all smiles for her then, always at hand to assist in whatever task she undertook, that was in the past.

A fortnight earlier, he had issued a challenge to the knight her father had chosen to become her husband. Sir Michael had wanted her for himself and been prepared to do battle to win her hand. However, Edward Charwyck had remained adamant that she wed Sir William Rotwyld, the knight who had retrieved her from the abbey.

Sir Michael had hurled insults at her betrothed, pointing out that the man's great age might prevent him from fathering the heir Edward badly wanted.

Graeye would have preferred the kind young knight over the repulsive man Edward had chosen for her, but to avoid bloodshed, she had declared she was content to wed William.

She had succeeded in preventing the two men from taking up swords, but Sir Michael was no longer her champion. He had no warm words for her, nor smiles, and had become conspicuously scarce in the days since. She missed him.

"There is a merchant at the postern gate who says he has cloth for you," he said, halting before her.

"Cloth?" Graeye pondered when and for what purpose she had ordered it. "Ah, for the tables." She gestured toward their bare, unsightly tops. "Do you not think coverings will brighten the entire hall?"

Mouth grimly set, he turned and tossed over his shoulder, "I will send the man to you."

Once more pained by his indifference, she hurried after him and caught his arm. "Sir Michael, do you not understand why—?"

"Perfectly, my lady." His gaze was stony.

"Nay, I do not think you do. Will you not let me explain?"

He shrugged her hand off. "A lowly knight deserves no explanation."

So he thought she had rejected him because of his rank. "You are wrong. I—"

"Pardon me, but I have other tasks to which I must needs attend." He bowed stiffly and walked away.

Graeye watched him go. Though she could not say she loved him, he was much like the brother she had once imagined having. Perhaps love would have grown from that, but she would never know.

"He is the one you want, is he not?"

She spun around. "F-father!"

His lips twisted into a knowing smile.

Trying to gauge his mood, she took in the sour smell of alcohol carried upon his breath, the sound of his shallow, labored breathing, and the gray, sagging features set with reddened eyes. It was a common sight, for he was more often drunk than sober, but she had yet to become accustomed to such a state.

His mood was harmless, she decided. Blessedly, with each passing day, he became more genial, but it had not been like that when she had first arrived. Then he had been half-mad with grief over Philip's death, had called her the devil's daughter, had—

She did not want to think on that first night, for it chilled her to relive the memory. Fortunately, now he mostly named her *Daughter of Eve* when displeased. Not that she cared to be blamed for the sins of man alongside Eve, but it was better than the alternative.

"The cloth has arrived," she said, hoping he would not pursue the matter of Sir Michael. "By tomorrow eve, the tables will all be covered."

He glowered, then slurred, "William will make you a good husband. That pup Michael knows nothing of responsibility or loyalty. And, I assure you, he knows little of breeding."

Blushing, Graeye averted her gaze. "Aye, Father."

"But still you want the young one, eh?"

She shook her head. "I have said I am content with Sir William."

"Content!" he spat. "Yet you would choose Sir Michael if I allowed it. Do not speak false to me."

Reminding herself of the vow she had made weeks earlier not to cower, she lifted her chin. "It is true Sir Michael is young and handsome, and he is soft of heart, but—"

"He is a weakling, that is what he is. He has no property and very little coin."

Though Graeye knew it was unwise to defend him, she said, "He is still young, and what would William have if you had not given it to him?"

Surprisingly, Edward seemed to consider her argument. "True," he mused, "but he earned it, something Sir Michael has yet to do. If ever."

"Methinks he will."

"Not with my daughter. I want an heir—and soon—and your union with William will ensure that."

"How can you be certain?"

He grinned. "William made seven boys on his first two wives—not a single girl." He let that sink in, then added, "It is a son you will bear come spring."

Then it was not the knight's possessions, nor his years of loyalty that had decided Edward. It was his ability to produce sons. She suppressed a shudder at the thought of the man making an heir on her.

Edward turned and surveyed the hall. "You have done well, Daughter."

He had turned the conversation so abruptly that it took her some moments to realize he referred to the improvements made to the hall.

Happily abandoning all thoughts of her future as William Rotwyld's wife, she said, "I thank you." All the hard work was worth it for just those few words of praise. Had he also noticed the improved foodstuffs at table? Or had drinking numbed his sense of taste?

"Methinks I shall have to reward you," he said.

She blinked. "'Tis not necessary, Father."

"Of course it is not! Were it, I would not do it."

Realizing he teetered on the edge of a black mood, Graeye merely nodded.

Edward grumbled beneath his breath, studied the floor and, a short while later, smacked his lips. "A new wardrobe! Aye, it would not be fitting for a Charwyck to go to her wedding dressed as you are." Sneering, he slid his gaze down the faded bliaut she wore.

Graeye smoothed the material. Having no clothing other than what she had worn as a novice at the abbey, she had taken possession of the garments that had belonged to her mother. Though aged, they fit well, for she was nearly the same size as Lady Alienor had been, just a bit shorter.

"I would like that," she said and indulged in imaginings of the beautiful fabrics she might choose.

"It will be done." Edward swung away and stumbled in his attempt to negotiate the level floor. Though he scattered the rushes beneath his feet, he somehow managed to remain upright.

Graeye hurried forward and caught his arm. "You are tired," she said, hoping he would not thrust her away as he often did when she touched him—as if he truly believed the devil resided in her.

He looked down at her hand but did not push her away. "Aye, most tired."

She urged him toward the stairs. "I will help you to your chamber."

The wooden steps creaked alarmingly beneath their feet, soft in some places, brittle in others, reminding Graeye that she needed to set men the task of replacing them.

Up a second flight of stairs they went, down a narrow corridor, and into the lord's chamber where Graeye tossed the covers back from the bed. "I will send a servant to awaken you when supper is ready," she said as her father collapsed on the mattress.

"Supper." He grunted. "Nay, a wench and ale will far better serve me."

He asked for the same thing each evening, and each time she sent a manservant to deliver him to the hall. It was bold, but thus far he had allowed it.

Graeye pulled the covers over him, but as she straightened, Edward caught hold of her hand. "A grandson," he groaned. "'Tis all I ask of you."

Pity surged through her as she gazed into his pleading eyes. He was vulnerable, pained, heartbroken. Here was a man of whom she was no longer frightened—the one who should have been her father these past eleven years. Perhaps it was not too late.

Graeye knew she should not entertain such thoughts. After all, had she not been Edward's only chance for a male heir, he would not have sent for her. Knowing this should have been enough to banish false hope, but she could not help herself.

She bent, kissed his weathered cheek, and whispered, "A grandson you will have. This I vow." When she lifted her head, his eyes shone with gratitude amid brimming tears.

"I thank you," he muttered, his fingers gripping hers tightly. Moments later, he fell asleep.

Graeye withdrew from his chamber and quietly closed the door. She had taken but a single step toward the stairs when a sound drew her attention. Chills pricking her skin, she slowly turned toward the small chapel at the end of the corridor. As no torches were lit beyond Edward's chamber, she squinted to see past the shadows, but they were too deep.

As much as she longed to return to her chores belowstairs, she knew she must eventually face the memories that had haunted her dreams since that first night at Medland. Determinedly squaring her shoulders, she drew a full breath and walked forward.

What had caused the noise? she wondered, refusing to allow her imagination to believe it had anything to do with her brother's death. A rat, perhaps, or a breeze stirring the rushes about the chapel.

As she drew near, the sound became that of scratching and quick, shallow breathing.

Heart feeling as if it tested the bounds of her ribs, Graeye halted and peered into the shadows. "Who goes?" she demanded.

Silence, then a deep groan. An instant later, a large figure leapt out of the darkness and skidded to a halt before her.

Mouth wide with the scream she had nearly loosed, she stared at the great, mangy dog. "Oh, Groan!"

Tongue lolling, he wagged his tail so vigorously his backside jerked side to side.

Graeye sank to her knees and slid an arm around him. "You are naughty for frightening me," she scolded and turned her face away when he tried to lick it.

As she stroked his head, she remembered how frightened of the beast she had been when he had introduced himself during her first meal at Medland. She had rarely been around dogs, certainly never one of such grand proportions, and had shrieked when he had laid his slavering chin upon her lap. That had gained her nothing but humiliation, for her father's men had roared with laughter.

She had dislodged the dog by tossing food to him, but always he returned to her and Edward had advised that if she beat him rather than feed him, he would not bother her. Such callous words had replaced her fright with a longing to protect the animal.

Since that day, Groan—as she had named him due to his penchant for making that horrible sound—had attached himself to her. And he had more than once proved valuable.

Recalling the night, a sennight after she had returned to Medland, when Sir William had cornered her as she readied to bed down in the hall, she shuddered. The vile man had taunted her with cruel words, and his hands had bruised her as he familiarized himself with her cringing body. Though he was to be her husband, and she had known it was unlikely she could prevent ravishment, she had fought him. It had not deterred him. In fact, he had seemed to enjoy her resistance. Even as he had torn her bliaut and laid hands to her flesh, he had threatened that if she bore him a child with the same mark she carried, he would kill it himself.

That had frightened her more than the inevitable violation of her body. She had been about to scream when Groan appeared. Snapping and snarling, he had circled William, bunching his body as he readied to attack.

The man who had thought nothing of exerting his greater strength over a frightened woman had retreated, leaving Graeye to offer profuse thanks to her unlikely champion.

Now, conveniently forgetting her resolve to face the memories that had been birthed within the chapel, she straightened. "Come," she said. "I will find you a nice morsel."

The dog looked over his shoulder, back at her, then returned to the chapel door and resumed his scratching and sniffing.

Graeye pulled her bottom lip between her teeth. Sooner or later, she would have to go inside and brave her fears. It might as well be now.

She stepped forward. "Shall we see what interests you, Groan?" When she pushed open the door, he rushed in ahead of her.

It was not like that first night when a profusion of candlelight had greeted Graeye. Today, the chapel was dim, its only source of light that which shone from the small window that had been opened to air out the room.

Crossing herself, Graeye stepped inside. Instantly, her gaze was drawn to the high table that stood against the far wall. Her brother had been laid out on it that first night, his ravaged, decomposing corpse emitting a horrible stench. She could still smell it. And found herself reliving when Edward had brought her here. She had been unable to cross the threshold for the smell that assailed her, and so he had thrust her inside.

"I would have you see Philip with your own eyes," he had said, "that you might know the brutality of his murder." He had pulled her forward and swept aside the covering to reveal the festering wounds and Philip's awful death mask.

"See the marks on his hands and chest?" He had run his fingers over the stiffened corpse. "These he survived. 'Twas the arrow that killed him."

Battling nausea, Graeye asked, "Arrow?" She saw no evidence of such a wound.

"Took it in the back!" Edward's face turned crimson as he stared into his son's sightless eyes.

Anxious to withdraw, Graeye touched his sleeve. "Let us speak elsewhere. This is not the place—"

"The Balmaine witch and her brother did this to him!"

Graeye's head snapped back. Balmaine? Was that not the family under which Philip had completed his knighthood training, the same whose properties bordered those of Medland?

"I do not understand, Father. The Balmaines are responsible for this?"

He looked up, the hate upon his face so tangible it gripped a cold hand about her heart. "Gilbert Balmaine challenged your brother to a duel, and when Philip bettered him, his wicked sister put an arrow through his back."

Graeye gasped. Though her familial ties were strained by the long years of absence, she was appalled to learn of the injustice done her brother.

"Why?" she whispered.

Edward gripped her upper arm. "'Twas the Balmaine woman's revenge upon Philip for breaking his betrothal to her."

Graeye had not known her brother was to wed. Despair over the lost years gripping her, she wondered if things would have been different had her mother lived and Graeye had been allowed to grow up at Medland.

"Why would Philip break the betrothal?" she asked, and flinched when Edward's fingers bit into her flesh.

"She was a harlot—gave herself to another man days before she was to wed Philip. He could not wed her after such a betrayal."

Graeye clenched her hands. What evil lurked in a woman's heart that made her seek such means of revenge? "When did he die?"

"Over a fortnight past."

She glanced at his corpse. "Why has he lain in state so long?"

"He was returned to me nine days ago over the back of his horse," Edward said, the corners of his mouth collecting spittle.

"Whence?"

"One of the northern shires—Chesne."

"The north? But what was he—?"

"Be silent!" Edward gave her a shake. "The Balmaine is my enemy—ours! Do not forget what you have seen here, for we will have our revenge."

"Nay, we must forgive, Father. 'Tis not for us to judge. That is God's place."

"Do not preach at me!" He drew an arm back as if to strike her and she instinctively shrank from him. Then, abruptly, he released her. "I will have my revenge," he barked. "And you, Daughter, will pass the night here and pray Philip's soul into heaven."

She shook her head. It was too much to ask. If there was not yet disease in this chamber, soon there would be. She pulled free, spun around, and ran for the door.

With a gasp, Graeye dragged herself back to the present. She did not need to relive any more of that night to exorcise her memories. There was not much else to them other than endless hours of prayer. Locked in the chapel, she had knelt before the altar and prayed for her brother's soul and her own deliverance until dawn when a servant had let her out. Since then, she had not come near this place.

Groan's bark brought her head around. "What have you found?" she asked.

Crouching low, he pushed his paws beneath the kneeler and swatted at something that gave a high-pitched cry.

"Is it a bird?" No sooner did she ask it than a young falcon flew out from beneath the kneeler and swept across the chapel.

Had it slipped free of the mews? Graeye wondered as she rushed to close the door so it would not escape into the rest of the castle.

It took patience and effort, but between her and Groan chasing it about, the falcon finally found the small window and its freedom. Gripping the sill, Graeye watched the bird arc and dip in the broad expanse of sky.

How would it feel to have wings? she wondered. *To fly free and—*

She chastised herself for such yearnings. There was nothing she had wanted more than to come home to Medland and assume her place as lady of the castle. In spite of the obstacles encountered these past weeks, and that she must wed a man she loathed, she had never known greater fulfillment.

With the abbey forever behind her, her future was assured. That, no one could take from her.

3

AN AIR OF import surrounded King Henry's knight as he strode into the hall five days later, his armed retinue following and positioning themselves around the room. Clothed in chain mail, none wore smiles nor a congenial air that might mistake them for visitors passing through.

Realizing something serious was afoot, Edward ordered all, except his steward and William, from the hall in order to receive the king's missive in private.

Graeye did not have long to learn the effect of the news delivered to her father, for his explosion was heard throughout the donjon. She ran into the hall and stumbled at the sight of two knights struggling to hold her red-faced, bellowing sire from the messenger.

Fear thrumming through her, she searched out William where he stood beside the steward. His expression reflected the other man's— shock, disbelief, outrage.

She veered in the direction of the messenger. "What has happened, Sir Knight?" she asked, halting before him.

He swept his gaze down her faded bliaut, then back up and settled it on her face framed by its concealing wimple. "Who are you?"

She dipped a curtsy. "Lady Graeye."

His eyes narrowed. "Sir Royce Saliere, here by order of the king. You are a relation?"

She glanced at her father. "I am the baron's daughter."

Surprise transformed his dour face, but he soon recovered. "No longer baron," he said with what seemed a token shrug of regret. "By King Henry's decree, all Charwyck lands are declared forfeit and returned to the sovereignty of the crown."

Edward roared louder, raising his voice against God as he struggled to free himself.

Feeling as if the air had been sucked out of her world, Graeye shook her head. It could not be. The king would not take from the Charwycks that which had been awarded the family nearly a century past. This had to be some trickery by which another sought to steal her father's lands now that he was without an heir.

"Methinks you lie," she said.

Sir Royce raised his eyebrows. "Lie?"

"King Henry would do no such a thing. My father is a loyal subject. He—"

"Can you read?" His tone was patronizing.

"Of course." She took the document he thrust at her, and her gaze fell upon the broken wax seal. Though she had never seen the royal signet, she did not doubt this was, indeed, from the king. With dread, she unrolled the parchment and read the first lines. And could go no further.

"Why?" she croaked, reaching for something to brace herself against but finding only air. If the Charwyck lands were lost, what was to become of her father, an old man no longer capable of lifting a sword to earn his living? And what of her? She would not be needed to produce a male heir—of no value since William would not wed her without benefit of the immense dowry she would have brought to their union.

"For offenses committed by your brother, Philip Charwyck," Sir Royce said as he pried the document from her fingers.

Graeye swayed, glanced at her father who had quieted. "I do not understand. Of what offenses do you speak?"

"Murder, pillaging…"

Recalling her brother's disposition, the accusations should not have surprised her. Still, she said, "Surely you are mistaken," desperation raising her voice unnaturally high. "'Twas my brother who was murdered. Why do you not seek out the perpetrator of that crime?"

The man raised his eyes heavenward as if beseeching guidance from above. "As I have told your father, Philip Charwyck was not murdered. His death is a result of his own deceit."

"What did——?"

Sir Royce held up a hand. "I can tell no more."

"You would take all that belongs to the Charwycks and refuse to say what, exactly, my brother is accused of having done?"

He folded his arms over his chest. "Your fate rests with Baron Balmaine of Penforke. As 'tis his family the crime was committed against, King Henry has given this demesne into his keeping."

Graeye barely had time to register this last shocking news before her father renewed his struggles. "Curse the Balmaines!" he shouted. "I will gut that miscreant and his sister!"

Sir Royce signaled for his men to remove the old baron.

Graeye rushed forward. "Nay!" she cried, following the knights as they half dragged, half carried Edward across the hall. However, her efforts to halt their progress were to no avail, for they thrust her aside each time she stepped into their path. Neither William, nor the steward, were of any help. Like great pillars of earth, they remained unmoving.

She hurried back to Sir Royce and gripped his arm. "My father has committed no offense. Why are they taking him away?"

"He must needs be held whilst he is a danger to others," he said and looked pointedly at her hand upon his sleeve.

She dropped it to her side. "He has been dealt a great blow," she entreated. "Not only has the king taken everything he owns, but he has given it to his enemy."

The man considered her, then ran a weary hand through his cropped, silvery hair. "Lady Graeye, I do not fault your father for his anger. 'Tis simply a measure of safety I take to ensure Medland passes into Baron Balmaine's hands without contest."

Simply...There was nothing simple about it, certainly not where the Charwycks were concerned.

Wishing she had the luxury of sinking to the floor as she longed to do, Graeye said, "The baron will arrive soon?"

"A sennight." Sir Royce turned and strode to where his knights were gathered near the doors.

So many questions swirled through Graeye's mind that she thought she might go mad in the absence of answers, but she knew the man would give her no more.

She turned to William and the steward. "All is lost," she said, and at their continued silence, withdrew from the hall.

Without a mantle to protect her against the lingering chill of morning, she set out to discover her father's whereabouts. Not only was she aware of the precipice upon which the old baron's mind balanced and worried for him, but she needed to know whether she would be allowed to remain at his side to care for him, or if he intended to return her to the abbey.

It was no great undertaking to discover his whereabouts. With expressions of concern, the castle folk pointed Graeye to the watchtower.

Along the way, she became increasingly uneasy over the great number of the king's men positioned around the walls. They were alert, ready to stamp out any signs of uprising. That unlikely possibility gave rise to a bitter smile. Not only had the ranks of Edward's retainers been depleted from Philip's foray to the north, where he had given up his life for a cause yet unclear to her, but few would be willing to challenge the king's men for their lord. They disliked him that much.

At the watchtower, a surly knight halted Graeye's progress. "You would do well to return to the donjon, my lady. No one is allowed to see the prisoner."

"I am his daughter, Lady Graeye. I would look to his needs."

He shook his head. "My orders are clear. No one is allowed within."

"I beseech you, let me see him for a short time only. No harm will be done."

She thought his eyes softened, but he said, "Nay."

Without considering the consequences, she snatched up her skirts, ducked beneath his arm, and managed to make it up the flight of steps before encountering the next barrier. With a small sob, she halted at the sight of the two who guarded the room where her father was surely imprisoned. Undoubtedly, they had heard her advance, for their swords were trained upon her.

Though the knight behind did not need to seize hold of Graeye, as she could go no farther, he turned a hand around her arm. "You—"

"Just a moment," she choked, peering up at him through tears. "'Tis all I ask."

The angry color that had brightened his face began to recede and, to her surprise, he sighed and said, "A moment only," then released her and motioned the guards aside.

After a brief hesitation, during which Graeye feared he reconsidered the wisdom of allowing her to see her father, the knight threw back the bolt and opened the door.

With a murmur of gratitude, she entered the cold room. Though she had expected to be granted a private audience with her father, the knight's great bulk shadowed the floor where he positioned himself in the doorway.

Graeye crossed to where Edward huddled in a corner with his forehead resting on arms propped upon his knees. As she sank down beside him, her heart swelled with compassion for the pitiful heap he made. True, he had often been unkind, had never loved her, had not inquired as to her welfare at the abbey, but he was her father. And now he had lost everything—his son, the grandson who would have been his heir, his home, his dignity. Everything gone. Would what remained of his mind go, too?

Though she longed to embrace him, she first tested a hand upon his shoulder. "Father?"

He did not move.

She scooted nearer and tentatively slid an arm around him. "'Tis I, Graeye."

Slowly, he lifted his head. For a long, breath-holding moment, he stared at her, then he jerked free and so forcefully landed a hand to her chest that she toppled backward. "'Twas you who brought this upon me!" He lurched upright. "You, spawn of the devil!"

Dragging in air that had been lost to her, Graeye peered up at him.

"I should have left you to the Church!" He pointed a shaking finger at her. "For this offense, I am to be punished to everlasting hell."

Graeye glanced at the knight who had not moved from the doorway, though he was tense as if he struggled against coming to her defense. Fearing his interference would portend ill for Edward, she quickly gained her feet.

"Father," she said softly, "I have come to see to your needs. Pray, let me—"

"My needs?" Edward thrust his face near hers. "What else have you come for?"

She held his stare. "I would know what is to become of me."

His laughter was cruel. "What do you think your fate should be, Daughter of Eve?"

"I would stay with you."

"Ha! Of what use are you now that all I possess has been stolen?"

"I shall care for you. You will require—"

He seized hold of her. "The last thing I require is the devil on my shoulder."

"'Tis not true—"

"Did you know that twice your mother bore me sons? Sickly things that lived no more than a few days? And then she bore you, a healthy girl child with the devil's mark full upon her face. And afterward...no more."

Graeye had not known. Never had her mother spoken of those children who had come before. It explained much of her father's feelings for her.

"Nay," he continued, "you will return to the abbey. As the Church has already received your dowry, your place there is secure. *That* Balmaine cannot take from me."

She pulled free of him. "I do not wish to return."

"Do you think I care what you wish?" he snarled. "Many a daughter would vie for the soft life of a nun, but the devil in you resists. Thus, as my final offering to God, you will return."

"You need me!" It was true. What would become of an old man alone in a world so changed from what he had known? And what of her? Though determined she would not spend her life at the abbey, she could not do so outside of it without a man to protect her.

"*I* need you?" Edward crowed. "'Twas your body I needed. Blood of my blood. A vessel for the heir you would make with William. Now"—he snorted—"you shall either return to the abbey or go back to the devil whence you came. That is the only choice I grant you."

The air of hate upon which his words were delivered stank, and Graeye began to back away.

"And do not let me see you again without your nun's clothing!"

She was surprised when she came up against the knight in the doorway. Without a word, he drew her outside and closed the door on Edward. Almost immediately, a clamor arose as the old man threw himself against the door, pounded and kicked, cursed and spat.

"My lady," the knight spoke to her bowed head, "you ought to return to the donjon." At her nod, he gently guided her forward.

If not for his support, she thought she might not have made it down the steep stairway, so blurred was her vision. When they reached the bottom, he showed her further kindness. Rather than send her on her way, he led her past the curious stares of the soldiers and castle folk and did not relinquish his grip until they stood within the hall.

She tried to smile, but she knew it was a sickly attempt. "My thanks, Sir…?"

"Abelaard." He gave a curt bow.

"If you will wait"—she stepped away—"I will gather blankets that you might deliver them to my father."

A thick silence descended, and she turned back. Too late, she realized it was beneath the man's rank to perform such a duty.

"My apologies," she said. "I shall send a servant."

Looking relieved that he did not have to refuse her, he offered an uneven smile. "My sister is a nun. 'Tis not a bad life she has."

Graeye stared at him as he grew visibly discomfited with the effects of his poorly timed, though well-meaning disclosure. "I fear you do not understand, Sir Knight," she said and turned away.

Desperate to escape the curious regard of the castle folk and the king's men, she climbed the stairs. Shortly, she entered the small chapel whose only other occupant was the dark, lingering presence of Philip Charwyck whose actions, whatever they were, had brought this day crashing down around her father and her.

Kneeling before the altar, she clasped her hands and tried to offer up prayer. But now that her hopes were dashed by the coming of the treacherous Baron Balmaine, there seemed no place for such devotions. With a great, soulful sob, she cried as she had never cried—and vowed she would never cry again.

4

With all the extra mouths to feed and bodies to bed in a hall that suddenly seemed inadequate, Graeye had little time throughout the day to dwell on the misfortune that had befallen her father—and the fate that awaited her.

Now, however, as night deepened and sleep refused to soothe her churning thoughts, she kept the confrontation with Edward as far out of reach as possible by fixing instead on the events that had preceded and followed that heart-rending exchange.

She recalled Sir Royce's veiled revelations, Sir Abelaard's kind and well-intentioned words, the emotions that had assailed her in the chapel, and afterward her encounter with William—one that might have gotten out of hand had she not put a quick end to it.

Amid the preparations for the noon meal, she had come face-to-face with the angry knight who had sought no cover in which to deliver his hateful words.

Without thought, and in front of the servants, she had struck him across the face with all her strength. Fortunately, he had been too surprised to retaliate, allowing her to flee the hall and seek safety in the kitchens.

During supper, the tables overflowing with the addition of the king's men, she had spent an uncomfortable hour beneath the watchful eyes of William and Sir Michael. Afterward, the young knight had twice attempted to corner her, but she had evaded him, certain no good could come of allowing him near.

The most difficult day of her life had been made all the worse by the amount of pity heaped upon her. It shone from the eyes of the castle folk, as well as several of Edward's knights. Even the king's men cast it upon her. But it was not what she needed, and she had determined she would waste no more time on the useless emotion, not when a plan that would make it possible for her to remain at her father's side would serve far better. Somehow, she must find a way.

Turning on her bench to get more comfortable, she winced at the rumble that drifted up from beneath her.

Throughout the day, Groan had become increasingly testy at the changes wrought in his home. There were too many people, too much commotion, and the air of gloom that hung over all was as unsettling as the morsels the dog had been denied due to the shortage of viands. Nevertheless, he had not strayed far from her side—except the one time William had caught her alone.

Groan rumbled again.

Graeye leaned over the side of the bench and searched out the dog's glowing eyes. "Shh," she breathed and reached to him.

"Lady Graeye," a man whispered.

Stifling a yelp that might have awakened those in the hall, Graeye pressed herself back on the bench and peered up at the still figure that stood a foot away.

Was it William come to seek revenge for her striking him earlier? If so, she would gladly awaken all to avoid whatever the wicked man had in mind.

"Who goes?" she whispered.

Groan rumbled deeper.

Ignoring the dog's threat, the figure stepped forward and bent near. "'Tis I, Sir Michael."

Though relieved, Graeye was still alarmed that he sought her out in the middle of the night. "What is it you want?"

"I must needs speak with you."

"We can speak on the morrow."

"Nay, we must speak now."

"Shh," she hissed. "Lower your voice, else you will awaken the others."

"Then come with me."

She drew back from the hand he reached to her. "Be gone, Sir Michael. On the morrow will be soon enough to talk."

Without further word, he slid an arm beneath her and scooped her from the bench. Her immediate response was to protest his boldness, but she checked the indignant words lest she roused the others. Fortunately, though he presumed where he should not, she did not fear him as she feared William. Too, the scrape of claws over the floor assured her Groan would not leave her to fend for herself should she have misjudged the young knight.

Resigned to the conversation, she grabbed fistfuls of his tunic and held to him as he picked his way over the sleeping bodies toward the stairway.

Sir Michael was not of a great height or build, but he proved surprisingly strong, easily negotiating the stairs to the first landing where a torch flickered. There, he lowered her to her feet. "Forgive me, my lady."

Graeye jerked the blanket closed around her shoulders. "'Tis unseemly behavior, Sir Michael," she whispered, comforted by the press of Groan's body against her side.

"I saw no other way."

She glared at him a long moment, then sighed. It was, after all, her fault. Had she given him the time he had sought earlier in the day, this would have been unnecessary. "Well, speak," she said.

He shifted his weight as if uncomfortable, then said in a rush, "I would have you go away with me."

She blinked. "What?"

He set a hand upon her shoulder. "There is naught for you here, as there is naught for me. Though I am the fourth of five sons, I have not much to offer, but 'tis more than the abbey can give you. Surely you do not wish to return there?"

She leaned back against the wall for support. "Of course not." Was this the answer she sought? "Is it marriage you speak of, Sir Michael?"

He slipped a hand beneath her chin and tilted her face up. "I offered once before and you denied me." There was a bitter edge to his voice. "Should I offer again, would you refuse?"

She stared into his imploring eyes. "Surely you know the reason I denied you. Even had I expressed a preference for you, my father would not have agreed, and I did not wish blood spilled for a lost cause."

"Then you thought I could not best Sir William."

"I did not know," she said with apology, "but 'twas not worth the risk."

"I am not a child unable to defend myself!" he snapped. "'Twould have been William's blood spilled, not mine."

Hoping to soothe his injured pride, she said, "I am sorry."

His indignation was slow to ease, but when it did, he lowered his head and touched his mouth to hers. "Will you marry me, sweet Graeye?"

Surprised at the gentleness of that fleeting kiss, she lowered her gaze. He was a better man than William, and what he proposed held more appeal than returning to the abbey and leaving her father to fend for himself among enemies—providing Edward was included in the offer.

She looked up. "What of my father?"

"Your father?" His disbelief boded ill. "Your loyalty is misplaced, Graeye. You owe him no allegiance. Allow Baron Balmaine to decide his fate."

Leave him to the mercy of one of those responsible for Philip's death? No matter what he felt for her, he was still her father. "I cannot desert him."

Sir Michael gripped her shoulders. "Can you not see the evil in him? You, my family would accept, but Edward?" He shook his head. "I will not ask that of them."

She pulled out of his hold. "And I will not leave my father to the greater evil of Balmaine. Good eve." She turned and placed a hand on the wall to guide her down the steep steps.

Groan followed, but Sir Michael made no move to detain her. Clearly, his desire for her was not strong enough to cause him to change his mind about Edward.

Upon regaining her bench, Graeye huddled against the wall and tried not to question if she had made a mistake in refusing the young knight. Failing, she acknowledged that her only other option was to return to the abbey. Whether she went with Sir Michael or back to the Church, the result was the same. Edward would be alone to face the cruelty of Baron Balmaine.

Unless you make it impossible for him to return you to the abbey, whispered a small, desperate voice.

She frowned. What would cause him to——?

Chastity, the voice came again. *The breaking of that vow is unforgivable. Lacking purity, you cannot be professed a nun.*

Feeling the moral foundation upon which her life was built shudder, Graeye clasped her arms around herself and tried to push the wicked idea down by naming it ungodly...blasphemous...wanton, but it kept rising to the surface. It even struck her that, had she not escaped William when he had tried to force himself upon her weeks earlier, there would be no question regarding the taking of vows. Edward would have to keep her with him.

If Sir Michael——

She shook her head, squeezed her eyes closed, and began to pray away the evil thoughts. If there was a way out of the Church, it was not in that direction. Never that direction. She must trust in the Lord, not herself.

"Dear God, help me believe it," she breathed. "Pray, help me."

5

IN THE LATE afternoon of the fourth day following the arrival of the king's men, Sir Royce ordered that Edward Charwyck be released from the watchtower.

Immediately, the old man sought out Graeye and told her arrangements had been made for her return to the abbey the following morning. He was calm, almost emotionless, until she tried again to convince him to allow her to remain with him. Then he had raged so terribly that he might have done her injury had Sir Abelaard not interceded.

Thus, a defeated Graeye slipped out the postern gate late that evening and headed for the one place that might offer solace—the waterfall where she had spent sunny days with her mother before an untimely death had stolen away the one person who had loved her unconditionally.

She was not running away, for life in the Church was less daunting than the prospect of being on her own in a world she did not know. She but longed to see the falls one last time and revive the memories made there so that, come the morrow, she could carry them with her back to Arlecy.

Leaving the castle walls behind, she entered the wood and made her way over the debris-strewn ground and among towering trees whose branches had begun to shed their colorful leaves. She made good progress until night began to creep across the blue sky and she had to slow to ensure her footing and direction. When, at last, the ground began to slope away from her, she paused and listened. Catching the distant sound of falling water, she corrected her course, and it was not long before the wood opened up to reveal a glorious white veil that swept from on high into a large pool below.

As she stared at it, memories sweetly drew her back to a time when she had mattered to someone, when she had been happy, when she had known love. It was more than some ever had.

She ventured forward and, shortly, knelt upon the pool's upper bank. As she dipped her fingers in the cool water, she told herself to forget the castle and those who dwelt within—to be here and nowhere else.

"Such a night as this will not come again," she whispered. "Not ever."

She stood, dragged off the heavy habit, and entered the pool clad in her thin chemise. The water was not frigid, but it was chill enough to make her limbs quake and teeth chatter until she began to exert herself.

With the moon and the awakening stars her only witnesses, she attempted the strokes her mother had taught her years ago. They were not graceful, nor efficient, but they allowed her to cross the deepest stretch of the pool and venture into the falls' biting spray.

For what must have been an hour or more, as told by the dark of the sky, she became so immersed in her solitude that, had the animal not whinnied loudly, she might not have noticed the trespasser until it was too late.

Returned to the present, she treaded water as horse and rider halted upon the grassy bank near the lower portion of the pool.

Water lapping at her shoulders, she berated herself for lingering so long and glanced at the half moon that had traveled some distance since her arrival. Praying its dim light would not reveal her, she turned and slowly pulled herself through the water until she reached the long shadows where she had entered the pool on the opposite side.

Though instinct begged her to flee, fear of discovery stayed her. Even with the length and width of the pool separating her from the trespasser, there would be little to deter him if he decided to give chase.

Thus, submerged up to her neck, she knelt in the shallows and used the cloak of darkness to appraise the one who had happened upon her.

He was no wayfarer. With his fine, glittering vest of chain mail and highly prized white destrier, he had to be of the nobility. Dark of hair and beard, he sat tall in the saddle and appeared every bit the gentleman warrior. But gentleman or not, with the breadth and certain height of him, he would be a formidable opponent. Indeed, he exuded something more ominous than strength, something that caused disquiet to skitter up her spine. Anger?

Rubbing her hands over her arms beneath the water, she wondered if he might be one of her father's former retainers who had heretofore gone unnoticed.

She rejected the idea, certain she would remember such a man, even had she only glimpsed him from afar. Neither did she think he was one of those sent by the king. One of Balmaine's men, then? Nay, the new lord of Medland was not expected for three more days. Thus, the man was likely a knight-errant passing through.

When he swung a leg over the saddle and dropped to the ground, Graeye fought the urge to flee and pressed herself more deeply into the shadows.

As he descended the bank, she thought she detected a limp, but she could not be certain, for it took only two strides to carry him to the pool's edge where he dropped to a knee to quench his thirst. Perhaps he had simply partaken of too much drink, she considered, and conjured a vision of her father.

The knight rose and surveyed the pool.

Though she assured herself he could not see her amid the shadows, fear rippled across her skin. Did he sense her presence?

When he finally returned to his destrier, she sighed. However, rather than mount, he unbuckled his belted sword and draped it over the saddle. Then he began to remove his chain mail.

Graeye held her breath for fear he intended to bare himself. But even when he drew the armor off over his head, she found herself transfixed by curiosity that Mistress Hermana would have severely punished.

Amid moonlight and above the pour of the falls, came the gleam and metallic peal of thousands of joined rings as the chain mail was draped over a large boulder. Next, he drew off his tunic.

Though her maidenly senses protested that he should so boldly disrobe, she reminded herself that not only was she scantily clothed in a chemise, but he had come upon her sanctuary unwittingly—was unaware he shared with another the dark-mantled sky that danced stars upon the tumbling water.

But when he removed the padded undertunic, leaving nothing save the gloss of night upon a broad, tapering back above the waistband of chausses, a gasp escaped her.

He swung around, and she nearly cried out when she saw he had brought his sword to hand.

With a snort and a toss of its massive head, the great animal echoed its master's disquiet as the knight peered into the darkness where Graeye knelt.

She stared at him, told herself he could not have heard the small sound she had made above the tumult of falling water. And yet, it seemed he had. If she ran, would he pursue her in nothing save chausses and boots?

After an interminable time that had her chest burning from lack of sufficient air, he turned to his destrier, slid the sword into its sheath, and belted a dagger at his waist. Then he shed his boots and hose, leaving only his chausses.

Though Graeye was grateful for that one item of clothing that covered his lower torso and legs, she flushed so deeply she momentarily warmed. This was far more of a man than she had ever seen.

When he entered the water without pause, as if unaffected by the temperature, she slowly threaded breath into her lungs and prayed he would keep to the lower portion of the pool and be quick with his bath. Having grown chill from the lack of exertion, she feared that if he had heard her gasp, he would more easily pick out the sound of chattering teeth.

His great height had been obvious at the outset, but when he stood at the center of the pool, she was better able to gauge his measure. Head and shoulders above the surface where she had earlier treaded water, she guessed he would stand a foot or more above her head.

A moment later, he dived beneath the surface.

Though tempted to take the opportunity to flee, Graeye doubted he would stay under long enough to allow her to slip away.

When he reappeared, relief swept her. Not only had she been right not to risk leaving the shadows, but he had returned to the lower portion of the pool. What might have happened had he ventured toward the upper end did not even bear thinking upon.

Go, she silently entreated, holding herself tighter, clenching her teeth harder. *Pray, go.*

Rather than accommodate her, he turned onto his back.

As moonlight traveled across his chest, she once more found herself warmed by embarrassment—a brief respite from the cold. Though she hated to admit it, even if only to herself, it was interest as well as fear that made her follow his movements.

This is as much as I will ever know of a man, she attempted to soothe her conscience. *Never will I wed. Never will I lie in a husband's arms. Never will I hear the laughter of children I might bear. Never.*

Her throat tightened and she felt the sting of tears. Now that she was no longer a pawn upon which to get heirs, she was to be tossed aside. On the morrow, she would journey back to the abbey where she would profess herself a nun and live out her days beneath the disapproving regard of Mistress Hermana.

All was hopeless. There was nothing left to her—

The thought that broke free of the depths to which she had pushed it did so with such force that she jerked. As when the idea had first occurred to her on the day the king's tidings had caused her world to collapse around her, her conscience screeched and named her every vile thing for thinking the unthinkable. What would it name her if she did what she should not do?

I ought not, she told herself. *It is wrong. But...*

Before her was a man to whom she could give her virtue. An unknown—here this night, gone come the morrow. Once all that remained of him was proof she was no longer worthy of being professed a nun, she could stay at her father's side.

Do not, Graeye! her conscience cried. *'Tis sin most foul. Turn from such thoughts. Pray! Pray hard!*

She nearly sought the Lord's help to fight the temptation to do what was settling far too comfortably into her, but her baser, desperate self whispered that, in this, she must trust Graeye Charwyck.

But would the knight be willing? If men were as lecherous as Mistress Hermana warned and William would have proved if not for Groan, then the trespasser would take what she offered. Unless...

She raked her teeth across her lower lip. If he saw the mark upon her face, he might reject her. She glanced at the half moon. Perhaps he would not notice. But perhaps he would.

In that moment, she longed to fling the idea back to its pit, but as she was swept with equal parts regret and relief, she became aware of the sodden weight of her hair. She pulled the mass over her shoulder, raked it forward, and smoothed the wet strands over the mark at her temple. Then she considered and considered again. With a painfully hard swallow, she once more gave herself over to the idea.

Forgive me, Lord, she silently prayed. *Forgive me, though I know what I do.*

It was surely blasphemous to try to gain His ear, and foolish to think to gain forgiveness of a sin from which she could still turn away, but she had to ask.

She looked to the trespasser who was now swimming toward the bank where he had entered the pool. Shortly, he rose up and stepped from the water.

"Ah, nay," she breathed and pushed forward. The silt and mud sucked at her feet as if to keep her from committing the wicked act, but she freed herself and, when the ground fell from beneath her, fanned her arms out and swam forward.

As she drew near the knight where he stood near his destrier, he dragged his undertunic on over his head.

Graeye was still several yards away, heart pounding furiously, when he swung around and wrenched his dagger from its sheath.

"Who goes?" he demanded as his gaze settled on her where her chin bobbed on the surface. His dark expression turned to disbelief, then he blinked as if to dispel a vision and leaned forward to better see her.

She saw then that his short hair was not simply black, but pitch—so much that night bestowed a blue cast upon the unruly locks. Though more handsome than she had gleaned from her hiding place, he looked every bit as hard and dangerous as first thought. And he frightened her nearly as much as a lifetime spent behind abbey walls. Nearly...

Pressing her fear down, she raised her gaze to glittering eyes that held no kindness. What color might they be, and did they ever shine with the light of a smile? She shifted her scrutiny down the length of his body, the lower half of which was clothed in wet chausses that clung to his legs.

Oh, Graeye, what are you doing? Stop this now!

But even as she tensed to abandon her plan, that other side of her told that it was the only way—just this one thing, this one night, and she could remain with her father.

You assume he will wish a wanton at his side, her conscience argued.

Of course he would not, but what other choice would he have? And even if his wrath left her bruised, in the end he would be glad of the succor she provided. Thus, she must finish what she had begun.

Assuring herself her hair hid the mark, she lowered her feet, crouching so that only her shoulders and head were visible above the water.

"Who are you?" the knight asked again, his voice deep and resonant and without slur that would have evidenced he had imbibed too much.

Not knowing how she should answer and wary of other questions he might put to her, she shook her head.

His eyes narrowed.

Once again, her resolve began to fray, causing her breathing to turn shallow. Then something taut and trembling snapped within her.

He is dangerous. This is wrong!

She pushed backward, but before she could turn away, he lunged into the water, gripped her arm, and dragged her to her feet.

She cried out and threw a hand up to balance herself. It landed on his chest, but though she was taken aback by the feel of his muscles beneath the undertunic, she held her hand there to maintain distance between them.

"What are you?" he asked, his warm breath reaching her from that great height.

The question confounded Graeye so much that she momentarily forgot she was clothed in a wet chemise that clasped itself close to her body. With a shaky breath, she peered up at him.

"Perhaps you are a fairy turned woman, come to tempt me with your wiles," he mused.

His face had softened, the corners of his mouth curving toward a smile. And beneath her palm, his muscles eased. It seemed the danger was past.

But the wrong of it is not, her conscience once more asserted itself.

Perhaps if that voice had been louder—more forceful—she would have heeded it, but the other voice was too convincing.

Just this one thing, this one night.

She lowered her gaze to the dagger he clutched, then drew her hand from his chest to his shoulder and down his arm. He did not resist when she loosened his fingers from the hilt, nor move to prevent the weapon from falling to the water.

Though Graeye had no experience with seduction, she was certain it started with a kiss. Thus, she breached the space between them, slid her fingers over his crisp beard, and looked to his mouth. Then she rose onto her toes. Finding he was yet too tall, she curled a hand around his neck and urged his head down.

Only when he released his breath did she realize he had been holding it, then he encircled her waist and drew her close. When his mouth covered hers, Graeye was jolted by sensations she had not felt with William's fumblings and Michael's brotherly peck. And suddenly she was wonderfully warm—until he pushed his fingers through her hair.

She jerked her head back, swept up a hand, and was relieved to discover the mark had not come uncovered.

Frowning, he reached to her hair again.

She shook her head.

His frown deepened, but he shrugged and contented himself with running his fingers through the tresses that swept her hips as he once more claimed her mouth.

And then Graeye was lost. Completely, devastatingly lost.

"Forgive me," he spoke into the hair atop her head. "I did not know."

He could not have, surely would not have considered that the woman who so brazenly offered herself had never lain with a man. But there had been no way to hide it, for she had not known there would be pain, so much that she had wondered why women subjected themselves to it at all—at least, until the hurt subsided.

He drew back from her where they lay on their sides in the grass facing one another and lifted her chin to peer into her face.

Grateful the mark was not only in shadow but her hair yet clung to it, she gazed back at him and consciously made a place in her mind for his face so it would ever be with her.

"Forgive me?" he said again.

Though it was not for her to do, she nodded.

"There should be no more pain," he said, and it took her a moment to realize his assurance was meant to ease any misgivings should they lie together again. They would not.

"You are not going to tell me who you are?"

She shook her head, then, impulsively, touched a finger to his chest and raised her eyebrows.

To her surprise, he grinned and his eyebrows jauntily rose and fell. But he also shook his head.

She knew it was best not to know his name, for she would not see him again. Still, such cool logic did not stop her from wishing it could be otherwise.

When his thumb began drawing lazy circles over her jaw, she once more yielded to impulse and pressed her mouth to his palm.

"You are real?" he asked in that deep voice she found so pleasing. "Not some spirit come to distract me from my labors?"

She smiled, shrugged.

Though his eyebrows gathered, he did not coax her further. "You are beautiful, little one," he rumbled.

Truly? She recalled her reflection in the pool. She was not unbecoming, but to be told she was beautiful...

Were it possible, she thought she could stay with this man forever. Though unfamiliar with the notion of love beyond what she had felt for her mother, there was something here she longed to hold to. And she was swept by sorrow that it could not last, that it ended this night.

Suddenly, he raised his head, then his body followed. Moving swiftly, he retrieved his sword, and it was then she heard what had stolen him from her.

She sprang to her feet, but there was no cover to be had, and whoever moved through the wood made good progress. Knowing he would be upon them shortly, she stepped back into the water.

"Wait!" the knight called.

Graeye glanced at him, then waded farther out. She could not be discovered, especially if the one who approached was one of her father's or the king's men come to battle the trespasser. The knight had given her what she required, and she would not have him pay for a sin that was far more hers than his.

She looked around one last time and gasped when she saw he followed, and again when he caught her arm and pulled her back.

She shook her head, silently entreating him to release her.

"My lord!" a voice called from the trees.

The knight's tension dissolved. "'Tis but my squire," he said low. "You need not fear."

Finding no comfort in his words, she tried to pull free, but he held fast. "Duncan!" he called. "Come no nearer."

The crackling of leaves ceased, and a short-lived quiet fell over the wood. "But, my lord——"

"Remain where you are!" The knight looked back at Graeye. "Stay with me."

If only her life was such that she could, that she could know him in truth and he would accept her no matter the mark she bore. But that was fantasy. And fantasy was folly.

She shook her head again.

He lowered his face and recaptured her mouth beneath his with an urgency that made her long to lean in and not think on the morrow. Instead, she forced herself to remain still.

When he drew back, his expression was puzzled. "I will release you so that you might seek cover," he said, "provided you stay near until I have finished with my squire."

Graeye hated the lie, but as she could see no other way past him, she nodded.

After a long silence that bespoke doubt, he released her.

Fearful he might change his mind, she lowered herself into the water and hurriedly swam to the opposite side of the pool. There, she boosted herself out, snatched up her outer garments, and ran for the trees. Amid the tall shadows, she peered back at the pool and saw the knight had not moved from where she had left him.

She would have donned her clothes then, but she sensed he was as aware of her presence as she was of his. Unmindful of the chill that raised the fine hairs across her body, she turned and ran deeper into the wood, her vow to the knight shredded upon the breeze stirring the leaves.

So he had sinned. Again. More, he regretted not having been cautious in the sinning, for he was not one to beget fatherless children. It almost made him wish she had not been real. And, perhaps, she was not.

"Mayhap 'tis an undine I have seen," he muttered, imagining those mythical water spirits who, it was told, could earn a soul by marrying a mortal and bearing his child.

She had certainly deceived him. She of the witching mouth and beguiling curves had dismissed the vow she had made and disappeared as easily as she had appeared.

Curses! he silently fumed. *If she is real, I will find her. If not—*

Ridiculous! Of soft flesh and warm blood she had been. No wraith, but a woman. And he *would* find her.

Leading his destrier into the clearing where a camp had been erected for the night, Gilbert Balmaine headed for the large glowing fire at its center. There, the messenger he had sent ahead awaited him.

Immediately Squire Duncan appeared at his side and began a recounting of the messenger's call upon the castle.

But Duncan was not the one Gilbert wanted to hear from. He threw a hand up, bringing a halt to the young man's ramblings, and thrust the stallion's reins at him. "See he is properly fed and watered."

"Aye, my lord," Duncan said, poorly disguising his frustration at Gilbert's strange mood.

As the squire led the destrier to where the others were penned for the night, Gilbert drew a hand through his damp hair and began kneading the back of his neck as he unhurriedly advanced on the group of men gathered around the fire. Though the news he awaited was important, it seemed less so since his encounter at the waterfall. And it nearly angered him that he should be so affected.

"My lord," Sir Lancelyn called as he disengaged himself from the others. "I bring tidings from the king's man, Sir Royce."

Gilbert halted and set his feet apart. "And?"

"All is secure. There will be no resistance. On the morrow, all of Medland will be given over to you."

"What of the old man?"

The knight shrugged. "Naturally, Edward Charwyck would challenge you for Medland, but he is without recourse. Nearly all his men have deserted him, and I am told his vassals are eager to pledge themselves to you."

This pleased Gilbert. He could think of nothing better than ridding the world of that family and their influence, and the old man was the last of them. With a grunt of discomfort, he shifted his weight off his aching right leg. "Then Charwyck will not give me his oath of fealty?" Not that he expected it—or wished it.

"Highly unlikely, my lord."

"Good." Gilbert ground the heel of his hand into his aching thigh.

His vassal stepped nearer. "My lord, methinks it best you expel Charwyck from Medland at the first opportunity. He is certain to prove difficult."

Gilbert raised his eyebrows. "Then, as expected, he is of the same bent as his son, Philip."

"This I do not know, but Sir Royce believes he is mad. The man raves with threats against you and your sister."

Gilbert narrowed his lids. "He has been detained?"

"He was. However, this morn Sir Royce granted him his freedom. Although he does not think the old man is much of a threat, he says he is not to be trusted."

Gilbert sighed. "He is old and now without an heir. What can he gain by resisting? Even had King Henry not given Medland into my keeping, 'twould likely return to the crown upon Charwyck's death."

Lancelyn's face lit.

Gilbert raised an eyebrow. "Tell me."

"'Tis not as thought. The old man does have another heir—or nearly so."

"Baseborn?"

"Legitimate."

Gilbert tensed. "I have heard of no other. There was only Philip."

Lancelyn shook his head. "Unbeknownst to all, Edward Charwyck has a daughter."

This puzzled Gilbert. The lands of Penforke and Medland were so close that he was certain he would have heard of the existence of another offspring. "Still a child, then," he concluded.

"Nay." The knight's lips twisted wryly. "A woman. And a nun, no less. The old man brought her from the abbey more than a month past. It seems he intended to wed her to one of his vassals so she might give him a male heir."

"A nun?" Gilbert exclaimed. "She would break her vows? What manner of woman is she and why would the Church allow it?"

Lancelyn's shoulders rose and fell. "This I do not understand, but 'tis said she bears the mark of the devil upon her face. Mayhap the Church is grateful to be rid of her."

"Mark of the devil," Gilbert mused. Though it fit with what he knew of the family, he could not bring himself to believe in the absurdity of such a thing. "I will see her returned to the abbey at once," he decided. "Providing, of course, the good sisters will accept her back amongst them after such a betrayal."

"It would seem her father is of the same mind, my lord, for he has asked Sir Royce to arrange an escort for her on the morrow."

"As it should be," Gilbert said. "Now, let us talk of the state of the demesne. Is it in as poor a condition as I have heard?"

6

Wʜᴇɴ Gʀᴀᴇʏᴇ ᴀʀᴏsᴇ from a nearly sleepless night, she learned Balmaine was to arrive that day rather than several days hence. As the news had surely been brought during her venture to the falls yestereve, she had been none the wiser until the talk of servants reached her.

She was stunned, then dismayed at the realization she had little time in which to reveal the sin she had committed. Her father would have to release her from the obligation of taking the veil, but how would he receive the news?

Badly. Very badly. But she would not think on it now.

It was not until she returned to the hall following matins that another implication of the baron's untimely arrival struck her—with such force that had there not been a table nearby on which to brace herself, she might have sunk to the floor.

The man to whom she had given her most precious gift was likely among Balmaine's men.

It was true her father would know of her sin soon enough, but the possibility of others learning of it nearly made her retch. What could she do?

Hope. That was all. Hope the knight would not recognize her, and it was possible he would not, for it had been dark.

She had no time to worry further, for Edward appeared at her side, evidence of a night of heavy drinking all about him. He swayed, his face was florid, and the odor of his breath and that which wafted off his clothes further stirred up her belly.

"Where is your habit?" he demanded. "You dare defy me in this?"

Feeling the gaze of those in the hall who gathered for the morning meal, she looked down at her rumpled clothing. As it had seemed sacrilegious to wear her habit after breaking the vow of chastity, she had chosen to wear the brown bliaut. And now she must reveal the reason, must confess all. "Father, I—"

"This day you are to return to the abbey, and you walk about as if you have time for a hunt!" Edward pushed her toward the stairs. "Dress yourself ere that knave Balmaine arrives and starts slavering over you."

"Will you not accompany me, Father? I must needs speak with you on a matter of—"

"Go!"

His shout caused those in the hall who had not been openly watching to look their way.

She ground her teeth. Her confession would have to wait.

Abovestairs, in the small room where her mother's belongings were kept, she pushed back the lid of the old chest and dug down to where she had buried the habit earlier this morn. Having thought never to wear it again, she had bunched it into a ball and secreted it beneath the other clothing.

She shook it out now, and the veil and wimple dropped to her feet. She stared at the latter a long moment, then shifted her gaze to the robe that would cover her neck to toe. Not only was it terribly wrinkled, but it was far from clean. She should not have been so careless in tossing it to the ground on the night past.

With dread, she stripped off the brown bliaut, reached for the robe, and hesitated. Other than appeasing her father, nothing good could come of donning it. Indeed, it might make her impending confession worse. She was on the verge of defying Edward's order when the veil and wimple once more drew her regard, and it occurred to her the habit might serve as a disguise if the knight to whom she had given herself was among Balmaine's men. He would certainly not expect her to be a nun.

Quickly, she donned each piece of the cumbersome habit, all the while mumbling prayers of contrition for daring to clothe herself as a bride of Christ. Nevermore. And yet, once the wimple was in place, she had the sickening feeling she had sealed her fate.

Not so, she told herself. *Edward will have to allow me to remain with him. He cannot return me to the abbey.*

When she descended to the hall that should have been teeming with those breaking their fast, she found the room deserted. Certain it meant the baron would soon be within the castle's walls, Graeye hurried across the rush-covered floor and stepped out into the morning air where the king's men and her father's former retainers bustled about.

But where was Edward? He had such an obvious presence that, within moments, she knew he was not in the inner bailey, and she guessed Sir Royce had once more imprisoned him in the watchtower now that Balmaine's arrival was imminent.

She lifted her skirts, hurried down the steps, and broke into a half run to overtake those surging forward. Though she pretended not to notice the curious stares that followed her, she felt every one of them.

Flushed, she crossed the inner drawbridge into the outer bailey just as a procession of armored and mounted men passed beneath the portcullis in the outer wall.

Balmaine had arrived.

Fighting panic, Graeye slipped among the chattering, raucous castle folk who pressed and surged against one another in their eagerness to view the impressive spectacle and greet their new lord. Not until she found adequate cover, the stark white of her habit hidden amid the dull colors of the common folk, did she venture another look.

She grimaced. Though she had managed to make herself less obvious amid the others, her short stature forced her to stand on tiptoe to catch a glimpse of the retinue as they surged forth. Jostled side to side, she took hold of a nearby arm to steady herself. Having gained a small vantage, she scanned the mounted knights in search of one who was dark of hair and beard.

With each elimination, relief swept her. They were all either too short, hair too long or straight, or faces too soft.

"Milady." A tall woman touched her shoulder.

Graeye recognized her as a serving wench from the hall and was embarrassed to discover it was her arm she clutched. She removed her hand. "I am sorry," she murmured and started to turn her attention back to the riders.

"Nay, milady, I do not mind. I only thought to point out the baron."

Odd, Graeye thought. She had been too intent on discovering whether or not the man of the night past was among Balmaine's men to seek out the baron himself. She thanked the woman, took her proffered arm again, and craned her neck to look where the servant pointed.

The moment her gaze settled on the great white destrier that advanced on the inner drawbridge, it was as if ice had poured into her veins. With the horse's purity of white, it was a rare animal, so rare that she had only ever seen one so untouched with any color other than white.

Having forgotten how to breathe, Graeye forced her eyes over long, darkly clad legs, a vivid red-and-gold tunic, and up a bearded face to eyes that stared back at her.

Time yawned, and for those long, torturous moments, it was as if the world had paused in its toils to take note of the occasion.

Forcing air into her lungs, Graeye tore her eyes free and landed so heavily on her heels she stumbled back. The man behind steadied her and grunted when she trod upon his feet in her haste to push past him. She barely noticed the offense, though she was all too aware of the commotion that followed her slow progress through the crowd.

When she finally broke free, the white destrier was before her. As a murmur of interest rose from the onlookers, she ventured a glance at the rider. The contemptuous look with which he swept her spoke more than words could.

Eager to escape the black-hearted cur responsible for her brother's death, Graeye lunged to the side, skirted the horse, and ran to the community chapel. In her haste to ascend the steps, she stumbled but managed to keep her legs beneath her. Once inside, she thrust the door closed. Though tempted to press her body back against it, she knew it would be futile. If a man such as Baron Balmaine wanted in, there would be no keeping him out. As she hurried toward the altar, the chaplain appeared.

She halted, lowered her gaze, and tightly clasped her hands before her. "F-father."

"What is it, my child?"

How she wished his voice did not proclaim his usual lack of interest in the members of his flock, that he was someone in whom she could confide. "I must needs pray," she muttered and stepped around him.

Hardly had she settled on the kneeler before the altar than the door of the chapel was thrown open and issued in a swell of light that rarely knew the darkened interior.

Graeye bowed her head and tried with all her might to block out the sound of boots upon the floor.

"Out!" the baron commanded.

As the chaplain sputtered and muttered, Graeye fingered the knots of her leather girdle and offered prayer for each one that slid through her fingers.

Then there was silence. Though the exchange behind her was unspoken, she knew something had passed between the two men. A moment later, she heard the shuffle of feet, followed by the groan of hinges as the door was drawn closed.

With the sanctuary returned to its usual gloom, one minute after another dragged by, during which the presence at her back became increasingly tangible. Fervently, she prayed the man away, but he persisted. She prayed this was all a terrible dream, but she was fully awake. She prayed herself to another place and time, but there was only the here and now. Thus, when she was empty of prayers and all hope of convincing the Lord she was worthy of a miracle, there was nothing left to her but to brave the encounter and be done with it.

She crossed herself, rose from the kneeler, and turned to face the one responsible for her brother's demise—the same to whom she had unknowingly given herself on the night past.

Baron Balmaine stood in the center aisle that divided the benches into left and right. Countenance hard and expressionless, he slowly lowered his gaze down her disheveled habit, more slowly raised it back to her face. Despite feeling thoroughly degraded, she did not look away from the piercing eyes that held no hint of mercy or tenderness for the night past. This was not the man who had loved her yestereve, though his likeness was none other's. This was a man who looked as if he might knock her senseless before deigning to kiss her again.

"'Tis obvious," he said at last, his voice deep and clear in the silence of the chapel, "you are unaccustomed to keeping your vows, Sister—sacred or otherwise."

His words jolted her, though she was not surprised that he saw her in the worst light. She had offered her body to him, then made a vow she'd had no intention of keeping. And today she stood before him clothed as a nun.

As he stepped forward with a slight limp of which she had been uncertain on the night past, she steeled herself for what was to come by stiffening her spine, straightening her shoulders, and instructing herself not to cower.

When he stood a reach away, he halted and looked down his long nose at her.

Graeye braved his stare and was taken aback by the most amazingly blue eyes she had seen. In the darkness of the night, they had been unknowable, and she had been too frightened when she had encountered him in the bailey to take note of their color. But there was no mistaking the summer sky in them now.

"By what name are you called, daughter of Edward Charwyck, faithless bride of Christ?"

Her mouth having gone dry, it was some moments before she could answer. "I am—"

"Ah, so you can speak."

Yet another mark against her already maligned character. Feeling warmth steal up her neck, she said, "I am Lady Graeye Charwyck." She winced at how husky her voice sounded, and again when he narrowed his lids. "But I am not——"

"Graeye," he said and tested the name a second time. "Appropriate. What is your name in religion, Sister?"

She shook her head and took a step back when he moved nearer. As she did so, it occurred to her she was forever running from those who threatened her. And she hated herself for it. Still, when he continued his advance, she once more retreated, and her calves came up against the kneeler. "I am not of the sisterhood," she declared, throwing a hand up to ward him off.

The words stopped him, and he searched her face. "I spoke literally when I afforded you the title of Sister. I was not speaking of your genuine disposition. We both know what that is."

She raised her eyebrows into the crisp band at her forehead. "I am not a nun."

"Not after last eve." He took another step forward and his leg brushed her skirts.

Straining her neck to peer up at him, she said, "I do not play with words. I speak true when I say I am not of the sisterhood. I have not yet made my profession."

His hands descended to her shoulders, and she nearly shrieked. Fear threatening to reduce her to something small and pitiful and keening, she bowed her head and stared at the bare space between them as she struggled for composure.

Giving no quarter, he pulled her chin up and forced her to look upon him. "If you have not taken your vows, why do you dress as a nun?"

"I am..." She swallowed hard. "I was a novice and was to have been professed the day my father sent for me. This is my bridal habit."

His brow furrowed. "You speak true?"

"I do."

He considered her, then gave a bark of laughter, released her, and swung away. "Quite the burden you have lifted from me," he said and dropped down upon the nearest bench. "Certes, if there is a God"—he stretched his long legs out before him—"He would not be kindly disposed toward one who claimed the virtue of His son's bride."

Graeye gasped, took a step forward. "*If* there is a God? You speak heresy."

"Heresy?" The corners of his mouth crimping, he gripped his thigh and began to knead it. "I merely question His existence. Do you believe in Him?"

Indignation displacing fear, she hastened forward and halted before the blasphemous man. "Of course I believe in God!"

His dark eyebrows arched. "And here I thought I had found myself one of kindred spirit. Tell me, is your sexual proclivity typical of all members of the clergy? If 'tis, I shall question God's existence no longer. I will simply deny it, *Daughter of Eve.*"

The anger that had granted her strength those few moments ebbed, and she was horrified to feel the heat of tears. It was as her father called her when angered, and though it was better than being named one sired by the devil, it further wounded.

"Do not call me that," she said low.

He sat forward. "It offends?"

"I am Lady Graeye."

"Ah, then rather than Daughter of Eve, I should call you Lady of Eve?"

"You should not!"

"You are saying it does not fit? You who tempted a man to sin last night and this day plays the good sister?"

"I—" Her voice cracked. "I would have you know that what I did yestereve was done with the intention of refusing to take the veil."

"Truly?" He put his head to the side. "Then this day you wear the habit simply for the privilege it affords you?"

Holding his gaze, she said, "My father ordered me to don it. He does not yet know of my sin."

Something glimmered in Balmaine's eyes a moment before his hand shot out and caught the skirt of her habit. With a hard yank, he dropped her onto his lap.

"And when will you tell him you are no longer eligible to become a nun?" he demanded as she strained against the arm clamped around her waist. "Or perhaps he does know of your sin—condoned it as a means of entrapping me. Was it he who sent you?"

Graeye stilled. Did he truly believe Edward and she had conspired to entrap him? That she would sell her virtue in hopes of gaining... What? Concessions?

Swiping aside the veil that had fallen across her face, she looked across her shoulder and was struck by how attractive he was despite the wrath he wore so well. And how she hated that she should notice. "Release me, knave!"

His lids narrowed. "What did you hope to achieve by seducing me?"

She twisted toward him and thrust her hands against his chest, but there was no dislodging his hold.

"To force me to marriage?" he persisted. "Is Medland so important you would sell your body for it—perhaps even your soul?"

Suffused with anger of a depth she had not experienced before, she said, "Never would I marry you! Had I known who you were when you came upon my sanctuary, I would not have done what I did."

He snorted. "I am to believe you?"

She stared into his cold eyes and determined that whether or not he condemned her for a liar, he would hear the truth. "I did not give myself to you to capture a husband. I did it to renounce the possibility of becoming a nun so I might remain at my father's side and help his people—"

"*My* people."

Of course they were. "Their needs are great, their fields—"

"Think you I cannot see to them myself?"

The question was—would he? This man who had shown her brother no mercy?

"Even if you speak true," he continued, "and I were fool enough to believe you, you would be little better for having used me to attain your goal."

It hurt that he was right. "I know I did wrong yestereve, but I do not wish to live out my days at the abbey, and it seemed the only way to ensure I would not be made to return there."

His eyes probed her face, and she became aware of how askew her wimple was. But though tempted to straighten it, she feared drawing attention to what may or may not have come uncovered.

"I do not believe you," he said, "for I have heard life among the clergy is far preferred over the toil of everyday life—even if one's days are spent in the comfort of a castle."

Graeye unclenched her teeth. "Hearing is but a shallow reflection of reality. I was sent to the abbey at the age of seven, and in all the years since, I knew little happiness. Mayhap such a life is desirous for others, but it was not so for me."

Only when he intercepted the hand with which she reached to smooth the linen about her face did she realize she had succumbed to the nervous habit. He pushed it aside. "How touching your tale," he murmured, then further trespassed by fingering the wimple's chin strap.

Thinking he intended to snatch it from her, she drew her head back.

He lowered his hand. "I was told Charwyck's daughter bears the mark of the devil. Is that what you hid yestereve?"

She steeled herself. "It is."

"Show me."

Graeye blinked. Clearly he could uncover it himself. Why did he not? Consideration? Or merely an attempt to further humiliate her?

"I would see it," he said again.

She bowed her head and removed the veil, freeing her hair that had dried into a mess of intertwined tresses following her visit to the waterfall. Next came the wimple. Gripping the linen pieces tightly in her fist, she raised her chin, but not her eyes.

"I thought it a game you played," he said as she felt his gaze move over her face. "I should have guessed."

"It was...necessary."

"Then you misjudged me," he said so softly—so strangely—that she looked up.

She thought she glimpsed the man of the night past, but if it was him, he was too soon gone.

"You see," he said, "I have as much belief in the devil as I do God." He reached up and lightly touched the stain.

Though Graeye's heart plummeted further, she did not flinch, nor when his fingers moved to her hair and drew a tress through them.

"I would not have guessed it to be so golden," he murmured.

He could not have, for on the night past it had been darkened by the damp of her swim.

Coming to the end of the tress, he let it fall against her bodice, then he shrugged almost wearily and once more considered the stain. "Still, considering your deception, I daresay there might well be something to this. That it is, indeed, the mark of—"

"Enough!" she cried. All of her life, she had been looked upon with suspicion, and now, with her world in a shambles, she could bear no more accusations, especially from him. Thus, when his expression turned derisive, she did not check the impulse to wipe it from his face and was amazed at the ease with which she struck his cheek.

"I am but a woman cursed to bear a mark set upon me—not by the devil but by God," she spat as his face brightened where her slap had landed. "'Tis a mark of birth, naught else. You have nothing to fear from me that you would not fear from another."

"So the little one has claws." His spectacular eyes bored into hers. "Had I the time or inclination, I might try to tame that temper of yours. But as I have neither, you will have to content yourself with this."

Temper? She did not have a—

His hand curved around her neck and drew her face toward his, then his mouth was upon hers and she was swept back to the night past when she had longed to stay with him. Ignoring the voices that urged her to resist—to bite, kick, and scratch—she sighed.

Just as abruptly as it had begun, it ended. He lifted her off his lap, set her on the bench, and stood.

Graeye peered up at the man who had so effortlessly disengaged himself from her. How had he such control over his emotions when she had none?

"I may have fallen prey to your wiles last eventide," he said, straightening his tunic, "but I have no intention of paying your price for such an unfortunate tryst. Your scheme has failed, Lady Graeye."

It was no easy thing to gather her wits about her after such an attack upon her senses, but his words made it less difficult than it would otherwise have been.

She pushed up off the bench. "You err." How she wished her voice did not sound so small. "There is naught I want from you that you have not already given me."

His lids narrowed. "What do you think you have stolen from me?"

Refusing to be drawn into an argument over whether she had stolen or been given his caresses, she said, "Though you do not believe me, I tell you true that I did not know who you were until this morn. It was freedom from the Church I hoped to gain, not a husband. *That* you have given me."

Balmaine laughed. "Be assured, Lady Graeye, you will return to the abbey." He adjusted his sword belt. "Though you now lack the purity to become a nun, there will be a place for you at the convent. Thus, you will go, even if I have to drag you there myself."

She took a step nearer him. "'Tis not your decision—"

His hand sliced the air. "Everything that has anything to do with Medland is under my control. You had best accept it and prepare to enter the convent."

Her heart lurched. Was what he said true? Could he usurp her father's rights over her? If so, all she had done was for naught.

Though it nearly made her sick to humble herself, she said, "Then I ask you to reconsider, Baron Balmaine. My father is not well and requires someone to—"

"The decision has been made." He strode away.

Even if Graeye could have contained her anger, she did not think she would have, for she had nothing to lose. "You have a nasty penchant for rudely interrupting when one is trying to speak," she snapped at his retreating back. "'Tis something you ought to work at correcting, *my lord*."

He pivoted and returned to her. "In future, if you have anything to say to me, Lady Graeye, address my face rather than my back."

Though she knew he could crush her between his hands, and at that moment he looked tempted to, she drew herself up to her last hair of height. "In future? As we have no future together, Baron, 'tis an absurd request. Or should I say *order?*"

A muscle in his jaw convulsed. "Sheathe your claws, little cat. The day is young and we have games yet to play."

Then he once more strode opposite, leaving her to stare after him as fear bloomed anew in her breast.

7

IT WAS MIDDAY before Graeye summoned the courage to leave the chapel. With her veil and wimple in place, she set her chin high and stepped out into the gloom of a day draped with heavy clouds.

Many of the castle folk who had resumed the labors to which she had set them weeks ago, paused to look upon her. Doubtless, they speculated over their new baron's interest in her—something he had made abundantly clear when he had followed her into the chapel. Though she told herself she did not care what any thought of her, she knew it was a lie.

But at least now she had a plan—or the beginnings thereof, she reassured herself as she put one foot in front of the other. Having used her time of prayer to seek guidance, the idea had slowly unfolded. It was not necessarily a good one, but no others had presented themselves.

Resolutely, she crossed to the watchtower where she hoped to find Sir Abelaard. If anyone knew where her father was, it would be the king's man whose responsibility it was to make certain Edward caused no further trouble.

So many new faces, she noted of those she passed. Balmaine had brought a great number of men with him, likely having anticipated resistance. It must have amused him to simply ride in and have the castle handed over without a scrap of opposition, the king's men having made the road smooth for him.

To her relief, Graeye found Sir Abelaard just inside the watchtower where he spoke with a knight who wore the colors of Balmaine.

"Lady Graeye." He disengaged himself from the other man and strode toward her. "You seek your father?"

"I do. He is above?"

"Nay, he has been taken to the hall."

Graeye had not thought Balmaine would so soon turn his attention to Edward. With greater foreboding, she asked, "Do you know what is to become of my sire?"

The knight's brow furrowed as he considered her silent appeal for reassurance, then he looked back at Balmaine's man.

The other knight strode forward. "Lady Graeye, I am Sir Lancelyn." He reached to take her hand.

Graeye stepped back and laced her fingers at her waist.

Her snub raised an eyebrow. "The baron is a fair man, my lady," he said. "I am certain he will deal justly with your father."

"My father has done no wrong."

He shrugged. "'Tis up to the baron to determine that."

Graeye swung away.

"My lady," Sir Lancelyn said, following, "if the hall is your destination, I am fair certain you will not be received within until Baron Balmaine has concluded his business."

She turned to him again, but he was so near she had to jump back to better see him. "When will that be?"

"I fear I cannot say, though I expect many hours yet."

She inclined her head, exited the watchtower, and was relieved when he did not follow.

Upon reaching the inner bailey, Graeye saw that several men-at-arms stood in the open doorway of the donjon with their backs to her. So engrossed were they with the goings-on in the hall that none noticed her ascent of the steps.

As she neared, Balmaine's deep voice sounded from within. She faltered, pushed aside the voice that urged her to retreat, and slipped unseen past the men into the great room that had been set fully to light with torches.

Beyond the wall of people that obscured her view, the new baron of Medland stopped speaking. After a long silence, his voice once more swelled around the hall. "Sir Edward Charwyck"—

Sir, not Baron…

—"will you be the first to give your oath of fealty?"

Graeye almost spilled bitter laughter, for her father would never make such a pledge. Knowing his response would not be good, she pushed her way through the gathering to the front.

At the raised dais at the far end of the hall, Edward stood silent before the man who had usurped his place.

What would happen when he refused the oath? She shifted her gaze to her father's former retainers who waited to pledge themselves to their new lord. William Rotwyld, no longer her betrothed, numbered among them.

"I would sooner die," Edward finally answered, "than pledge myself to my son's murderer."

Balmaine looked down upon him a long moment, then stepped from the dais and halted before him. "I have told you, old man—"

Edward swept up an arm and lunged. For a moment, Graeye thought it was a fist with which he intended to strike at the other man, but silver flashed from his hand.

Balmaine did not have time to evade the attack, for he had drawn too near, but he did have the presence of mind to sidestep. Thus, it was his shoulder that took the blade rather than his heart. With a roar, he threw Edward away from him, then tore the dagger free.

As his knights rushed to his aid, he drew his sword and strode to where the old baron lay sprawled upon his back. Setting a booted foot on Edward's chest, he swept the point of his sword to his prey's neck. "I now see from whom Philip learned his treachery," he growled.

Graeye returned to herself with a gasp and ran forward, but hardly did she make it to the center of the hall than Balmaine swept his sword back to deliver a killing blow.

"Do not!" she cried, but the weapon had begun its descent. She stumbled, dropped to her knees, and buried her face in her skirts to block the sight of the rushes soaked through with her sire's blood.

Her again! Gilbert silently cursed, then demanded, "What is *she* doing here?" When no answer was forthcoming, he strode toward the woman heaped upon the floor.

As he neared Lady Graeye, so focused on her he was only vaguely aware of the stirrings around him, he realized he was more angry now than when her treachery had first been revealed. If not for the pleading in that husky little voice, he would be done with the Charwycks forever—the father dead with just cause, the daughter returned to the abbey on the morrow to live out her miserable days.

But this woman had denied him the drawing of blood, causing him to pull up just as his sword neared its destination. Thus, the curses he silently hurled were not only against the Charwycks but himself.

He shoved his sword into its scabbard and, pressing a hand to his shoulder to stanch the blood, leaned down to take hold of Lady Graeye's arm. But before he could clamp a hand around her, a mangy dog bounded forward and placed itself between Gilbert and the woman. Growling, its sparse coat standing on end, the animal thrust its great head forward.

Slowly straightening, Gilbert reached for the dagger at his waist.

The beast bared its fangs, growled louder.

A movement beyond drew Gilbert's attention, and he saw one of his knights had removed his own dagger and drawn his arm back to hurl it. Gilbert caught his eye, shook his head, and said, "Lady Graeye, you will stand. Now."

She lifted her face from her arms and stared up at him with vast silvery eyes that shook him to the core. It was unsettling that she could have such an effect upon him after what he had discovered about her true character. Indeed, it almost sickened him.

Holding his stare, she gripped the dog's shoulder and raised herself.

Though her eyes were bright, Gilbert noted there were no tears upon her face. He wondered at that, for he had expected hysterics. What exactly was the relationship between father and daughter?

"You are satisfied?" she asked in a voice as tremulous as it was challenging. "Or am I to be next?"

"Satisfied?" He stepped aside and nodded to where Edward was supported between two of his knights. "I am not."

Graeye startled. Though her father's chin was upon his chest, he was alive without a spot of blood to attest otherwise. Why? How? She had seen—

It mattered not. Silently thanking the Lord for this answer to her prayer, she started toward Edward.

Balmaine pulled her back.

As gasps and murmurings went up around the hall, Groan barked and bunched in readiness to pounce upon the one whom he perceived as a threat to his mistress.

"Nay, Groan!" she commanded and met the baron's gaze. "You had best unhand me."

Even under threat of attack by a dog that obviously wished to tear out his throat, he did not release her.

Noting the clench of Balmaine's teeth and the deepening grooves that revealed he was in pain, she lowered her gaze to the shoulder of his tunic. It was torn and soaked through with blood where Edward had driven a blade into him, and when she looked to his hand upon her arm, she saw it was coated in crimson fingertips to wrist from where he had first held it to the wound. It was surely this—the blood staining her white habit—that so roused the others in the hall when he had taken hold of her.

Graeye glanced at her father. Though she longed to go to him, she said, "Come, Baron Balmaine, I will tend your injury."

Surprise flickered in his eyes before indifference fell into place. "Methinks you should first call off your dog." He jerked his chin toward Groan.

"Nay, he shall stay with me," she said, having once more discovered the value of his loyalty.

Balmaine looked as if he might refuse her, but then he shrugged his uninjured shoulder. "Very well," he said and released her.

Graeye turned from him and, with Groan following, made for the stairs.

"Take Charwyck to the watchtower and hold him there until I decide what will become of his miserable person," Balmaine commanded.

Hands clenched, Graeye veered toward Sir Michael, braved the compassion of his stare, and asked him to send a servant with water, strips of clean cloth, needle and thread, and salve. Then she mounted the stairs ahead of the baron.

With the arrival of the king's men, she had forgotten how badly in need of repair the steps were. However, Balmaine's weight and that of the squire who followed reminded her of their poor state.

Her father's chamber being the most adequate room abovestairs, she led the way to it. As she stepped inside, the thought struck her that Balmaine would not clear the doorway. She looked around to warn him, but he had already ducked beneath the lintel. Clearly, he was accustomed to his height.

She was grateful she had seen to the freshening of the rushes, the cleaning of the sparse furnishings, and the placement of oiled linen over the narrow window. Still, it was a dismal, dank room, the brazier having long ago radiated its last ember of comforting heat.

She pulled a three-legged stool to the center of the chamber and motioned for Balmaine to seat himself. As he did so, Groan drew near, securing a vantage from which to attack, if necessary.

Graeye turned to the squire who stood in the doorway surveying her with distrustful eyes. "I will need light," she said. "Fetch some torches."

The young man propped himself against the door jamb.

"Duncan," Balmaine said, "do as the lady says."

The squire cast Graeye a look of warning, straightened, and pivoted.

She turned back to Balmaine. Though unsettled by the prospect of seeing his torso bared, the tunic and undertunic would have to go. "You must needs remove these." She touched the material.

"With your assistance," he said.

Her unease must have shown, for amid the ashen color of his face, his mouth took a derisive turn.

After he had removed his belt with its sword and dagger and lowered them to the floor, Graeye moved only as close as was required to grasp the garments and draw them up over his chest.

Balmaine made no sound when the material pulled from the wound, but his stiffening evidenced discomfort.

As she carefully drew the tunic and undertunic off over his head, she noted the injuries carved into his flesh, from the bloody one recently dealt by her father to a jagged ridge that slashed across his breast to a wickedly curved scar upon his lower abdomen. And still there was the unseen scar that was surely responsible for his limp.

Lord, he has so many.

She took a step back. "Hold your hand to it," she said, then shook out his garments and laid them on the rumpled bed.

When she came back around, his squire had reappeared. As the young man set about placing torches in wall sconces around the chamber, Graeye returned to the baron, bent over him, and examined the wound.

Though she had spent time in the infirmary at the abbey, she had rarely been responsible for caring for the sick and wounded unless another had first seen to the stitching, medicating, and bandaging. Still, she had watched the sisters perform the duties required to mend such injuries and was certain she could see to this one.

"Milady," a young voice called.

She looked to the two serving girls in the doorway whose arms were laden with the items she had requested, eyes wide and round as they stared at the baron's bared chest. Behind them stood Sir Michael.

"Come," Graeye beckoned.

The girls entered with a provocative swing in their hips that made Graeye wonder how they were able to make their bodies flow so smoothly. Could she do that?

Immediately, she chastised herself. For what purpose would she wish to do so? To again seduce this man who thought her the vilest of beings?

"Baron Balmaine," Michael said, "with your permission, I would have a word with Lady Graeye."

Astonished that he should be so forthright with the man who was to become his lord, Graeye turned to catch Balmaine's reaction.

Save for the narrowing of his lids, he gave nothing away. "Be quick about it," he said.

Reluctantly, Graeye stepped out into the passageway. "You should not have done that," she said low.

Michael took her elbow and led her from the doorway. "There is no need for you to tend him," he whispered. "There are others capable of the task."

Taken aback by his concern, she stared at him. Why did he seek her out after avoiding her for so long? Had he changed his mind about Edward?

"It was my father who did the deed," she said, "and so it is I who shall mend it."

He sighed. "Still you make yourself responsible for that old man. Is there naught you would not forgive him for? He tried to murder the baron, Graeye."

"'Tis Philip's death that—"

The appearance of the serving girls halted the words with which she had intended to defend her father's madness, and she took a step back.

Once the girls disappeared down the stairs, Michael resumed their hushed conversation. "Graeye, your father will likely be sentenced to death. Come with me this night, and you will not have to witness his end."

Death? Not if her plan went well. "I have told you," she said, "I will not abandon him to the likes of Baron Balmaine."

Face reflecting frustration, Michael stepped near and cupped her chin in his palm. "You are being foolish, sweet Graeye."

Perhaps, but she would not give up so easily. "I—"

"Are you finished?" Balmaine asked.

Graeye spun around.

He leaned in the doorway, a forearm against the frame. Though his eyebrows were raised and a smile curved his mouth, he looked ominous.

How much had he heard? Angry at herself for allowing Michael to pull her into a conversation with the baron so near, she said, "We are finished," and stepped toward the chamber.

Balmaine remained unmoving, his great bulk denying her access while his gaze probed Michael's face, then hers.

"If you will step aside," Graeye said between her teeth, "I will tend your wound now."

His eyes that seemed more black than blue at the moment, returned to Michael. "Await me belowstairs," he told the knight, then stood aside to grant Graeye entrance into the chamber.

She checked the items the serving girls had laid out on a table beside the stool, then cleaned her hands in the wash basin, all the while aware of the eyes boring into her back. The tension grew worse when Balmaine resumed his seat upon the stool and his outer thigh settled against her leg.

Though she longed to step back, she determined he would not know the effect he had upon her and dipped a strip of cloth in water. She wrung it out and wound it about her hand.

"Duncan," Balmaine said, "leave us."

"But, my lord—"

"Leave us!"

"I suppose I should be heartened to know I am not the only one you treat so rudely," Graeye observed once the squire had gone. Still, she was sure the young man lingered not far down the corridor, prepared to defend his lord should she make an attempt upon his life. As if she posed a threat to a man such as he...

Withholding her gaze from him though she certainly felt his, she moved his hand aside and set to cleaning the wound. It was seeping now, the flow having been suspended by the pressure he had applied. Careful lest she start it welling again, she lightly wiped the cloth over it.

And still he stared at her, and still she refused to meet his gaze.

Once the wound was cleaned, she retrieved the needle and thread and turned back into the light. "I have not done this before," she murmured as she attempted to thread the elusive eye.

"What?" Balmaine barked.

She glanced over her shoulder at him. "I have seen it done. 'Tis simply sewing, and I am proficient at that."

His jaw convulsed, but he said no more.

"What is to become of my father, Baron Balmaine?" she asked, touching the thread to her tongue before making a second attempt to force it into the small eye.

"You ask that before laying a stitch to me?" he demanded.

Her second attempt failed, and she sighed. "I assure you, your answer will have no bearing on my handiwork. 'Tis what you imply, is it not?"

"What is your relationship with your father?"

She met his gaze. "He is my father."

"'Tis not what I asked."

Beside her, Groan growled.

"Nevertheless," Graeye said, "'tis the only answer you will have from me. There!" She held the needle up for him to see the thread that dangled from it.

Balmaine groaned.

"So what is to be my father's fate?" she persisted as she bent over his shoulder.

"Stitch first," he said, "then we shall talk."

Graeye drew a deep breath, pressed the pieces of flesh together, and pushed the needle in with a hand that was far from steady. To her relief, it easily slid in and out, the only sign of the baron's discomfort the rigid hold of his body.

With great concentration, she continued to ply the needle.

"The stitches need not be so small!" Balmaine snapped when she was barely halfway through. "Space them farther apart."

Frowning, she lifted her head and looked into fiery eyes that were too near her own, then quickly resumed her stitching. "You would not want there to be a great, ugly scar, would you?" she asked.

"One more will do me no harm. Do as I say."

She ignored his order and, for some reason, he allowed it.

After tying off the last stitch, she straightened and flexed her shoulders to ease the tightness that had settled into them, then she opened the pot of salve. As she rubbed the ointment over his stitched flesh, the tension once more escalated and she was grateful when the wound was finally bandaged.

She retrieved his clothing and dropped them in his lap. "Now I would know my father's fate."

Balmaine lifted the garments and inspected the damaged linen. Then he tossed them at Graeye.

Reflexively, she caught them.

"Hold them open over my head," he said.

Grudgingly, she stepped near and lifted the garments.

Immediately, his arm came around her waist, and he pulled her between his thighs.

Her cry of surprise had Groan rushing forward, snapping and growling.

"Back!" Balmaine shouted.

As if he understood the danger this man represented, Groan came no nearer, but neither did he retreat.

Heart beating so frantically that Graeye feared it might burst, she continued to hold the garments above Balmaine's head. "How long do you expect me to hold these for you?" she demanded.

He was silent so long that she was finally compelled to look at him. It was a mistake. Staring into wide pupils rimmed with incredible blue, she felt herself drift to the night past. Remembering his kiss and his arms around her, she nearly closed her eyes.

"Has Sir Michael touched you as I have?" he asked, and began stroking the small of her back.

Telling herself she felt nothing, she strained against his hold. "Let me go."

"Has he touched you?"

"You know that is not so!"

"Do I?" He raised his eyebrows. "I know only that he did not gain your virtue."

Shame flushed her with heat.

"Has he never touched your soft skin nor tasted your lips, *sweet* Graeye."

This time it was anger that warmed her. "Methinks you are jealous, Baron Balmaine."

His nostrils flared. "You have not answered me."

"And I will not."

He held her stare a moment longer, then released her and raised his arms.

Graeye hurriedly lowered the garments over his head and jumped away lest she suffer further assaults upon her wayward senses.

Balmaine rose and smoothed his tunic. After retrieving his belt and fastening it about his waist, he strode to the door.

"What of my father?" she spluttered.

He turned, raked his gaze over her, flexed his injured shoulder. "I have been thinking on him."

"And?"

"I have not decided."

She gasped. "You kept me waiting for that?"

He shrugged. "I must needs think on it more, but for the offense committed, it would not be undue punishment to take his life." He let that sit, then said, "Of course, there are other ways to ensure he never troubles me again."

"Then I pray God lightens your heart."

"Were you true and virtuous, Lady Graeye, I might feel compelled to believe prayer alone could do that, but I fear you will have to look elsewhere for a means of convincing me to have mercy on a man such as Edward Charwyck."

Heart feeling as if it were breaking into a thousand pieces that she would never be able to put together again, Graeye turned her back on Balmaine, leaned down, and stroked Groan between the ears.

Gilbert did not immediately retreat. Staring at her, he acknowledged that he did not understand this enigma who had earned his wrath with her cunning seduction. And frowned as part of him defended her, pointing out that she appeared a gentle soul, that her heart did not seem corrupt as he was so ready to pronounce it. Had not the servants been quick to defend her, bearing witness to the changes she had made and the compassion shown those in need of food and shelter? Had not her healing touch been gentle when it should have been anything but?

For answer, the greater part of him shouted that she was a Charwyck and her show of kindness was self-serving.

He nodded. She was not to be trusted. Ever.

Firm in his resolve, he turned away.

Graeye did not need to hear Balmaine's footfalls to know he had left, for it was well told in the easing of Groan's body. She sighed, crossed the chamber, and went directly to the room containing her mother's effects.

After removing the habit for the last time, she stood in her thin chemise and considered the blood Balmaine had left upon the white fabric. If she did not see to the stains immediately, the garment would be forever marked.

"So it shall," she whispered and folded it and placed it in the chest.

Once she had laced herself into the brown bliaut she had worn earlier that day, she returned to the hall. In the shadow of the stairway, Groan at her side, she went unnoticed as Edward's former retainers entered into the ceremony of homage, offering oaths of fealty to Baron Balmaine. Sir Michael was the last to pledge himself.

Graeye craned her neck to better see him when he stepped to the dais and, with great sorrow, watched as he knelt and placed his clasped hands within the baron's.

"Lord, I become your man," he said, voice strong with conviction.

Balmaine answered him.

Still kneeling, Sir Michael recited his oath of fealty. "Baron Balmaine, I vow to love what you love and loathe what you loathe, and never by word or deed do anything that should grieve you."

Balmaine answered him again, raised him to his feet, and bestowed a ceremonial kiss as he had done with the others. Then the servants hastened forward and began to position the trestle tables for the midday meal.

In the ensuing commotion, Graeye took the opportunity to leave the donjon without drawing notice. When she entered the outer bailey a short while later, she was disappointed to discover Groan had left her side.

Missing his companionship, she turned her thoughts to the two options available to her. She could search out her father or escape to the falls. She was debating the merits of each, her feet carrying her toward the postern gate, when the knight whom she had encountered earlier at the watchtower appeared.

She faltered, but when he did not attempt to detain her, she continued walking, and he kept pace with her. She glanced at him and thought him passing attractive. He had none of the dark attraction of Gilbert Bal—

She halted her thoughts. Of all the men who surrounded her, why had she chosen the heartless baron against whom to measure others?

She halted and turned to the knight. "What is it you want?"

His eyebrows shot up. "The baron thought you might require an escort. As he feels obliged to offer his protection until you return to the abbey, I am it."

She drew a deep breath. "When will I return to the abbey? Today?"

"'Tis too late now for the journey. I would guess first thing on the morrow."

Then she had the remainder of the day to set her plan in motion. "Sir...?"

"Lancelyn."

"As I do not require an escort, I ask that you allow me my privacy."

"Would that I could." He smiled apologetically. "I follow my lord's orders."

It was on her tongue to tell him what she thought of his "lord," but her training as a novice kept the words from her lips.

"Then I will not see you put out, Sir Lancelyn." She turned and retraced her steps.

She had thought he might let her go her way, but it was soon obvious he had no intention of allowing her out of his sight.

"Truly, is this necessary?" she demanded.

He drew alongside her. "Simply a precaution, my lady." He nodded at the donjon. "'Twould not be unseemly if you joined the others for dinner."

"If you are hungry, Sir Knight, pray, satisfy yourself. As for me, I have no appetite that would compel me to share a meal with your lord."

His lids narrowed. "You are working very hard at being a true Charwyck, Lady Graeye."

She halted, glared at him, then lifted her skirts and hurriedly mounted the steps.

Sir Lancelyn followed at a more leisurely pace.

Her rashness was a mistake, Graeye realized, for when she entered the hall, all eyes turned to watch her progress along the perimeter of the room. Though she did not intentionally seek out the baron, her gaze fell straightaway to his.

Eyebrows lifted, he nodded at her.

She lowered her chin and lengthened her short stride. When she reached the stairs, relief washed over her, for it was there Sir Lancelyn ended his pursuit.

She went directly to the small chapel and closed herself in. Here it was cool, the uncovered window allowing the breeze outside to stir the air within.

On her knees before the altar, she assumed the familiar position of prayer. But though she knew she ought to set herself to that most exalted task, she turned her thoughts to the plans that must be enacted this night if there was any possibility of saving her father and herself. For certain, tomorrow would be too late.

8

For hours, Graeye feigned sleep upon her bench in the hall. And was miserable for it. She kept her breathing deep and even and mumbled incoherent words when it was necessary to shift upon the hard surface. But though she felt guilty over the deception practiced upon Sir Lancelyn who had positioned himself on a straw pallet not far from where she lay, she more resented his interference and the man who had ordered him to it. If not for his night vigil, she was certain she would have found her way to her father hours ago. Perhaps they might even now be free of the castle.

Detecting a change in the knight's breathing, she turned her head and listened for some minutes to assure herself he had, indeed, fallen asleep. Once his state was confirmed, she turned her blanket back and rose from the bench.

With the exception of the wimple and veil, she had gone to bed fully clothed, wearing even her shoes so she would not have to search for them. Thus, she had only to make her way among those who bedded down in the hall.

As she lifted her skirts and cautiously stepped around the sleeping Sir Lancelyn, a low-pitched moan sounded from beneath her bench. She stilled, held her breath, and waited to discover if Groan had awakened the man. Blessedly, the knight's breathing did not change.

Graeye continued across the hall. Rather than risk the main entrance, she traversed the corridor through which servants carried the food from the kitchen in the inner bailey. As hoped, this door was unguarded, and she had only to lift the bar to let herself outside.

The air was brisk with the threat of an early winter, lifting her hair and stirring it about her face. It almost made her wish she had worn the wimple.

She gathered her tangled tresses, pushed them beneath the neck of her gown, and hurried to the front of the donjon. Keeping to the shadows afforded by cloud cover, she made good progress as she crossed the inner drawbridge to the watchtower where the glow of a lantern lit the lower floor.

Assuring herself all was quiet, she slipped inside. And paused at the sight of the unfamiliar guard near the stairs. Chin upon his chest, he barely retained his seat on a stool.

Slowly, she moved forward and peered closely at him. In his present state, he was harmless, but all would be ruined if he awakened.

Repenting as she went, she crossed to a second stool, lifted it, and returned to the guard. "Forgive me," she whispered and brought it down on the man's head.

With a grunt, he toppled to the earthen floor.

Graeye dropped to her knees beside him. After confirming he breathed without struggle, she regained her feet, pulled the lantern from its hook, and ran up the stairs.

She found her father in the cell he had earlier occupied. Curled on the straw pallet against the far wall, he remained unmoving when she set the lantern on the floor and crouched beside him. Gently, she shook his shoulder. "Father."

He shot up to sitting. Wild-eyed, he looked left and right of her before settling on her face and blinking as if to clear her from his vision.

"'Tis Graeye," she said.

He frowned, then demanded in a voice hoarse from ranting and raving, "For what are you here?"

She sat back on her heels. "I have come to release you."

He looked to the empty doorway. "How did you get in?"

Panged by her terrible deed, she said softly, "I rendered the guard unconscious."

"You?"

She nodded, but he appeared unconvinced. "Pray, Father," she beseeched, "let us make haste. We must be gone ere 'tis discovered what I have done."

"Gone?" He started to rise. "Not until I have my piece of flesh from Balmaine."

She grasped his filthy sleeve. "Would you be put to death before you can work your revenge?" It was the only argument that came to mind.

He laughed. "Certes, I shall have my revenge. And I shall have it now."

"You do not understand." She leaned near. "The baron is heavily guarded. It will do you no good to seek him this night."

To her relief, he seemed to consider her words, and after some moments muttered, "Mayhap you are right. And 'twould not satisfy me to simply slit his throat. I would have him suffer far longer—him and his murdering sister."

Though her stomach turned at the thought of the atrocity he hoped to visit upon the Balmaines, she was grateful to have gained the advantage. "Let us be gone from here." She urged him to standing.

Edward swayed, wrenched free of her hold, and lurched toward the door.

Graeye followed, only to collide with him when he came to an abrupt halt.

He swung around. "You shall remain!" He thrust a hand to the center of her chest.

She took two quick steps back to steady herself. But before she could appeal to him to allow her to accompany him away from Medland, he continued, "The king's man has assured me an escort will deliver you to the abbey—"

His words snapped off like the dry, brittle ends of a reed, lids narrowed as he lowered his gaze over her. On the return journey to her face, his mouth twisted and further bent out of shape when his eyes lit upon her uncovered head.

"Why are you dressed in this manner?" he rumbled, so dark and deep it struck her that if the devil were to speak, he would sound like the one who had fathered her.

Ignoring the inner voice that told her to retreat...to run...to put as much distance between them as possible, she said, "We must delay no longer. Once we are safely gone, we can—"

"I would know now!"

Of course he would, and it could mean the difference between escape and capture.

Graeye crammed her fingernails into her palms. "The habit became soiled," she said, fairly certain he had been unaware of what had transpired following his attack upon Balmaine when the baron's knights had supported him between them. "It must needs be laundered."

Edward was slow to respond, his enraged deliberation eating up moment after moment that could be put to better use. At last, he said, "Do not move from this cell until they come to return you to Arlecy."

"Nay!" The word burst from her, and she immediately regretted it.

Edward lunged forward and thrust his face so near hers she nearly gagged over the foul breath that sought to enter her every pore. "You dare defy me?"

Dear Lord, she whispered into herself, *he frightens me so.*

Keeping her eyes turned up to his, she said, "I beseech you, do not send me back to Arlecy. I would better serve you at your side."

"Serve me? Of what use could you possibly be?"

"I can cook and sew and write and, together, we will find another to whom you can pledge your services."

"Nay, *we* will not. You will take your vows and do penance for the devil that dwells in you."

Realizing the truth could no longer be avoided, and knowing it might unleash the devil in *him*, Graeye retreated a step, and another. "You have no choice but to take me with you. The abbey is no longer an option. One must be chaste to become a bride of Christ, and...I no longer am."

Silence. Dread silence that made her long to run for the door. And then the devil made an appearance.

"'Twas that dog, Balmaine, who spoiled you!" he roared.

Graeye was dumbstruck by the accuracy of his guess. How could he possibly know?

Then Edward was upon her, hands biting into her shoulders. "He violated you!"

"Nay!" She shook her head. "He did not force me."

His bared teeth bared further. "You gave yourself to him? Our enemy?"

"I did not know it was the baron. 'Tis the truth. I but wanted—"

One moment she was on her feet, the next sprawled on the musty straw pallet, one side of her face bursting with pain from the force of Edward's blow.

"Harlot!" he shouted, then wrenched her upright and landed the back of a hand to the other side of her face.

Graeye raised her arms around her head to protect it, but Edward knocked them aside and caught hold of her chin.

"The devil lurks in you," he spat.

Trembling hard, she peered into his mad, reddened eyes. "I am sorry, Father. I—"

He slammed a fist into her belly.

The pain was excruciating, and she would have doubled over had he not shoved her back onto the pallet.

Graeye rolled onto her side, drew her knees to her chest, and wrapped her arms around her head as she dragged in ragged breaths in an attempt to remain conscious. But the battle was likely lost, she realized as bright colors thrust against the backs of her lids and she registered that one of her hands was damp with blood. Would her father continue to beat her if she lost consciousness?

A shadow fell over her.

Forcing her lids up, she peered between her hands and saw Edward stood in the center of the room with the lantern held high above his head.

"From the devil you came, to the devil you shall return!" he shouted.

With darkness pressing in on all sides, promising the comfort of lost consciousness, she tried to make sense of his words—knew she must. And yet the temptation to sink beneath the black, swirling surface was so great she conceded it could do no harm to indulge herself a few minutes.

While you burn! a voice shrieked. *Look again, Graeye. Look!*

She blinked at her father, and it was then her eyes revealed what her mind refused to accept. He intended to burn her alive. "Nay!" she cried and struggled onto her knees.

Laughter swelled around the room, then the straw pallet burst into flames.

Graeye screamed and surged back onto her heels, pressing herself against the wall to avoid the hungry flames that did not seem to mind the damp, musty fuel it had been given.

"Burn!" Edward yelled from the doorway. A moment later, he turned his back on her.

Once more, darkness grabbed at Graeye. However, the breath of smoky air she pulled into her lungs made her cough so hard that she broke free of it. Opening her eyes wide, she stared at the fire to the front and sides of her and was surprised to find the flames were not yet high.

If I can make it to my feet...

As she inched her way up the wall, a long, low shape lunged through the doorway. It was followed by the figure of a man so tall he had to duck beneath the door frame to enter. Others came behind, but Graeye held her stinging gaze upon the impossible vision of Baron Balmaine until his image colored over into lovely blues, greens, and reds that shimmered like moonlight upon a veil of water.

Voices called to her. A dog bayed. Then, blessedly, the clamor melded into the thunder of water falling from a great height and she tumbled down...down...

She was not frightened when it wrapped around her, for it was warm and held her securely as it carried her through the winding currents. But then it turned cold, and the sudden change slapped her back to consciousness.

Graeye lifted her head to peer at the dark night and the people streaming around her, but her efforts were thwarted by a hand that pressed her face to a wonderfully solid chest.

She had just accepted it was not such a bad place to be when she realized she was being passed into another's arms.

She saw Balmaine's angry face a moment before it was replaced by Sir Lancelyn's.

"Take her to the donjon," the baron said. Then he was gone.

Struggling to make sense of what had happened, she lifted a hand and touched her face. Her breath escaped in a hiss as her fingers found the swelling alongside one eye and the gash on the opposite cheek.

She remembered. Dropping her hand, she turned her head and was horrified by the sight before her. The upper floor of the watchtower was ablaze, smoke billowing forth like a great, avenging storm.

Had Balmaine gone back into that? she wondered as she searched for him among the many who ran and shouted for water.

A moment later, the tower was swept from sight when Sir Lancelyn turned away. She had just resigned herself to darkness when she was shaken by a vision of the man she had struck senseless. Had he been discovered and pulled to safety?

"Nay!" She thrust a hand against the knight's chest. "The guard!"

He halted. "Guard?"

"Aye, he lies...within." She struggled to tell him more, but her tongue was too thick and slow.

Still cradling her, he swung back to face the fire. Then, with an angry exclamation, he set her on her feet.

She grasped his arm to steady herself.

"Give me your word you will stay here!" he commanded.

She nodded. "I vow."

Though he had to know the baron's wrath would fall upon him should she disappear, he loosed her hand from his arm and sprinted to the watchtower.

Graeye stared after him until he was swallowed by the smoke billowing out the door, then she dropped to her hands and knees. A moment later, something nudged her.

She pushed herself back to kneeling, lifted her head, and found her faithful companion before her.

"Groan," she whispered.

He licked her face, turned, and lowered to his haunches beside her.

Graeye draped an arm over his huge body and lightly explored her face as she watched the growing number of people who struggled to put out the fire. Nearly every place she touched was tender and swollen, especially around the eye whose vision was narrowing. Most confusing was the discovery that her cheeks were wet, but when she caught the sound of soft sobs and realized they were her own, she did not need to taste the salt upon her fingers to know she shed tears.

Shortly, two figures emerged from the burning building and took shape as they moved toward her. Not until they were nearly upon her did she see that one of them was Sir Lancelyn, and he had the unfortunate guard over his shoulder. The other was Baron Balmaine.

Swaying on her knees, she stared up at that blackened face, noting the flecks of ash in his hair and beard. Eyes like ice, he peered down at her from his great height.

It was the guard's moan that allowed Graeye to break eye contact. Where the man had been lowered to the ground beside her, he struggled to lift his head.

She reached to him, but the movement unbalanced her, and she tumbled forward. This time, she did not fight the dark but welcomed its comforting arms and thought it might be a good place to stay for a very long time.

9

W<small>HEN</small> G<small>RAEYE</small> <small>NEXT</small> looked out at the world, the light of dawn had turned the oiled linen golden, and there was evidence of an orange-streaked sky in the muted colors that filtered through the covering and glanced off the walls.

What was she doing in the refectory? She shifted her gaze to a flickering lamp. If discovered, Mistress Hermana would think it highly improper that she had made her bed in a room reserved for the taking of meals. And it would give the woman yet another excuse to assign Graeye additional chores and forbid her the gardens. Another excuse to lay a strap across her young charge's back.

Graeye considered sneaking back to her cell. However, though she might make it, her absence from morning prayers would surely be noticed.

Thinking it might go easier for her if she was presentable when she came face-to-face with that woman, she started to turn onto her side to raise herself up. But that small movement caused pain to rush through her head.

She dropped back, pulled her hands from beneath the covers, and touched her face. There was a gash over her cheekbone and a tender swelling above her left eye, which she only now realized was closed. And this was not the refectory. It was the chamber that had been her father's, that same room in which she had tended the baron's wound.

She lowered her hands and expelled a breath past a throat so raw and swollen she thought it must be nearly closed.

"'Tis more than you bargained for, eh?" a humorless voice said.

She swept her gaze up and to the left. Standing alongside the bed, a hand resting on a front poster, the baron looked down at her.

It was not merely his unexpected presence that shook her, though that would have been enough, but his state of undress seen clearly through the one eye she leveled upon him.

As if unaffected by the chill morning air, he wore an open under-tunic that allowed a glimpse of his chest and the edge of the bandage she had secured over his shoulder. Covering his lower body were loose chausses, the untied laces trailing as if he had recently donned them and in haste. For her benefit?

She briefly met his gaze, then turned her face away. Though she knew she must look horrible, it was not her vainglory that suffered when she peered into those probing eyes, but the vulnerable depths of her soul that this man seemed intent upon delving. She must protect herself from further hurt, and the sooner she erected the barriers that would stave off that event, the better her chances of coming out the other side of this deepening nightmare.

As she stared to the right, she reflected on the words the baron had spoken. It was true. It was all more than she had bargained for. In the space of a few weeks, a wondrous future had been placed in her hands, then cruelly snatched away. Desperate to reclaim some portion of it, she had given her body to this man only to be exposed and condemned. And now her father had tried to set her afire so he might return her to the devil.

Embittered by the next thought, Graeye almost laughed. Not even her worst day at the abbey had been so cruel.

Feeling the mattress sag as the baron lowered himself beside her, she turned her head farther to the side and fixed her gaze on the door.

Open, she silently implored. *Pray, someone—anyone—deliver me from this one's hate. I cannot bear it.*

When a hand cupped her chin, she did not resist its urging but moved her head back around to look at Gilbert Balmaine where he sat on the edge of the bed.

Once more meeting those unforgettable blue eyes, she was staggered by what seemed compassion in their depths. But even as she told her heart to find cover lest it be torn asunder, his eyes turned caustic again.

"You have discovered your father is a cruel man, hmm?" Balmaine narrowed his gaze on her swollen eye, then flicked back to the other to await confirmation.

Knowing she would gain little by defending herself, she determined that no matter what he faulted her with, she would maintain her silence.

He brushed his fingers over her jaw. "If not for that mangy dog of yours waking the donjon with his bellowing, you would have burned as your father intended."

She tried to pull her chin out of his grasp, but he held it firmly. Clenching her teeth, she lowered her gaze and stared across the foot of the bed.

Balmaine leaned into her sight. "Why did he do this to you?"

She had every intention of denying him an answer, and yet her hand lifted as if not her own and she touched his chest. "You," she breathed.

He was silent so long, one nameless emotion after another shifting across his face, that Graeye could only stare—until anger gathered upon his brow. She dropped her hand to her side and wondered at the wisdom of her disclosure. Yet another mistake?

He leaned nearer and set his other palm on the mattress beside her shoulder. "I tell you now, Lady Graeye"—his voice was dangerously soft—"your father's offense will not go unpunished. I will not rest until I have seen him join his son in hell."

She was stunned by his vehemence, but more so by his choice of words. Was it possible his anger stemmed from the harm done her?

Absurd, she chastised herself. *It is the damage to the castle that angers him, and most certainly the lives lost in putting out the fire.*

Tears stinging her eyes, sobs gathering below her throat, all of her aching beneath the burden of blame, she struggled to hold back the vulnerable expression of grief that must save until this man was gone from her.

"Naught to say?" he asked.

Slowly, she shook her head.

His gaze hardened further. "You are not even slightly curious as to the destruction wrought by your actions?"

She closed her one functioning eye so she would not be made to look upon his accusing visage. Nay, she did not want to know what her poor judgment had caused—could not bear to be told she was responsible for the deaths of others. Later she would face the truth, but God protect her from having to hear the details from this man.

"Graeye," he called to her, his voice oddly soft and insistent.

Had she heard right? The use of her given name without title brought her eye open again.

His face was nearer, his warm breath upon her lips causing her senses to spiral such that she momentarily forgot her body's aches and pains.

Lord, I hate myself for it, but how I long to feel his arms around me again...

As if he sensed her reaction to him, he drew back. "There were no deaths," he said.

"Truly?" she croaked and winced at the pain upon which that one word surged from her throat.

Something came and went in his eyes, then he nodded, released his hold on her, and rose from the bed. "Though the watchtower is destroyed, the fire was contained and the walls beyond salvaged." As he turned away, he drew a hand down his face. "Of course, it would have been of little consequence had it all gone up in flame."

"I am sorry," Graeye said, so low and strained she did not think he heard her, though she thought his back stiffened.

"There has been no sign of your father." He turned to her. "I would know where he has gone."

She shook her head.

He glowered. "For the love of God, you owe him no loyalty. Not only did he beat you, he tried to set you afire. Do you so easily forget that?"

As if she could...

It was not that she would not tell him, but that she was incapable of doing so. Still, she was loath to ponder what her answer would be if she did have the answer he sought. "Nay, I—" She swallowed on the pain searing her throat.

Balmaine's expression turned thunderous. "Protect him you may, but he will suffer my blade. This I vow."

"I do not know where he is," she whispered. "Truly, do you think he would tell me when he meant to..." Her mind flitted ahead to the words she had nearly spoken. It was one thing for another to speak of what her father had tried to do to her, quite another to acknowledge it aloud.

"Is it because you love him that you sought his release?" Balmaine asked.

"Love?" It was true she had longed for Edward's affection and would have given hers if he would have accepted it, but that sort of relationship he had refused her. "Nay, a man like my father has no need for love. I only wanted to help him."

Was it relief that softened Balmaine's eyes and relaxed his mouth? Not that it mattered. What mattered was what was to become of her. Did he still intend to return her to the abbey, or would he find another way to mete out punishment for her foolishness?

"You have said you will not rest until you have delivered my father to hell." She winced at how graveled her voice sounded. "I, too, am a Charwyck. Will you strive for my death as well?"

He gave a visible start of surprise, then narrowed his lids. "Were I so depraved as to wish your death, Lady Graeye, I would not have rescued you from the fire. Aye, you are a Charwyck and more than worthy of that name, but it will satisfy me well enough to see you back inside the walls of your abbey."

It should have been of comfort that he meant her no physical harm, but she could find little solace in his words. Not wishing him to see whatever ache might reflect upon her damaged face, she turned her head opposite.

Silence settled between them, then she heard Balmaine move away. The door opened and, after a brief pause, closed.

Groan was so quiet on his padded feet that Graeye was not immediately aware he had stolen inside. But when he trotted around the bed and propped his slavering chin on the coverlet to regard her with great, soulful eyes, there was no overlooking him.

She turned onto her side and laid a hand on his head. "Thank you, friend," she whispered, then curled into the tightest ball she could stand and yielded to the emotions she had held in check throughout her encounter with Balmaine.

Standing in the passageway, Gilbert's annoyance at having allowed the beast past him dissolved when he heard the sounds that slipped beneath the door.

He was alarmed by his reaction to the mournful sobs, for a woman's tears were a weakness he could ill afford. But neither could he deny their strong pull upon a heart that ought to be hardened against such.

He knew he should not mull what had just passed between Graeye Charwyck and himself, but the encounter disturbed him. Had she spoken true of her father's ignorance of their tryst—that the old man had not sent her to seduce him? Had revelation of her sin caused Charwyck to try to end her life?

It was believable that the man's hate for the Balmaines might be great enough that the loss of his daughter's virtue to the enemy would cause him to mortally turn against her. But still, that she had acted alone...

He recalled the explanation she had offered in the chapel but set it aside. It was too difficult to believe she had given herself to a stranger merely to avoid taking vows. Of course, perhaps there was more to it. Perhaps she had desired him as he had desired her when she had shown herself in the pool. As he still desired her.

He looked down at where her finger had grazed his skin when she had answered his question about her father's attempt to murder her. That singular contact had sparked his desire, and he had been furious that she could affect him so. Not even the beautiful Lady Atrice had elicited such a response.

Lust, he told himself. Animal lust that had nothing to do with the deeper emotions he had felt for that other woman who was now so far out of his reach he sometimes ached with longing. How different would his life have been if not for her death weeks before they were to wed?

The sobs from within the chamber quieted, or so he thought until he listened close. They were merely muffled, whether by a pillow or that great, hulking dog.

A woman's tears...

Memories of his sister, Lizanne, swept through him. Though seven years separated the siblings, he had been at her side to offer solace as she had grown from a babe into a young woman. She had needed him like no one else had—until recently. Married now, it was her husband, Ranulf, to whom she turned.

And who did Graeye Charwyck have to turn to? A dog.

Guided by emotions that strained past the barbed walls of his soul, Gilbert reached to the door. However, a sharp reminder of her deception pulled him back.

She had played him for a fool, used him to gain her own ends without thought for any save herself. She was a Charwyck through and through.

Clenching his hands, Gilbert strode opposite.

10

CLUTCHING THE COVERLET about her shoulders, Graeye leaned forward to better see out the window from which she had removed the oiled linen.

When the breeze took hold of her hair and swept it across her face, she pushed the strands behind an ear and continued to watch the stream of servants cross between the kitchen and the donjon bearing trays laden with food that sent savory scents wafting upward. Though she reached with her dulled senses to identify the various viands, she quickly lost interest in the dismal amusement.

She shifted her regard to the ominous structure being raised in place of the destroyed watchtower. Though it was far from complete, she was staggered by the efficiency with which it had been erected in a short time. Quite the feat, for only a sennight had passed since the fire.

What changes would Medland see come spring when the stage would be set for complete restoration of the castle? she wondered, grateful it no longer pained her that she would not be here to witness it. Surprisingly, it had not been as difficult as imagined to accept her fate. But then, considering the terrible events that had plagued her since departing the abbey, that place no longer seemed so unpleasant.

Blessedly, she had been left in peace these past days to work through her emotions and allow her ravaged face time to heal. Still, it had not been easy.

More than the loss of the future of which she had been allowed a glimpse, more than Balmaine's rejection and what he believed of her, and more than her pending return to the abbey, it had been hard to fully accept Edward's attempt to murder her. She had fought off the memories those first few days, but had finally found the strength to relive that night in all its grotesque detail.

She was grateful she had, for as painful as it had been, it had allowed her to see clearly what kind of man her father was—evil, of the same devil he accused her of being. True, he was very likely mad, but that did not excuse his actions.

That acknowledgement had freed her of the naiveté that had nearly ended her life, and she had vowed that never again would she leave herself so open and vulnerable to anyone.

Though she had dealt with her emotions on her own, her injuries had been tended by a healer named Lucy who had been brought from Penforke Castle—Balmaine's home—following the fire. The woman was kind and gentle, but Graeye closed her out, answering her questions only when a nod or shake of the head would not suffice. Fortunately, Lucy's services would not be needed much longer.

Graeye sighed, in the next instant startled.

"Then I shall drag her out myself!" Balmaine's voice carried down the corridor, announcing his advance toward her chamber long before his boots resounded on the wooden planks.

Dear Lord, he comes.

Although she had not seen him since the morning after the fire, each afternoon he had sent a servant to request her presence at the midday meal. Each day, she declined. Though she knew she only prolonged the moment when he would see her returned to the abbey, she had needed that time. Now it was at an end.

She grasped the edges of the coverlet closer but did not turn from the window, not even when the door was thrown open with nary a knock to announce her visitor.

An unnecessary courtesy, she mused. By din alone, the baron had announced himself.

Bracing an elbow on the embrasure, she rested her chin in her palm and wondered what it would take to teach manners to a man like Gilbert Balmaine. Reflecting seriously upon it, she nearly forgot he waited on her.

Gilbert was not averse to notifying the Charwyck woman of his presence when she persisted in feigning ignorance, for his tolerance of her continued refusal to come down from her chamber was a taut string ready to snap. He'd had enough of the game.

"Lady Graeye, methinks I should clarify myself." He crossed the room and halted behind her. "This time, 'twas not a request that you join me for dinner. It was an order."

He saw her shoulders rise with a deep breath, then she straightened and looked over her shoulder.

He should not have been surprised that she still bore the marks of her father's beating, but he was, and he hated that evidence of the cruelty visited upon her had yet to fade entirely. Still, she was much improved. The cut on her cheek appeared to be healing well, the swellings had gone down, the eye that had been closed was open, and the livid bruises had diminished such that they were mostly pale yellow and light purple.

"I have already eaten," she said and flicked a hand toward the tray that had been delivered this morn.

"Aye, and very little, I am told," he snapped, then gripped her arm and pulled her from the window.

Holding tight to the coverlet, she stumbled and nearly fell against him. Immediately, she jumped back as far as his hold on her allowed.

"Where are your clothes?" he asked, lowering his gaze down her and frowning over her bare feet.

"I am wearing all that I have."

He did not like her voice. It sounded almost lifeless. Thinking to rouse her, he pulled the coverlet from her shoulders, but though she should have been outraged to find herself standing in only a thin shift that clearly outlined her body, her only reaction was to protectively cross her arms over her chest.

"Considering there is less of you to see than what you previously revealed to me," he tried again, "your modesty is out of place."

Still no outrage. With another sigh, she dropped her arms to her sides and lifted her chin. "But I did not reveal myself to you, Baron Balmaine."

He was taken aback. "Truly? Who, then, did you seduce at the waterfall?"

She shrugged. "He did not tell me his name. I know only that he was a man who revealed nothing of the black heart that beats within his chest."

Gilbert was further disturbed by her behavior. He had heretofore glimpsed the tentative claws this small cat extended, but there had been little conviction behind her swipes. Now...

He berated himself for having left her alone so long. She had grown cold and indifferent, and it reminded him of the bitter years his sister had endured and which yet haunted him.

He did not intend to revisit those memories, but they dragged him back to when he had failed Lizanne. She had needed him desperately, and though he had fought to come to her aid, he had been struck down. The battle scars he bore and accompanying limp were all marks of shame for that night long past.

A touch upon his chest returned him to the present, and when he looked down, he saw concern in Graeye's eyes.

"Gilbert?" she said softly.

The sound of his name on her lips chased away memories of the distant past—and of her treachery. Remembering the softness of her body and their one night together, he pulled her close, lowered his head, and covered her mouth with his.

Graeye startled, in the next instant stiffened to ward off the traitorous sensations swirling through her. She knew what this man was capable of doing to her, and as there could be no outcome other than that which had already been dealt her, she would rather die than let him do it again.

She dragged her hands up his chest, pressed her palms to it, and thrust backward. "Nay!" she cried when her mouth came free.

"Graeye," he rasped and once more lowered his head.

She strained to the side, and it was her neck he fell upon, the touch of his lips stealing her breath and nearly scattering her resolve.

Do not, Graeye! she silently screamed. *You vowed you would not!*

Setting her teeth, she brought her knee up between his thighs.

He shouted and lurched back.

Knowing that when he recovered he would be furious, she strained to break free. And nearly made good her escape, but he caught her back and drew her with him to the bed where he dropped and pulled her down beside him.

She tried to sit up, but he held her fast and all she could do was lie back and await his wrath.

When several minutes passed and nothing untoward occurred, she grew more wary. What did he intend?

Slowly, she turned her face toward his. And her dread transformed into surprise.

Head resting on an outstretched arm, Balmaine stared back at her, countenance devoid of the anger she had been certain would be there. Indeed, one corner of his mouth was raised higher than the other.

"Where does a novice learn to do that?" he asked.

She frowned. "What?" Then, realizing what he meant, she said, "I am sorry you forced me to harm you, but 'tis all you deserved."

The other corner of his mouth lifted, and he rose up onto his side and propped his dark head on a hand. "Aye, it was deserved. And quite effective as you well know."

Graeye wondered what game he played—and how he would retaliate.

When he moved away from her, it was so sudden it took her a moment to realize he had risen from the bed.

"I owe you an apology, Lady Graeye." He adjusted his belt. "It was wrong of me to press my attentions upon you."

An apology? She sat up.

"In future," he continued, "I suggest you clothe yourself properly, use my title when you address me, and keep your hands to yourself."

She should keep her hands to herself? Anger once more an ally, Graeye glared at him.

He glanced at her. "You ought to know that such familiarity between a man and woman does not always go unanswered." He turned, strode to the door, and paused. "I will send a servant to aid in outfitting you for dinner. Do not keep me waiting long or I will see you clothed myself. Understood?"

How could she refuse such a threat? Graeye pushed off the bed, crossed to the window, and tossed over her shoulder, "Perfectly, my lord."

Behind, the door closed softly.

Attired in another of her mother's old garments and having eschewed the cover of a wimple, Graeye entered the hall just as Balmaine rose from his chair, surely to come after her as he had warned he would do.

He beckoned, reseated himself, and indicated the nearest of two empty places to his left.

As she was ushered forward by the young maid who had coaxed her into allowing her hair to be plaited, Graeye felt the curious stares that followed her progress across the stretch of floor.

She knew the sight she presented. Not only did she bear the "devil's mark," but ample evidence of Edward's beating. But though her humiliation should have been great, she was so curiously unmoved that she lifted her chin higher.

"You become more brave each day," Balmaine murmured as she lowered beside him.

She ignored his gibe and turned her attention to the trencher placed before her. Typically, she would have shared it with another, but as she had arrived in the midst of the meal, there was none with whom to divide it. She picked around the chunks of meat, looking for the bits of vegetables she preferred. As she indulged, she glanced at those seated around the hall and soon realized the king's men were no longer present. When had they departed Medland?

Does it matter, Graeye? she silently chided. *'Tis not as if it is your home any longer.*

Something landed in her lap, and she startled, but it was only Groan. Slobbery chin marking her skirts, he peered up at her.

She smiled and patted his head. Though he had been her constant companion during the first days of her recovery, he had grown restless and she had seen him only on the rare occasions when he wandered into her chamber for a quick stroke and the leavings of her meals.

Searching out a worthy morsel among those in her trencher, she slipped it into his mouth.

"Careful lest that animal grows any bigger," someone jested.

Until that moment, she had not realized someone had taken the seat to her left, but she knew the voice.

"Sir Michael," she said with a nod.

Why he would offer her the warmth of his smile she did not know, but she appreciated it.

He leaned toward her. "I had begun to think myself invisible," he said, then caught up her hand and brushed his lips across the backs of her fingers.

She returned his smile and slid her hand from his grasp.

"What do you at the lord's table?" she asked, surprised Balmaine should look kindly upon any of Edward's former retainers.

The young knight moved nearer, and his lips nearly touched her ear. "I have found favor with the baron."

Uncomfortable with his proximity, she drew back. "Pray, tell how you accomplished such a feat."

He grinned. "The supervision of the building of the new watch-tower was given to me. 'Tis a great responsibility, and for that, I am late to meal."

He did not need to elaborate further. Having seen that worthy structure, Graeye understood how he had pleased Balmaine. However, Sir Michael did elaborate, beginning with a narrative on the complexities involved with such a project.

She listened, made a few comments, and when he moved too near, scooted opposite along the bench.

Groan followed her progress, grumbling each time the man advanced on her.

After a time, Graeye found herself at the edge of the bench, one leg pressed against Sir Michael's, the other tight against Balmaine's chair. Making no attempt to mask her irritation, she looked around into angry blue eyes. And knew Balmaine had been following her conversation with Sir Michael.

But why did his anger seem directed at her? It was the knight who had encroached upon her, not the other way around. By neither manner nor word had she encouraged him.

Abruptly, Balmaine stood, declared the meal at an end, and ordered all but a handful from the hall.

"Lady Graeye," he said as she rose, "I would have a word with you ere you retire to your chamber."

Reluctantly, she lowered back to the bench while the others, including Sir Michael, exited the hall.

Groan, surely sensing there was booty to be had, trotted off to join the other dogs who followed the last of the serving wenches out. Though there was still much to be done to see the hall set aright, it had been cleared sufficiently for the lord to carry out his business.

Graeye watched as the half-dozen men instructed to remain behind, Sir Lancelyn among them, gathered at the far end to await their lord's summons. When they began talking amongst themselves, she supposed it was so they would not appear to be listening in on Balmaine's discussion with her.

She twisted around to face him.

Fastening his eyes upon her, he raised a booted foot to the edge of the table and pushed back in his chair until his weight was balanced on the rear legs. "Lady Graeye," he said, beginning to knead his thigh, "such behavior as I have seen displayed here today is unbecoming of a lady."

She was not surprised by his interpretation of what had transpired, but she was offended—and all the more so that the one who took her to task was tipped back in his chair like an errant boy. "As you obviously refer to Sir Michael's conduct," she said, "should you not take up the matter with him?"

"I will speak to him of it, but he is not entirely at fault for responding to your invitations."

Graeye jumped to standing and looked down at Balmaine where he perched precariously on his chair. "You see through the eyes of a man," she raised her voice, uncaring as to whether or not she drew the attention of the others. "And only that which you wish to see. I neither encouraged Sir Michael, nor invited his attentions. In the past, he has been kind to me. That is all. I was simply returning the courtesy."

Balmaine steepled his fingers before his face. "Then you would not be interested in him taking you to wife?"

Her breath caught, and she sank back to the bench. Why did his question dishearten her when it ought to be a light in her darkness? Though her mind immediately supplied the answer, she fiercely denied it. She had no liking for this black-hearted giant. None.

Determinedly shifting her emotions away from him, she pondered the reason Sir Michael still wished to wed her. Because Edward was missing, relieving him of the burden of also assuming responsibility for a man he detested? And what of her return to the abbey? Had Balmaine not made it clear he would be satisfied with nothing less than her confinement within those walls? If that was still the case, then he must be taunting her, dangling the possibility of marriage as revenge for the incapacitating blow she had earlier dealt him.

She searched his eyes for laughter, and finding none, said, "I do not understand."

"'Twould seem Sir Michael is enamored of you and wishes you for his wife. I was told he challenged Sir William for your hand, but that you refused him." He raised his eyebrows. "I am curious if you would do so a second time given the abbey is your only other option."

Graeye knew she did not owe him an explanation for the reason she had decided against the young knight, and yet she said, "As there would have been bloodshed had I not refused Sir Michael, I agreed to wed Sir William."

"You were content to do so?"

Suppressing a shudder at the thought of being that man's wife, she said, "Edward chose him for me."

"But now you would agree to take Sir Michael as a husband?"

After having accepted the abbey was a better place than this cruel world? Certainly not. And the sooner she left Medland, the better.

Still, she would play a bit longer. "Is it a choice you offer me, Baron Balmaine?"

"It is one I am seriously contemplating. *Would* you accept him?"

She made him wait on her answer, then said, "I would not."

Surprise momentarily recast his face, and she felt a prickle of satisfaction. If it was a game he played, she had won.

"Why?" he asked.

"As you have said repeatedly, my place is at Arlecy. Though I did not wish to return there, I accept it now—welcome it, even."

"Then you prefer the abbey to marriage?"

"I do. Too, I fear I would not make Sir Michael a good wife."

"For what reason?"

"I do not have the sort of feelings for him that would make for a satisfactory union."

Balmaine removed his foot from the table's edge, allowed his chair to drop onto its front legs, and sat forward. "Has no one told you 'tis not necessary to feel deeply for the man you wed?" he said low. "There is one purpose to marriage, and I am sure you would be able to fulfill that part of the contract, Lady Graeye."

She held her tongue, stared at him.

He stared back, then leaned so near his breath caressed her face. "Is there another you would choose?"

How she wished her heart did not so beat so hard, her gaze was not tempted to his mouth, memories of his kisses were not so eager to unfold. Pulling herself back from the edge over which she could easily plummet, she put her chin up. "There is no other."

Slowly, he sat back. "Then we are in agreement as to your future."

She smiled tightly. "We are."

"Good. See that your belongings are packed. You leave at first light on the morrow."

She was dismissed, as further evidenced when he turned his gaze from hers, motioned his men forward, and once more tilted his chair onto its hind legs.

Graeye rose and stepped away, but then something—some bit of mischief for which Mistress Hermana would have laid a strap to her—made her turn back. "Take care you do not upend yourself, Baron Balmaine," she said, "for it would hardly be becoming of a great baron such as yourself."

His eyes glittered, but he did not lower his chair.

She inclined her head, pivoted, and retreated to her chamber.

11

Among the generations of Charwycks long since departed, Graeye knelt before the grave of the one who had borne that name through marriage only. Clutching a spray of wilting flowers, scant survivors of summer's last harvest of color, she drew her mantle about her and bowed her head.

"I have missed you, Mother," she whispered, loath to speak too loudly in this hallowed place. "I…" Tears rushing forth, she could not utter another word for fear the sobs gathering in her chest would escape.

She breathed deep, swallowed, drew the back of a hand across her eyes, and flung away the moisture. When the constriction about her throat and ribs eased, she said, "Forgive me for failing you."

She remembered her mother's strength and determination, that she had been a woman who, even faced with one as daunting as Edward Charwyck, had not allowed him to trample her. Always, she had found a way around his anger and gained for herself and her unwanted daughter what they needed. But then she was gone, leaving her child to fend for herself.

Graeye closed her eyes, wished she knew how to handle opposition well enough to gain control over her own future. "I am learning," she murmured.

She laid the flowers on the grave and stood. Though the lower portion of her bliaut had become sodden from kneeling in the dew-laden grass, she paid it no heed and turned from the secluded grave.

As she neared the freshly turned ground where Philip lay, she slowed. Feeling a chill that made her long to hug her arms about herself, she crossed to her brother's grave. How long she stood there she did not know, but when she lifted her head, the first rays of the sun had struck the sky.

"You mourn for him?" a voice carried across the cool air.

She swung around.

Cloaked in a dark green mantle that hung past his knees, allowing only a glimpse of black chausses tucked into boots, Balmaine watched her.

She straightened to her full height. "You intrude, sir," she said and wondered how his mere presence could chase the chill from her limbs.

"My apologies." He bowed curtly and strode forward. "I would not have encroached, but your escort awaits."

Graeye turned her back on him and looked again at Philip's grave. "There is something that disturbs me," she said, "and I would have you tell me yea or nay."

Balmaine drew alongside her. "If I can answer it, I shall."

She looked up. "Did my brother accept the cross ere he died?"

A mess of emotions swept across his face before his expression turned stony. "It was not even a consideration. Philip Charwyck died a coward."

Her anger quickened, and she turned and walked opposite.

A moment later, he caught her arm and pulled her around. "Trust me in this," he said. "Even had a cross been thrust upon his shoulders, he would not have accepted it."

"As you would not?" she tossed back. "I hardly knew Philip, so I cannot judge him, but I have come to know your black heart, Gilbert Balmaine." She swiped at the hand with which he held her. "Be careful lest you suffer the same fate as the man you slaughtered."

His face suffused with color. "I will clarify one point, Lady Graeye. 'Twas not I who laid your brother down, though I would have welcomed the opportunity to do so."

She gave a short laugh. "Think you I do not know it was your wicked sister who dealt the killing blow? That she did it to save you from Philip's blade? Nay, no matter my brother's crimes, he was not the coward. It was your sister and you!"

"You are wrong."

"I saw the wound myself!" Her belly rolled as she was returned to the night she had spent with her brother's corpse. "Shot through the back like an animal."

Surprise spasmed across his face. "You saw? But your brother would have been dead near a fortnight when you were brought from the abbey. He would have been buried long before then."

"Ha! Do you think Edward would shield me from such an atrocity? He forced me—"

Realizing she revealed too much, she momentarily closed her eyes, then said softly, "Beware, Balmaine. For all the evil of which you accuse Edward, you do not know him. Do not feel bad, though, for I did not truly know him until recently. And he is my—" Again, she stopped herself, for she wanted never again to acknowledge him as her father.

Balmaine pulled her chin up. "What did he force you to do?"

She lowered her gaze.

"Tell me!"

She compressed her lips.

"I will know, Graeye!"

"Or what?" She lifted her eyes to his.

He stared at her. "I want to understand."

"Do you?"

"Aye."

"Very well. Then understand this. I spent a night with the rotting corpse of my dead brother, on my knees in the chapel, praying him into heaven and asking God to see justice done to those who had murdered him. So tell me again of my deceit, Baron Balmaine—after you repent of yours."

First anger, then compassion poured through Gilbert. Deep, red anger for Edward Charwyck's cruelty. Then that same compassion he had been fighting almost from the moment he had first seen Graeye Charwyck. And there was something deeper yet.

He ground his teeth. He did not want to care for this woman. He did not want to feel the pain she had suffered at her father's hands. He wanted her gone from Medland before she could weave another of her witching spells around him. He wanted her forgotten.

"You know naught of what transpired that day," he said and released her. "But mayhap it is best you think the worst of me than know the kind of man your brother was." He turned and started toward the castle. "Go back to your abbey, child," he tossed over his shoulder, then relinquished her to her fate.

12

Arlecy Abbey, England
Early Spring, 1156

"How long did you think to keep it from us?" the abbess asked as she lifted her hand from the softly rounded belly.

Graeye Charwyck lowered her eyes.

Settling in to await a response, Mother Celia clasped her hands at her waist and reflected on the young woman's return to the abbey nearly five months past. Though Graeye had always been a solemn soul, there was something changed about her—a sadness that often came with disillusionment of the heart.

From the day she had returned, she had been thus. When she had been urged to complete her vows of sisterhood, she had refused, offering only a tersely written note from the new baron of Medland to support her decision. Subsequently, she had entered the order of the convent and kept herself conspicuously absent from all but those activities she was required to attend.

However, there was also a quiet strength and resolve to Graeye's character that showed itself more clearly with each passing day. No longer did she seem ashamed of the mark upon her face, refusing to don a wimple despite Mistress Hermana's insistence. Chin high, she carried herself well among the others, paying little attention to their stares. Gone was the reserved young woman who had left the abbey with dreams in her eyes.

The abbess loosed a weary sigh. Though her instincts had proved correct regarding the loss of her charge's virtue, she had not expected this result. Irritated, she tapped a foot among the rushes as she once more settled her gaze on Graeye's waist which, beneath the voluminous bliaut, hinted at nothing out of the ordinary.

If not for Sister Sophia's experienced eye, it might have been several more weeks before any knew of her condition. But why had Graeye kept it to herself this long? After all, it was not unusual for daughters of the nobility to be sent to the abbey to birth misbegotten children to avoid dishonoring their families. Even now there were three others at the convent in various stages of pregnancy. Surely she had not hoped to give birth with none the wiser?

Graeye knew she owed the abbess an explanation and her silence was disrespectful, but though she had feared the revelation of her secret was behind her summons, still she was unprepared. But it was time.

She met the abbess's gaze. "Forgive me. I was ashamed," she spoke the words that best expressed the knot of anxiety that had settled within her when she had guessed her state three months past.

"Ashamed?" Mother Celia's eyes shone with kindness and understanding that made Graeye long to seek the comfort of her arms. "Methinks 'tis likely you have little to be ashamed of, Lady Graeye. This was, after all, a man's doing."

Since she had been a novice ready to take her vows, Graeye was not surprised the abbess believed her pregnancy was a result of forced intimacy. Though it would have been easier to let her continue to believe it, she could not lie to her, not even by omission.

She shook her head, once more averted her gaze. "'Twas entirely my own doing. I blame no one but myself."

Silence.

Venturing a look at the other woman, she was encouraged by the compassion upon Mother Celia's face.

"I shall leave here if it pleases you," Graeye offered.

"Where would you go, child?"

As she contemplated this question—and not for the first time since discovering the new life growing inside her—the abbess took her arm and led her to a bench. Graeye lowered to it and watched Mother Celia cross to a sideboard across the room. Shortly, the woman returned with a goblet of watered wine.

"Drink it all," she said and seated herself beside Graeye. "Then we will talk of your future."

Relieved that, at last, here was someone with whom she could speak of her fears, Graeye quickly drained the goblet.

A placid smile upon her lips, Mother Celia took the goblet and set it aside. "Now, tell me of the father. Is he wed?"

Graeye was painfully aware she did not know the answer. While at Medland, she had not thought to ask after Balmaine's marital status—had assumed he was without wife. "I do not believe he is," she murmured.

"Hmm. Think you he would be willing to wed you if he does not have a wife?"

Graeye nearly laughed. Gilbert Balmaine wanted nothing to do with her, misbegotten child or not.

"He would not." Her throat tightened. "Methinks he would first give himself to the..." Prudently, she withdrew the word that had nearly passed her lips.

Mother Celia nodded. "And he knows naught of the babe?"

"Naught."

"Do you fancy yourself in love with him?"

"Nay!" Graeye gasped. "He is the veriest of curs."

Mother Celia reflected on the note given her the day of Graeye's return. Though brief, the baron had been explicit regarding Graeye's entry into the convent. Because she had not wanted to read too much into it, Mother Celia had not understood then what she was fairly certain she understood now. There was no reason for the man to have concerned himself with this young woman's future at the abbey unless he had knowledge of her undoing—a knowledge, she suspected, that was of a personal nature.

"Worry not." She patted Graeye's clenched hands. "You will be provided for. Now seek your rest."

Her charge thanked her, rose from the bench and, moments later, closed the door behind her.

For some minutes, Mother Celia contemplated the best course of action, then she rose and crossed to her writing desk.

13

THE COLD WINTRY months that followed Graeye's return to the abbey did little to improve Gilbert's disposition. Not only were his days filled with the management of his newly expanded estates, but coordination of numerous forays against the brigands who attacked the villages.

Worse, the long nights dragged by on leaden feet. When sleep finally came, too often his dreams were touched by sad, silvery eyes, soft lips that rarely knew a smile, and silken strands that ran through his fingers in an endless stream of gold. But though he tried to banish his visions of Graeye by calling up the faded memory of Lady Atrice, it was futile. It made for a restless sleep and a foul temper when the morn finally presented itself.

Five months after Graeye's return to Arlecy, a messenger made his way through a frigid, pelting rain to Medland in search of Baron Balmaine, only to be told he had returned to Penforke. Sir Lancelyn, whom Gilbert had named the castellan of Medland, bade the man to pass the night at the castle and, before the sun rose the next morning, sent him on his way with a small escort to speed and ensure his safe journey. Thus, the disgruntled messenger seemed nearly in as foul a mood as Gilbert when he was ushered into the great hall at Penforke.

After an introduction that Gilbert cut short with an impatient wave of his hand, the man was led to a bench against the far side of the room to await an audience. The time lengthened, and when the messenger was finally called to deliver his message, it was found he had fallen asleep.

Having spent a good portion of the morning confined with his steward who had painstakingly cited the losses suffered from raiding brigands, Gilbert had little tolerance for the messenger's fatigue. Thus, he divested the man of his duty by retrieving the missive himself.

Without regard for the elaborate wax seal that held the parchment closed, Gilbert broke it and strode back to where his steward bent over the books. He thrust the parchment at the man.

Though Gilbert could read well enough, he found it and writing to be tedious work. Given a choice, he left it to his steward, or any other man capable of that rare talent with words.

Leaning back against the edge of the table, he drummed his fingers on its surface and waited for his steward to divulge the contents.

"'Tis from the abbess of Arlecy," the man said, squinting at the broken seal.

Gilbert stilled.

"She says, 'Baron Balmaine, there is a discreet matter of great import that I must discuss with you regarding Lady Graeye Charwyck." He cleared his throat. "She—"

Gilbert snatched the parchment from him. Ignoring the steward's stammered entreaty, he turned the missive toward the light of a torch and read: *She is many months with child.*

Gilbert struggled to get his emotions—anger, disbelief, suspicion, and something he refused to name—under control. Expelling his breath, he momentarily closed his eyes. Then he reread the message from the beginning. It ended with: *As she was last under your guardianship, I ask that you make haste to call at Arlecy so we might discuss this matter.*

Allowing the parchment to curl in upon itself, Gilbert drew a hand down his face and raked his fingers through his thick growth of winter beard. Was it possible Graeye carried his child—after but one night together? If she did, why had she waited so long to inform him of her condition? Was this another of her carefully worked deceptions?

In spite of his yearning for her, he knew he must not forget she was a Charwyck, and that it could as easily be another man's child she carried. If she carried a child at all.

Grudgingly, he acknowledged that even without the arrival of the missive, the unwanted bond between Graeye and himself would have had to be addressed eventually. There was unfinished business between them, and it must be seen through to its completion if he was to free himself of the stranglehold she had on him.

Still, if she did carry his child...

His thoughts turned to the trap he had planned to lay for the brigands two days hence. It was an opportunity he was loath to let pass, for if carried out without mishap, it would likely see Edward Charwyck, the brigands' leader, delivered into his hands.

Until that moment, he had thought there was nothing he wanted more than to apprehend the man. He was wrong.

He groaned, crumpled the crisp parchment, and called for his squire.

14

❧⁓❧

WITH GROWING IMPATIENCE, Gilbert paced the room he had been asked to wait in a very long half hour past. From time to time, he stopped before the window and scanned the courtyard below and the winter-ravaged garden beyond it that made one think spring had forgotten its place in the order of the seasons. Then he resumed his pacing.

What was keeping the abbess? Though he had given no warning of his arrival, he had been assured she would be along shortly. Considering the chill weather, his men were surely growing restless where they awaited him outside the abbey walls. Had he known the wait that lay ahead, he would have insisted they were brought inside as well.

He dropped down on the hard bench facing the door and began to massage his leg. Since he and his men had left Penforke two days past, nearly every waking hour had been spent in the saddle. Though that by itself did not usually trouble his old injury, coupled with the cold damp weather, it was nearly painful.

Perhaps the abbess was in the midst of none, that time of prayer taken shortly after dinner, he allowed, trying to reason himself out of the foul mood into which he was sinking more deeply with each passing minute.

Shortly, a light rap sounded on the door.

"Come," he called and stood as the door was pushed inward.

Tall and regal as any queen, the abbess entered and closed the door behind her. "Baron Balmaine," she said when she came to stand before him, "I am Mother Celia, Abbess of Arlecy."

Having expected Graeye to accompany her, he was disquieted by her absence. Was she in the corridor awaiting a summons? Or did she wait in one of those buildings where none but the clergy ventured?

He bowed, then removed the travel-weary parchment from his belt. "You wished to discuss this matter of Lady Graeye."

Smiling faintly, she took the missive and lowered to the bench. "I do. First, however, I must apologize for having begun to question your sense of responsibility, Baron. You see, I expected you sooner, and when you did not come…" She shrugged and gracefully raised her palms.

Irritated by the veiled reprimand, Gilbert crossed to the window and stared down at the small procession of nuns crossing the courtyard. They kept to a line so straight and unwavering he could have been watching a military parade.

"As I was not at Medland when your message arrived," he said, "it was delayed until it could be delivered to me at Penforke."

"Ah. Well, now that you are here, we have much to discuss. Come, sit beside me." She indicated the length of vacant bench.

He turned to face her, but remained at the window. "Where is Lady Graeye?"

She nodded at the window. "If she is not there yet, she soon shall be. After dinner, she feeds the birds."

Gilbert looked over his shoulder into the courtyard. For the first time, he noticed the mass of birds that walked the flagged stones and flitted ledge to ledge as they awaited their meal. Graeye was nowhere to be seen. He returned his regard to the abbess and shook his head.

"Soon," she said in a tone surely meant to reassure him but only further irritated him.

Did she think him anxious to catch sight of Graeye? It was mere curiosity that bade him search her out.

"I would have expected her to accompany you," he said, forcing indifference into his voice.

"Oh, nay." The abbess vigorously shook her head as if to impress upon him the error of his assumption. "I assure you, Lady Graeye knows naught of your coming, Baron."

He frowned. "Then?"

She pinned him with her serene gaze. "Upon discovering Lady Graeye's condition, I took it upon myself to contact you. You are responsible, are you not?"

Gilbert leaned a shoulder against the wall alongside the window. "She has said I fathered the child she carries?"

What seemed a self-satisfied smile flitted across the woman's face. "Nay, but I have guessed correctly, have I not?"

If she was to be believed, and Gilbert was reluctant to extend his doubt of God to this woman, then his conclusions about Graeye's character lost much of their credibility. It unbalanced him to hear she had not claimed him as the father and that she was unaware he had been summoned.

Still, he shrugged nonchalantly. "There is a possibility the child is mine, but only that."

The abbess inclined her head. "Then 'tis certainly yours."

Gilbert narrowed his gaze. "I do not know that." What trickery was she attempting to work upon him?

"I have long known Lady Graeye—though, I admit, not well. I was but a sister of the order when she first came to us…" The abbess paused. "…eleven years ago." She offered him a smile that lit her features and made her considerable number of years dwindle.

Settling in for the duration, he folded his arms over his chest and nodded for her to continue.

"Graeye has always kept to herself—a very sad child when she came to us. Most of the children sent to Arlecy do visit their homes, though it may be infrequently. But it was not so for Graeye. Not until her father sent for her last autumn did she leave Arlecy since arriving as a child. Indeed, never did she receive visitors. It is not an easy life she has had."

For an unguarded moment, Gilbert began to soften. However, he hardened himself by dragging forth the memory of Graeye's deception.

"Although I have never met the man," Mother Celia continued, "I have heard much of Baron Edward Char—"

"No longer baron," Gilbert corrected.

The woman nodded. "But this I know. Though the blood that runs through Lady Graeye is of her father, she is not of his ilk."

Determined to maintain his beliefs about Graeye, he stared at the woman and wondered what enlightenment she might use next to persuade him of whatever she aspired to.

"I had great hopes for her in your world, Baron," she said, "for I have always known it was not in her heart to join the sisterhood—"

"Then why did she consent to take the veil?" Gilbert interrupted and immediately regretted having once more stepped upon the woman's words.

She let his rudeness pass without reproach. "There was no other option for her, and it was her father's wish that she become a nun."

"Why?"

"The mark she bears." Mother Celia touched a finger alongside her own eye. "Though I know it is but a mark of birth, there are others who say it is of the devil. That was also her father's belief, and methinks he sought to appease God by offering Graeye to Him."

Turning this over in his mind, Gilbert looked out the window into the courtyard where a single figure had appeared. Though she was covered head to foot in a dark mantle and her back was turned to him, he knew it was Graeye. Vaguely aware he held his breath, he watched as she attempted to coax a bird down from its perch atop a roof. Unable to resist the offering of a crust of bread, it was not long in descending.

Gilbert felt not only a softening about his heart, but a crumbling of the walls that guarded it. Again, his mind threw up her deceit, but it was useless. It seemed she had not set out to trap him into marriage, but still she had used him to avoid taking vows. After a struggle so fierce he felt as if he had taken on wounds as formidable as the one that scarred his leg, he conceded to a standoff between heart and mind. But it was a confusion he could not afford—a tumultuous mix of antagonism and yearning that he could see no way to mesh.

"How many months is she with child?" he asked, frustrated by his inability to glimpse the shape of Graeye's body beneath the layers of winter clothing.

"It approaches five months since she returned here," the abbess said as she rose. "So she is at least that far along. No less, I assure you."

Gilbert worked his jaw as he followed Graeye's progress about the courtyard. He willed her to turn so he could gain a better view of her and see again the delicate beauty of her face. He was disappointed when she unknowingly fulfilled his desire, for her hair and features were hidden beneath her hood.

"She does not belong in a cloister of nuns," the abbess said where she came to stand alongside him. "Lady Graeye is of your world."

"You are right, she does not belong here."

"Then you will wed her and give her child your name?"

Without hesitation, Gilbert said, "It would be impossible for me to marry her."

Mother Celia frowned. "I do not see the difficulty. I have inquired and been told you are without a wife. Mayhap you are betrothed?"

"Nay," he ground out. "Were I of a mind to wed a Charwyck, there would be naught to prevent me from doing so, but I would never entertain such. Thus, 'tis not the solution you seek to this dilemma."

The woman studied him. "I know naught of your dispute with the Charwycks, Baron Balmaine, but I would ask that you not visit the sins of Lady Graeye's family upon her. She cannot be held responsible for wrongs done you by their hands."

"What of the wrongs done me by *her* hand?" he retorted.

"I know not of what you speak, nor can I guess what Lady Graeye might have done to earn your ire, but if you are set on condemning her, I would ask that you first consider your own conduct."

"Mine?"

She nodded curtly. "The lady was chaste when she left the abbey and spoiled when returned to us. That you would set yourself to seducing an innocent young noblewoman is most dishonorable—and then restore her to the Church with your child growing in her belly!"

Gilbert nearly choked. "She has accused me of seducing her?" He clenched his hands so tight he felt the bite of his nails in his toughened palms. "Truly, it surprises me she did not call it ravishment."

Anger flashed in the woman's eyes, but she looked away, and when she looked back, her gaze was clear. "As already told, Lady Graeye accuses you of naught, Baron Balmaine. Though I had initially thought she must have been forced, she assured me she was not."

But she had made it clear she had been seduced, Gilbert concluded. And it was obvious the abbess did not believe Graeye capable of deception. Bitter laughter and denial nearly made it to his lips, but he forced it down. Regardless of what lies she told, he would not reveal the true circumstances surrounding her pregnancy—though she certainly warranted no such consideration.

"I would ask that you reconsider and marry Lady Graeye," Mother Celia broke through his roiling.

"She is a Charwyck," Gilbert said again, "and every bit as deceitful as her brother and father. Look elsewhere, for I will not bind myself to that one."

This time, the abbess made no attempt to clear the anger from her eyes. "Then your taking of her virtue was merely a means by which to gain revenge against the Charwycks?"

Gilbert scowled. "In no way did revenge enter into it."

She sighed, stepped aside, and began pacing.

Leaving her to her plotting, Gilbert returned his attention to the courtyard, certain that in voicing his convictions he had strengthened his resolve to stay free of the treacherous bonds the abbess would impose upon him.

Disappointment swept him when he saw the place was empty save for a few remaining birds who foraged for scraps overlooked by the others. Where had Graeye gone?

"Then if you will not marry her..." the abbess said.

Gilbert did not move from the window. However, when several minutes passed and Graeye did not reappear, he turned back into the room.

"'Tis simple," Mother Celia said with a tight smile. "You must find another to take her to wife."

All of Gilbert balking at the suggestion, he crossed the room to stand before her. "It is not as simple as you say. Ere Lady Graeye was returned to this place, I did find a man eager to wed her, but she refused him." He did not tell her that, had Graeye accepted Sir Michael, he probably would not have consented to the match. Even then, when he had most deeply felt her deception, the thought of another possessing her had nearly infuriated him.

The abbess placed a finger to her mouth and pursed her lips against it. "It would seem, then, her heart lies elsewhere."

Suspicious, Gilbert stared at her.

Something other than anger glittering in her eyes, she patted his arm. "'Tis a great burden you bear, Baron Balmaine, but if you set yourself to discovering to whom Lady Graeye has given her heart, there you will find the husband she would have, and all your problems will be solved." She shrugged. "And if you cannot find it in you to do that, then look for another more acceptable to her. However, I warn you to be careful lest you choose a man unworthy of raising your child."

Knowing she dangled bait, Gilbert resentfully took the hook, though he did not for one moment believe the words he next spoke. "You imply Lady Graeye thinks herself in love with me."

She laughed. "Nay, Baron, I would not suggest such a thing, especially now that I have met you and seen for myself the embittered man you are. It must be another to whom she has given her heart."

Though vexed by her effrontery, Gilbert did not take the bait a second time. She was correct, after all. He was not an amiable man. His every day was shadowed by constant reminders of the wrongs done him and his family by Philip Charwyck. Still, he resented the abbess's meddling and wanted nothing more to do with it.

He turned, snatched up his mantle, and secured it with a simple brooch. "I will be taking Lady Graeye from here. See she is ready to depart within the hour." He threw the door wide.

"Her sanctuary is here at Arlecy, Baron Balmaine."

He turned in the doorway and leveled his gaze on the woman.

"If Lady Graeye does not wish to go with you," she said, "naught can be done to remove her from this place. Hence, you may have to set yourself the task of convincing her otherwise."

In his eagerness to depart, he had not considered the possibility Graeye would choose to remain at the abbey. If she did, he could not simply subdue her and carry her away. The protection afforded by the Church denied him that course of action. And though he would willingly risk its wrath, he would not risk the king's.

"Come," the abbess said. "I will take you to her."

Gilbert stepped into the corridor and allowed the woman to precede him from the guest house. In silence, she led him across the courtyard to the gardens where she clearly expected to find Graeye, but she was nowhere to be seen.

"Wait here." Mother Celia waved at an arbor enclosed on three sides. "I will send for her."

Gilbert stepped into the shelter but declined a seat on the bench. How would Graeye receive him? he wondered, feeling his pulse quicken at the thought she would soon stand before him.

It was not long before the abbess reappeared. "She is at prayer, but I have asked Sister Sophia to send her along."

"She will know the reason for her summons?"

"Nay, for I do not know that she would come if she knew."

Gilbert inclined his head and turned toward the walkway to gauge Graeye's reaction when she discovered him in this place.

When a handful of minutes passed and she had yet to appear, he muttered, "She is not very punctual."

The abbess looked up at him. "As told, this is not her world. Too, the babe has been troubling her some—"

"Something is wrong?" he pounced.

She nearly smiled. "I do not think so. 'Tis likely a malady of pregnancy that many women experience."

Regardless, Gilbert was keenly troubled.

Carefully picking her way over the frozen ground to ensure her footing, Graeye faltered upon hearing the abbess's voice carry across the long, narrow strip of garden. She was with someone.

Quickening her pace, she admonished herself for forgetting her gloves in the chapel. Though her hands had grown cold in the short time she had been outside, she held them out to her sides lest she slipped.

As she rounded the corner, a fluttering in her belly reminded her of the necessity to slow her advance. Smiling, she pressed a hand to the subsiding movement and continued forward with greater care.

Two stood within the shelter of the arbor—one well known, the other striking a chord of familiarity. Curious as to the identity of the dark-haired visitor, she stepped nearer and considered the clean-shaven face, then the eyes that shifted to her. Startling blue.

She stumbled, but kept her feet beneath her. When she looked again, Balmaine had closed much of the distance between them.

It was no wonder she had not recognized him immediately, for he appeared much younger and less ominous lacking a beard, even with shadows beneath his eyes. She had thought him attractive before, but now she was struck nearly breathless by the face revealed to her.

Though fewer than two of his long-legged strides separated them, he halted and neither attempted to bridge the remaining gap.

"I believe you know one another," Mother Celia said. She came alongside Graeye, leaned near, and pressed a kiss to her cheek. "Think of the child," she whispered and turned away.

She had told him. Graeye watched the abbess depart, staring after her even when the older woman went from sight.

It was the babe's movement that pulled her from her stupor. Keeping her gaze averted from the eyes she felt through every pore of her being, she slipped a hand beneath the mantle and smoothed it over the swell.

"The child you carry," Balmaine's deep voice strummed the strings of her emotions, "is it mine?"

How she longed to flee, to be far from this disbelieving man who posed such a hurtful question. Instead, she lifted her chin and met his stare with one of her own, putting into it all of the loathing she could summon before pivoting and heading down the path the abbess had taken.

When she heard Balmaine's footsteps, she had to struggle to quell the impulse to run. It was too dangerous, and she would do nothing to harm her child.

Accepting that she could not escape, she swung back around just as Balmaine reached to her.

As she peered up at him from beneath her hood, he lowered his arm to his side. "Is the child mine?" he asked again.

"Nay. Another fathered it. Thus, you need not concern yourself."

He appeared momentarily stunned, then said, "You must apply yourself more diligently if you wish to become an accomplished liar, Graeye Charwyck." Without warning, he swept back the hood to reveal her face and the tawny, gold-streaked hair she had not bothered to tame into a braid this morn.

Graeye reached to retrieve the hood, but before she could take hold of the coarse material, he enveloped her cold fingers in the warmth of his.

Quivering with anger, she glared up at him and said, "Has it been so long since last we met that you should forget how deceitful I am? Had I acknowledged you as the father of my child, I feel certain you would have denied it." She raised her eyebrows. "Be warned, Baron, such a bent toward believing the opposite of what one is told could place you at a disadvantage against those who seek to deceive you."

His eyes searched her face, and there was satisfaction in knowing he stared at a stranger.

"Consider this," she continued. "Mayhap my denial is but a means of maneuvering you into accepting responsibility for my child." She shrugged. "Or perhaps I speak the truth."

He grunted. "I refuse to play games with you, Graeye——"

"Graeye?" she snatched up the rare opportunity to interrupt him as he had so often done her. "Such familiarity, my lord?"

She was entirely unprepared when he pulled her against him, slipped a hand inside her mantle, and settled it upon her belly.

She started to resist, but his gentle touch stilled her, and her breath caught when his long fingers began an exploration of her pregnancy that incited an awareness of him she had thought long dead. How was it this man whom she had convinced herself to hate could still rouse such a response?

"Tell me again this is not my child," he said.

Pulling free of her mind's desperate wanderings, she tilted her head back. "You would believe the words of one so deceitful?"

He brought his face nearer hers. "Only if you confirm what I know to be true."

Then he meant to acknowledge her child as his? She searched his face, lingering over features that had heretofore been hidden behind a beard. His mouth was wider than she had thought, and there was a slight indentation visible below one cheek. It would be a dimple if he ever smiled. And his smooth skin offered testament to having recently had a blade set to it.

Before she could think better, she lifted a hand to his jaw. The muscles beneath her fingers leapt, reminding her of the inappropriateness of such a gesture. She dropped her hand, slid it beneath her mantle, and gripped his wrist. He did not resist when she lifted it from her belly.

"'Tis my child, Gilbert Balmaine. Mine."

His eyes narrowed. "And the father?"

Refusing to give him the grudging admission he believed she owed him, she said, "Who scattered the seed by which my babe grows is of little consequence. You would do best to—"

He swung her up into his arms, the surprise of it making her cry out, then he was carrying her from the garden.

Though Graeye was sensible enough not to struggle, she loudly demanded, "Know you the sin you commit by taking me against my will? Arlecy is my sanctuary, and there is naught you can do without risking the Church's wrath."

He did not falter.

"Nor King Henry's!"

She felt him tense, but he did not stop, and as he stepped from the garden onto the path leading to the courtyard, the lengthening of his stride made his limp more pronounced.

"Do not do this," she protested. "God will visit this trespass upon you tenfold."

"God!" he rasped. "Let Him do His worst. I have endured all He has hurled at me thus far. I will endure what is to come."

Breathe, Graeye, she silently implored. *If there is any hope of reaching him, you must calm yourself.*

She dragged a deep breath through her teeth and pressed a hand to his heart. "Though you may deny Him," she said, "you are not godless, Gilbert. Now release me ere the damage is done."

At the edge of the courtyard, he halted and looked down at her. "For months I have longed to feel you again as I did that first night. You are a scourge to my soul, and yet I cannot empty you from it no matter how often I remind myself of your deceit. But I intend to try."

Shocked by his declaration, she could find no words that would lend themselves to a response.

"You are mine, Graeye," he asserted, "and the babe you carry is mine. Now will you come willingly or have me risk your God's wrath yet again?"

That he would lay claim to her, as well as their child, sent shivers of uncertainty through her. But what, exactly, was he saying? That he would not abandon her as she had supposed he would once she delivered his child? Dare she hope that what he offered was of a permanent nature rather than an expedient one?

"If I go with you," she ventured, "will you wed me so the child may be made legitimate?"

"Nay, Graeye. Though I offer you and the child my protection, 'twould be impossible for me to wed you."

A dark pall fell over her. "Then you already have a wife."

"I do not, and 'tis not likely I ever shall. I will have my heir from you, and that will suffice."

Hope kicked out from under her, she forgot her earlier caution and threw her hands against his chest. "Release me, infidel! I will not become your leman merely to quench your desire. Find another to beget a child upon and leave me be."

He enfolded her more tightly against his chest and stepped from the path into the vacant courtyard.

Feeling another flutter from her child, reason returned, but though Graeye stilled, she protested more loudly.

In answer, the abbess appeared in Gilbert's path. "Baron Balmaine," she said, "it is clear Lady Graeye has chosen to remain at Arlecy. Be so kind as to set her to her feet."

Gilbert came back to earth with a thud. Previous to this most recent encounter with Graeye, he would not have believed himself foolish enough to seize her from her sanctuary. It was terribly imprudent, especially since there were other avenues yet to be explored.

He lowered Graeye to the uneven stones and stepped back.

Immediately, she hastened around the abbess, placing the woman before her like a human shield.

"Lady Graeye," Mother Celia said, "return to your room. I will speak with you later."

When she had gone from sight, the abbess stepped near Gilbert. "Baron, that you dared such a thing is quite beyond me. What could you have been thinking?" She tossed her hands up as if to ask God to deliver her from such stupidity. "Are you so bereft of words that might persuade her to go with you that you must resort to force?"

He held her steely gaze. "My apologies, Abbess. I fear I acted without thought when she refused me. It was, indeed, foolish."

She considered him, then sighed heavily and waved for him to follow. Shortly, she led him back into the room in which they had first met. "Now that you have seen her again, what are your intentions?" she asked.

He lifted a hand to run fingers through his beard, but his face was bare, having been scraped clean just this morn. "I do not know. Though I would have her and the child with me, I cannot take her to wife, yet neither can I give her to another."

"You told her this?"

At his nod, the abbess shook her head. "Then I understand why she refused you. 'Tis unseemly what you propose." She stepped nearer. "Tell me, do you love her?"

Gilbert was so astonished he nearly choked. "Love her! A Charwyck?"

She raised her eyebrows. "Then what will you do, Baron Balmaine?"

"There are other ways." He began to pace. After several crossings of the room, he returned to her. "I will petition King Henry for charge of my child once 'tis born. I do not think he will deny me my heir."

Once more, anger flashed in her eyes. "That could take a very long time."

He shrugged. "Providing it achieves the same end, that is all that matters."

"Is it? What of Lady Graeye? You would take her child from her? Without remorse?"

He smiled ruefully. "I do not believe that will be necessary. Indeed, I am fairly certain she will then come to me of her own accord."

Her nostrils flared. "It will not only be the ruin of her, but of any possibility of there being peace between you."

He feared that as well. "I hope you are wrong, but I see no other course."

This time it was Mother Celia who took up pacing, and when she returned to Gilbert, there was determination in her eyes. "There is one other course."

He narrowed his gaze upon her. "What course is that?"

"I shall repent for breaking this confidence, Baron Balmaine, but I am told that, following matins, Lady Graeye is wont to slip outside the walls. She walks along the river that lies beyond."

It was no feat to make sense of what she implied. The feat was in believing she had done so.

At his continued silence, which he was certain she interpreted as ignorance of what she was telling him, she added, "Alas, 'tis lamentable, but the Church cannot extend its protection outside the walls."

He delved her face. "Why do you tell me this?"

"Lady Graeye is not the same young woman who left Arlecy six months past. She is much changed, that soft heart of hers hardened and bound up in sorrow, disillusionment, and anger. Thus, methinks she could more easily forgive you the trespass of carrying her away than of stealing her child by decree of the king."

Gilbert had only to remember the way Graeye had received him to know the abbess was right. When he had asked if the child was his, she had warned him of how deceitful she was, forcing him to examine the underlying meaning of her words and try to understand the anger emanating from her. He had previously glimpsed that emotion and discovered those sharp claws of her, but this day it had reminded him far too much of his own embittered self. And it had disturbed him to find himself mirrored in her.

Thus, he inclined his head and said, "Tell me, how goes she?"

The abbess smiled thinly. "By way of the postern gate."

15

ANGERED AT BEING a party to what he perceived as trickery, Gilbert once more considered his plan of petitioning the king.

For four long, wet days, he and his men had concealed themselves in the wood surrounding the abbey, lying in wait for their prey to venture forth. In all that time, Graeye had not left her refuge.

Gilbert was certain of this, for he was not foolish enough to completely trust the abbess. Hence, he had set men to watch the comings and goings through all the gates of the walled sanctuary lest an attempt was made to spirit Graeye away while he watched for her at the postern gate.

It was well past the hour of matins on that fourth day when he and a handful of his men once more returned to camp empty-handed. Barking off orders, he lent his shoulder to hastening their departure the sooner to reach London.

When they were finally ready to ride, Gilbert's destrier, sensing anger, shied away from his master.

Forcing himself to a calm he did not feel, Gilbert slid a soothing hand over the animal's quivering neck and wondered where his squire had wandered off to. As he thought further on it, he did not recall the young man accompanying them back from the river.

Once the destrier calmed sufficiently to be mounted, Gilbert grabbed the saddle's pommel and put a foot in the stirrup.

"My lord, she comes!" Squire Duncan sprinted out of the trees to the center of the disassembled camp. "She comes!"

Gilbert turned from his destrier, caught hold of the young man's shoulders. "To the river?"

"Aye, my lord, though she does not venture far out of sight of the abbey."

Though it would be best to approach Graeye without the clamor of horses, there was no time to waste lest she too soon returned to her sanctuary.

Gilbert slapped Duncan on the back. "Good man. Gain your horse. You shall ride with me." Smiling for the first time in days, he vaulted into the saddle and motioned three others to follow.

With no regard for the noise they made within the deep of the wood, they sped toward the river. However, as they neared the clearing beyond the dense grouping of trees, and through which the river snaked, Gilbert instructed his men to spread out and proceed with caution.

He guided his horse to the edge of the wood and peered around, but there was nothing that would indicate Graeye's presence. He glanced at the abbey, thinking she might have started back, but saw only an empty stretch of land laden with recent rainfall.

Then he heard the trill of a bird, one he knew well. Farther up and nearer the river sat Duncan, a smile splitting his youthful face as he gestured to a place hidden from his lord's view.

Gilbert gave the signal and prodded his destrier out from amid the trees.

Though the noise of their approach no longer mattered since Graeye could not possibly reach the abbey before they were upon her, they kept to a trot lest she was too soon alerted to their presence and took a risk that would harm her or the babe.

Nevertheless, Gilbert's impatience was great, for he could not remember ever wanting anything as badly as he wanted to once more hold Graeye in his arms.

Hardly had Graeye settled on a large, flat rock alongside the river than she heard the sound of approaching horses.

With dread, she pushed upright and turned. Immediately, her gaze lit upon a handful of riders. And Gilbert was in the lead, so tall and broad in the saddle, hair so deeply black, it could be no other.

"Dear Lord," she breathed.

These past days, she had kept to the safety of the abbey, knowing that if she were caught outside its walls, the Church could do little to aid her. But this morn, restless and thinking to take advantage of the break in the rain, she had decided the risk was past.

But he had lain in wait all this time.

She gauged the distance to the abbey and, with sinking heart, acknowledged it was too far, especially in her condition. Still, she hauled up her skirts and hurried toward it along the river's bank, determined that this lamb to slaughter would at least make it difficult to lead her to the altar.

As she traversed the undulating ground, keeping her eyes lowered to ensure a secure footing, she heard the riders draw nearer and resented that they continued to advance at an almost leisurely pace that bespoke confidence in her capture.

Sparing a glance over her shoulder, she saw Gilbert's men were moving outward on either side of her. Soon, they would enclose her.

And so she had reached the altar on her own.

Out of breath and warmed by the spurt of exertion, she turned, gathered her mantle around her, and curved an arm over her belly.

Gilbert arrived too soon, affording her little time in which to compose herself.

Though unnerved by his gaze, she stared back. "You are a more patient man than I would have thought, Gilbert Balmaine."

"And you are very stubborn."

"You expected otherwise?"

"Nay, but I would have preferred your willingness to this."

"This," she repeated and looked to the abbey. "It was Mother Celia, was it not? She who betrayed me?"

He raised his eyebrows. "What makes you think she would care to aid me?"

Graeye smiled tightly. "She brought you to the abbey."

He shifted in the saddle. "She did."

"Then it follows that, in her eagerness to see me gone from Arlecy, she would stop at nothing to achieve that end."

Gilbert shook his head. "You judge her wrongly, Graeye. If it was not this way, it would have been a far less desirable means by which I laid claim to my child. Truly, she has done you no disservice. You should be grateful for her wisdom."

At that moment, she could see nothing good coming of the betrayal, nor did she believe she ever would. Well-intentioned or not, it injured her and stole the future, albeit uncertain, that she had begun to plan for herself and her child.

Would she never be free of the domination of others?

Though she longed to scream at the injustice, she looked to Gilbert's mounted knights and gave a short, harsh laugh. "What warrants my pursuit by so many? Am I truly such a dangerous beast that all this is necessary?"

"I take no chances with that which belongs to me," Gilbert said.

She narrowed her lids. "I do not belong to you."

"That could be argued, but what cannot is that the child belongs to me. And I will not be denied its upbringing."

"What of when he is born?" Pain jabbed her heart. "Will you take him from my breast and cast me aside?"

"He?" Gilbert leaned forward in the saddle. "How know you 'tis a boy you carry?"

Though she sensed it was a son growing in her, she would not admit it. "I speak in general terms. It may just as well be a girl."

He looked unconvinced, but he held out a hand. "Come, Graeye. Your rebellion is at an end."

She took a step back. "You have not yet revealed your intentions toward me."

"We will speak of it later." He motioned her forward.

She shook her head. "We will speak of it now."

His gaze shot heavenward, and then he threw a leg over the saddle and dropped to the ground. "Otherwise?" he said as he advanced on her.

She looked more closely upon the men flanking her, and her eyes lit upon the familiar visage of one positioned directly in her path to the abbey. Though he was distant enough that his features were indistinct, she knew it was Sir Michael. Disconcerted, she looked back at Gilbert. "Otherwise, I will resist you no matter the odds," she bluffed.

A corner of his mouth rose. "Why do I not believe you, Graeye?"

"Because you do not know me. 'Tis simple enough for you to take me from here, but I will not make the journey to Medland easy for you." As he neared, she took another step back and another.

Gilbert halted, and was grateful when she did as well, for he did not think she realized she was near the edge of the bank. Though the river was not overly deep in this spot, it would be chill and even a short fall could injure her or the babe.

He drew a deep breath. "I have told you, Graeye, I will not marry you."

"And I have told you I will not be your leman."

As much as he longed to know her again, it was not in his nature to force himself on any woman. Thus, if it was assurances she sought, she would have them. However, they would be on his own terms, for he saw no reason to hold himself from her should her resolve weaken.

"So be it," he said. "You will serve as mother of my child, naught else."

"I do not believe you."

He ground his teeth. "I give you my word. You will suffer no unwanted attentions."

When her eyes continued to reflect distrust, he drew his sword and lowered its tip to the marshy ground. Gripping the hilt tightly, he recaptured her gaze. "I give my word, Lady Graeye. I will not force myself upon you. May God take note."

She scoffed. "I am to believe such a vow when you make no secret of your aversion to a belief in the Almighty?"

He resheathed his sword. "'Tis a knightly vow I have made, the ceremony of which is of less consequence than the words I have spoken. However, I give notice that if ever we come together again out of mutual need, I will not likely refrain from taking what you offer. And then you will be mine as much as the child you carry."

Though apprehensive about that last bit, Graeye said, "It appears I have naught to fear from you, then."

"Naught."

Feeling as if she were stepping into an abyss, she walked forward and, when he held out a hand, placed hers in his.

His gaze lowered to where his fingers closed over hers. Then, slowly, he drew his thumb across the back of her hand.

Disturbed by the caress, she tried to pull free, but he tightened his grip.

"Release me," she hissed.

He did not look up, his gaze intent upon her small hand trapped in his.

Graeye loathed herself for the surge of feelings she had vowed never again to allow herself. Why could she not hate him? Why could she not disassociate herself from this man as she had done her father?

"Beautiful," he murmured, then lifted her hand, pressed his lips to the inside of her wrist, and captured her wide-eyed gaze.

She floundered in the depths of those incredible blue eyes that regarded her with such intensity it was as if he sought to gain her soul. Knowing he felt her response against his mouth and desperate to keep hold on her convictions, she tried again to pull free.

He did not release her but lowered their hands between them. "'Tis time we ride," he said and drew her toward his destrier. Shortly, he gripped her thickened waist and, in spite of her added bulk, easily lifted her into the saddle. Then he swung up behind her.

Graeye would have liked to resist when he pulled her back against his chest and draped his mantle around her, but she was suddenly too tired to fight anymore.

16

"I MEAN NO disrespect, my lord, for she is welcome, but if 'tis your child she carries, why do you not take her on to Penforke?"

Coming up out of sleep, Graeye latched on to the hushed words and ran them backward and forward through her mind in an attempt to attach meaning to them.

They speak of me, she realized.

Careful to keep her breathing even, she opened her eyes to narrow slits and peered at her surroundings while she awaited Gilbert's answer.

It was the deep of night, though she knew not what hour it was, and she lay abed in one of the smaller rooms of the donjon at Medland. This last she knew instinctively, for the chamber appeared much changed from what she remembered of the dank, foreboding place.

Though muddled from sleep, she had no difficulty recalling the circumstances that had led to her being taken from Arlecy. However, she recalled very little of the ride to Medland, having slept through much of it.

"I do not want her at Penforke," Gilbert finally answered.

She frowned. Though he had mentioned returning her to Medland, she had not thought he meant to abandon her here. Did he also mean to hold himself from the child once it was born?

"And when the child is born?" the other man, whose voice she now recognized as Sir Lancelyn's, asked the question for her.

"I will decide then."

Though the tightening skin of her belly began to itch, Graeye fought the urge to scratch it.

It was Sir Lancelyn who changed the subject. "That girl you sent to serve her—Mellie, is it? She arrived two days ago. Though I have heard nothing of it myself, I am told she objects to serving Lady Graeye."

Graeye's eyes flew open. Was there no end to the passing of judgment against her before one even knew her?

"She was Lizanne's maid," Gilbert said. "Though I would have it otherwise, it is now common knowledge what Philip Charwyck set out to do to my sister. I daresay the girl remains loyal to her former mistress and is as distrustful as I am of any bearing that particular name."

"Think you it prudent, then, to give Lady Graeye into her care?"

"I will speak with Mellie and make clear my desires with regard to the handling of her new mistress. She will do as told."

"There are others, my lord, who would make a better maid."

Surprisingly, Gilbert did not rise to anger at his vassal's continued opposition. "Nay," he said, "Mellie will do fine."

"Is it loyalty you are concerned about?" the other man pressed.

"Aye, without question, I have the girl's loyalty. I cannot be so certain of those who have previously served the Charwycks."

"Then you think Lady Graeye might attempt to return to the abbey?"

"I do not know what she will try, but Mellie will not aid in such an undertaking."

Graeye bristled. Had she not agreed to adhere to the conditions set forth only that morning? Providing he kept his side of the bargain, she would keep hers. And as for this Mellie, the girl would soon discover Graeye had well and truly had the last of being trod upon. The chit would not undermine her.

Graeye was so gripped by indignation that it took her a moment to notice Gilbert had come around the end of the bed. What had given her away? Her breathing? Aye, those quick, shallow breaths of anger that even now panted from her.

"Lady Graeye has awakened," he blandly informed Sir Lancelyn.

"Then I will leave you to your privacy, my lord."

Graeye rolled onto her back and caught sight of the other man as he slipped through the doorway.

"You have been awake long?" Gilbert asked.

She shifted her gaze to where he stood alongside her. "Long enough."

To her dismay, he lowered to the edge of the bed. "Then you know of my plans to maintain you at Medland."

"Why do you not tell me more of it?" she invited, making no attempt to disguise her anger. "I may have missed some ere I awoke."

He ignored her barb. "I doubt there is much more to tell than what you overheard. What else would you like to know?"

"Naught. Though, mayhap, there are things you would care to know."

His lids narrowed. "Aye?"

She pushed an elbow beneath her to raise herself up and, when Gilbert reached to assist her, brushed his hand away.

"You should know, Gilbert Balmaine," she said as she dragged the coverlet up over her thick chemise that, blessedly, had not been removed along with her other garments, "I will not be bullied by anyone—especially that maid you think to have dog my every step. And if you are of a mind to take my child from me once he is born and leave me at Medland, then I give notice I will use every deception at my command to escape you ere the birth to ensure you never lay eyes upon my child."

At the conclusion of her tirade, a muscle jerked in his jaw. "I have not lied to you," he said. "Though there remains the question of where the child will be raised, wherever he goes, so shall you."

She attempted to discern the truth beneath his expression, but it was not possible. "I have no choice but to take your word on that, but if you renege, you will find me all you have thus far wrongfully accused me of—and more."

Abruptly, he stood from the bed. "I do not doubt you, daughter of Edward Charwyck," he said and turned away.

As he strode across the chamber, she felt a peculiar sense of disappointment that he was leaving.

At the door, he looked over his shoulder. "I depart for Penforke at first light."

"So soon?" The words tumbled from her before she could call them back.

He raised his eyebrows. "I had thought it would not be soon enough for you."

Embarrassed, she dipped her chin and studied the pink ovals of her fingernails. "It is. 'Tis just that your haste surprises me considering all the time and effort expended to achieve your end."

"For that reason, I must return posthaste to Penforke. I have been gone too long, and there are matters more deserving of my attention than verbal sparring with you, my lady."

Graeye could not suppress the rejoinder that flew to her lips. "Then it would not be soon enough for you to leave this night."

He momentarily closed his eyes. "I have placed you in Sir Lancelyn's care. Do not vex the man overly much. As the new lord of Medland, he is heavily burdened with the duties of keeping all in order." He pulled the door open.

Graeye panicked at the realization this might be the last time she saw him for a long while and called, "Gilbert!"

He turned. "Graeye?"

"Will you visit?" Though she was not sure what, exactly, she wanted from him, she felt a pressing need for him to stay.

Detesting his rumpled emotions, Gilbert stared at her. Then, not knowing what possessed him, though he would later question how he could have once more allowed himself to fall prey to her wiles, he pushed the door closed and returned to the bed.

When she lifted her pale gaze to his, he pulled her up into his arms. Molding her sweet new curves to him, he took possession of her mouth.

He was allowed only a taste of her before she thrust her hands to his chest. "I will not become your leman!" she cried, eyes bright with fury.

What had come over him? Gilbert wondered. Her eyes, he realized, their silent pleading. But perhaps he had imagined it. Feeling as if burned, he lowered her back to the mattress.

She snatched the covers up over her chest. "Leave," she said in a hard little voice. "Now."

He inclined his head. "My apologies. 'Twould seem the right decision for you to remain at Medland."

For answer, she turned her back to him.

Gilbert pivoted and crossed to the door. *It is the right decision*, he told himself. *No peace will I have if I take her with me to Penforke.*

And he so longed for peace.

17

Emerging from a profusion of covers, Graeye rubbed her eyes before venturing a look at the world. It was the same one in which she had fallen asleep yestereve.

She inched up onto her hands and knees and sat back on her heels. The chill morning air struck her and sent a shiver of discomfort through her.

Frowning, she looked down and was alarmed to discover she was unclothed, but then she remembered how she had come to be so.

Having awakened in a sweat during the night, she had thrown off the covers, but that had not been enough. After tossing and turning, she had finally discarded her chemise and dragged the light sheet over her. Only then had she slept.

As she pulled the covers around her shoulders, she pondered Gilbert's whereabouts. Had he left for Penforke as planned? The thought that he had, unsettled her in a way she refused to look too closely upon.

"Godspeed," she muttered.

A sharp knock sounded, but before she could call out permission to enter, the door opened and in stepped a rather pretty young woman not much taller than herself. Over her arm was a chemise, bliaut, and other items of clothing.

"Milady is awake," she said and closed the door and crossed to the bed. As she considered the stain marring Graeye's face, her eyes visually tracing its course, her lids narrowed to suspicious slits.

Graeye endured the scrutiny—until it became clear the woman had no other thought than to stare. "Are you quite finished?" she snapped.

A seemingly self-satisfied smile revealing crooked teeth, the young woman puffed out her chest with self importance. "I be Mellie."

The belated introduction was unnecessary, for Graeye had known beyond a doubt who this impertinent woman was the moment she had come unbidden into the room.

"'Tis the Baron Balmaine who assigned me to be yer maid," Mellie went on as she set her bundle upon the bed. "But I'll have ye know, 'tis a task I have no likin' for."

Graeye was grateful she had learned that much from eavesdropping upon Gilbert's conversation. Being forewarned of the maid's dislike took some of the sting out of it. "I am Lady Graeye Charwyck, and I would have you know that I resent the arrangements as much, if not more, than you."

Mellie's round eyes grew larger before she covered her astonishment with a scornful twist of the lips. "Ye Charwycks are all the same." She settled her arms over her chest.

Graeye feigned surprise. "You knew my brother?"

"Nay, but—"

"Then 'tis my father with whom you are acquainted." Graeye could not help smiling in remembrance of Gilbert's penchant for stepping on others' words.

"Nay, milady, I—"

"Then tell me how 'tis you can pass judgment on my family?" Graeye was pleased at the ease with which she had accomplished the rude feat a second time.

"'Tis no secret what yer brother did to my mistress, Lady Lizanne— and her brother." The maid thrust her small, pointed chin forward.

Graeye had no response for that, as she was still uninformed as to the exact crime that had persuaded the king to strip Edward of his lands. Was it possible the maid could be enticed to shed light upon the mystery? With such knowledge, perhaps she could better understand Gilbert's hostility.

"And already I have heard tale of how yer brother had done with his poor wife," Mellie continued. "Broke her neck, he did."

Graeye startled. When she had first arrived at Medland last autumn, she had heard the rumor Philip was responsible for his wife's death, but she had not known how the woman died.

"As long as we understand one another, milady," Mellie said and stooped to scoop up Graeye's chemise. Eyebrows raised, lips twitching, she brushed the rushes from the garment.

Graeye knew exactly what she was thinking and felt the heat rise in her cheeks. She was about to put Mellie straight on the reason she was unclothed when there came a scratching at the door.

The maid crossed the room and flung the door open.

"Groan!" Graeye called as the big dog bounded inside. Allowing herself the first real smile in ages, she scooted to the edge of the bed and took the animal's head in her lap. "You did not forget me, my friend!"

"Out!" Mellie ordered as she stalked toward the bed.

"Nay," Graeye said, "he may stay."

"But, milady, 'tis not seemly."

Graeye met the other woman's gaze. "He stays."

Mellie's lips tightened. "Baron Balmaine will not like this."

"I care not a whit what he does or does not like."

Groan yawned wide, ending on a moan that evidenced his namesake.

Muttering, Mellie folded the chemise and dropped it on a chair. "When is yer babe due, milady?"

Jolted by the bold inquiry, Graeye raised startled eyes to the woman.

Mellie spread her hands in mock apology. "Everyone knows. Baron Balmaine would have no other reason for consorting with a Charwyck, though 'tis odd he would ever have become involved with ye in the first place."

Anger was Graeye's saving grace, for it quickly replaced hurt and embarrassment. "Where is he?" she demanded as she dropped her bare feet to the prickly rushes.

"Gone." Mellie came to stand before her. "Left with the rising of the sun."

Feeling a pang in the vicinity of her heart, Graeye returned her attention to Groan who had settled back on his haunches.

Just as well, she told herself and stroked the animal.

"They are not very fine," Mellie said as she sorted through the clothing she had brought with her. "But they will have to do until the cloth the baron ordered arrives."

Graeye looked to her. "He has ordered cloth for me?"

"Aye. This morn he told the steward to see it done posthaste. When it arrives, we will be busy, you and I. You can turn a stitch, can't ye?"

"I can."

Mellie chuckled at some private humor. "Here now"—she held up a fresh chemise—"lift yer arms."

Not since Graeye was a child had she been assisted with clothing herself, and it seemed a bit late to resume the habit. Mostly, though, she did not care to bare herself in front of this woman. "I can dress myself," she said and reached from beneath the cover to take the garment.

Mellie drew back. "And have ye tell the baron I be wantin' in my duties?"

"I assure you, he will not hear it from me." She reached again, but the maid snatched it away.

"Do not fuss, milady. 'Tis a duty I am not averse to providin'. Besides, I'll be seein' much more of ye when I tend yer bath later. Now lift yer arms—unless ye prefer to break yer fast dressed so."

Graeye sighed, released the cover. Blessedly, the chemise dropped over her head without delay.

"Late spring, mayhap early summer," Mellie pronounced as she stepped back to eye Graeye's figure.

Knowing she referred to the arrival of the babe, having glimpsed her bare belly, Graeye's indignation flared. "'Tis no concern of yours," she said and grabbed the bliaut.

Seemingly content to let her new mistress finish clothing herself, Mellie skirted the dog and went around the bed to gather up the covers. "Lady Lizanne is also expectin' a babe," she said.

Graeye paused in securing the bliaut's laces. For some reason, she was hurt that Gilbert had not informed her of his sister's pregnancy, especially considering his own impending state of parenthood.

She jerked at the laces. "When is the child due?" she asked, hoping she surpassed Mellie's attempt at nonchalance.

"Early spring, milady." She gave a heartfelt sigh. "Would that I could be with her durin' her time."

Graeye turned to face her. "Why are you not?"

Mellie's mouth drooped. "'Twas planned that I would go to her come a break in the weather, but the baron decided I would better serve ye, milady."

In spite of her own petulant mood, Graeye pitied the maid who seemed devoted to her former mistress. "Then I understand your reluctance to serve me. My apologies that you have been forced into this duty."

Mellie harrumphed, then eyed Graeye's face amid her disarrayed hair. "Have ye a wimple?"

Graeye stiffened. "I do not wear one."

Mellie peered more closely. "Properly fit, it would cover the mark. And 'twould save us the worry of yer hair. I am not very good with hair, ye know. Lady Lizanne hardly ever allowed me to practice—"

"I will not be needing a wimple."

Mellie glowered. "As ye like, milady."

Graeye turned her back on the maid and began pulling on the thick hose laid out for her.

Aye, she thought, *Gilbert is right. I do have claws.*

Two leagues. That was all the ground they covered before Gilbert reigned in. "Curse all!" he shouted, surprising his men. Without further word, he wheeled his destrier around.

Curse her angry eyes, her witching mouth, her dainty nose, he silently cited. *Curse the curve of her neck, the silk of her golden hair, the small of her back. Curse her naiveté, her deceit...*

Graeye Charwyck had woven a powerful spell around him that had not lessened following her rejection of him on the night past. Indeed, it had made him want her more. Thus, in the dark of the first hours of morn, he had found himself in her chamber again.

He had been surprised to find her shoulders bare above the sheet drawn over her, the moonlight spilling in through the window allowing a glimpse of her new curves beneath the covering that molded itself to her lightly perspiring body.

It had been bold of him, but he had been unable to overcome the longing to rest his hand upon her belly. She had stirred at his touch but not awakened. He had held his hand to her and marveled at the fluttering movements of their child until, too soon, dawn arrived and ushered him from her room.

Nay, he could not leave her behind. Could not return to Penforke without her.

Having been alerted to the approach of riders, Lancelyn met Gilbert at the drawbridge.

"Say naught!" Gilbert ground out as he urged his destrier forward.

With a barely suppressed smile, his vassal nodded and followed his liege inside the walls. At the donjon, Gilbert dismounted and took the steps to the hall two at a time.

Minutes later, he exited the donjon and found Lancelyn scraping dirt from beneath his nails where he stood alongside his lord's destrier.

"Where is she?" Gilbert demanded. "By my troth, if you have allowed her to escape——"

"She is in the chapel, my lord." Lancelyn grinned and, when his liege roared his name, threw his palms up. "I but obeyed your directive that I say naught, my lord."

"As you are so well versed in obeying," Gilbert growled as he descended the steps, "obey this—wipe that smile off your face." He strode past the man.

Not since the day Gilbert had first cornered Graeye had he been inside the chapel. Swept with vivid memories of that confrontation, he paused before entering.

Lord, I was cruel! he silently admitted and dragged a hand down his face. But he could not wipe away memories that nicked at him, rapier-sharp. If only he could right some of the wrongs of that day...

Inside, she knelt at the altar, the same as that first day he had come within, but this time she was not clothed in the stark white nun's habit.

Preferring the light to shadows, he did not close the door behind him. Why a chapel should be so morose, he did not understand. Were not the heavens said to be bright and open?

Feeling his limp, he strode down the aisle and, as he neared, heard the softly spoken prayers she recited in Latin.

Why did she not turn around? She must know she was no longer alone. But even when he halted alongside her, her prayers did not cease.

Reluctantly, he lowered to the kneeler. As his leg brushed hers, he looked down upon her bowed head and wondered at the strange words that continued to spill from her.

He did not consider himself a patient man, but he waited on her rather than intrude.

When she finally crossed herself and turned to him, surprise flew across her face. Then her color drained and she swayed toward him.

Gilbert slid an arm around her and drew her against his side. "Graeye—"

"You came back," she whispered.

"Are you well? Something is wrong?"

"You came back," she repeated, and he was heartened when color began to return to her cheeks and a smile lifted her lovely mouth.

He pushed a lock of hair out of her eyes. "Aye, I came back. For you."

"Why?"

"I am taking you to Penforke."

Her smile slipped. "I do not understand."

He wanted that smile back. He curved a hand around her chin and lifted it. "You belong there."

Graeye waited, silently prayed he would speak the words she needed to hear—words that had resounded through her heart and mind when she had first found him kneeling beside her. Fight it though she did, she loved him. Loved this giant who rarely had a kind word for her.

"As your wife?" she ventured.

He drew back. "I want my son born there."

She felt as if struck. He had not come back for her, but for the child she carried. How foolish she was to hope he would ever feel anything beyond hate for a Charwyck. Would he be able to forget their child had half that blood in his veins?

Remarkably, it was not anger that worked its way toward her surface, but sorrow. "Will you pray with me?" she asked.

He dropped his arm from around her and stood. "I shall await you outside."

She turned on the kneeler and followed his progress down the aisle. "Gilbert," she called when he reached the doorway.

He turned, the daylight streaming in behind him rendering his face unreadable. "Aye?"

"I will go with you, but until you bring honor to this child, I will not share your bed."

"I have not asked you to," he said gruffly.

She nodded. "So long as you do not."

18

IT WAS WHITEWASHED and clean, rising gracefully into a sky beset by the coming of night. Seated before Gilbert on his white destrier, Graeye was glad he could not see the wonder she knew shone from her face. Penforke was no Medland. Indeed, it made that other castle look more like a hovel than the residence of a baron.

She grimaced. How appalled Gilbert must have been at his first sight of her home. It was a wonder he had not let it burn to the ground those many months past.

"What do you think of your new home?" he asked, his breath in her ear sending tremors of awareness up her sides.

Refusing to look around, she said, "It looks to be satisfactory."

"That is all?"

His disappointment at her lack of response nearly made her smile. Undoubtedly, he was proud of Penforke. "What else would you have me say?"

After a long moment, he said, "It is far more habitable than Medland. You will be comfortable here."

"Then I was not comfortable before?"

Suddenly, he laughed, a rumbling sound that rose from the depths of his chest. "You are trifling with me, Graeye Charwyck."

Abandoning her resolve to deny him her gaze, she twisted around. "Trifling with you?"

"Aye, the same as Lizanne. You are of a gentler temperament than my sister—though I have not seen evidence of that in some time—but you are also very like her."

It was not only the comparison to that other woman that rankled Graeye, but the sudden change in Gilbert's disposition. How was she to do battle with a man whose unexpected laughter warmed her and whose eyes reflected something other than contempt?

"I would thank you not to compare me to the coward who put an arrow through my brother's back," she said and turned forward again.

Though she should have been pleased, Graeye found no satisfaction in Gilbert's response—a stiffening that created a space between their bodies where there had been none. She knew she had pushed him too far, but it was too late to do anything about it now.

Determinedly, she fixed her attention on the castle. During the long ride, she had anticipated her arrival at Gilbert's home with dread, but now she was nearly eager to discover what lay within those walls.

When they entered the bailey, she felt none of the disappointment she had experienced upon returning to Medland. Indeed, it seemed a thriving community dwelled here.

Upon reaching the donjon, Gilbert reined in, dismounted, and lifted her down beside him. Then he turned to the dozens of castle folk who had converged upon the inner bailey to greet him.

Though Graeye felt a frisson of panic as she was drawn forward, she firmly took herself in hand. If this was to be her home and the place where her child grew into adulthood, it would bode ill for her to reveal any vulnerability to these people.

Blessedly, the introductions were brief, then Gilbert passed her into Mellie's care.

"See Lady Graeye is made comfortable in Lady Lizanne's chamber," he instructed and stalked away before Graeye—or the maid—could protest.

Grumbling beneath her breath, Mellie led her new mistress inside.

Though the many windows in the great hall were set high as added protection should an attack upon the fortress reach the inner bailey, there was so much of the setting sun's light inside that Graeye had to stop and look better at her surroundings.

"Something is amiss, milady?" Mellie asked.

Graeye shook her head. "Nay."

The chamber in which Mellie deposited her was not large, but it was well furnished and the light was plentiful.

Seeking the warmth of the window embrasure, Graeye slipped into it and drew her knees as near her chest as her belly would allow.

"'Tis also where Lady Lizanne preferred to sit," Mellie said.

Graeye met the woman's gaze. "Here?"

"Aye. Never a chair, as is fittin' fer a lady."

There was no mistaking the rancor in Mellie's voice, but Graeye decided to ignore it. "I would like a bath. Would you see to it?"

"There is not much time ere the supper hour, milady. Mayhap afterward."

Graeye nearly acquiesced, but she would not allow the maid to dictate what she could and could not do. "I would like a bath. Now."

Mellie might have argued further, but a tap at the door heralded the arrival of the chest containing Graeye's few belongings. The tub and water for the bath arrived shortly thereafter.

Fully dressed, hair neatly—though not artfully—arranged by Mellie, Graeye stood over the chest that had belonged to her mother. She shifted her gaze from the bridal habit that lay atop the lid to the pieces of linen in her hand.

Not once had she regretted discarding the wimple. It had been the beginning for her.

The door opened without benefit of a knock. Mellie again.

"I will be ready shortly," Graeye murmured as she fingered the yellowing chin strap.

There was no answer, but a moment later she was struck by a presence at her back that was too deeply felt to belong to the maid. Before she could react, Gilbert reached around and took the wimple from her.

"I will not have you wearing this," he said.

She turned to him. "I assure you"—she reached to regain possession of the item—"I have no intention of doing so."

He eyed her, then yielded the linen. "That pleases me."

Though he did not touch her, she felt as if caressed from head to toe, and as she stared up at him, she once more experienced the attraction she had first felt at the waterfall.

Why, now, did he allow glimpses of the man he had been then? Why could he not continue to be the blackguard against whom she had built her defenses? Did he truly desire her so much that he would set aside his dislike to have her in his bed?

Feeling her resolve weaken, she turned and crossed to the brazier. "'Tis not you I seek to please," she said as she set the linen atop the charred remains of the fire that had warmed her during her bath. "I seek to please myself."

She was a changed woman, Gilbert reflected as he watched the wimple smolder, then catch flame. Though part of him was proud of her embittered strength, another part mourned her loss of innocence. He— and Edward Charwyck—had done that to her. Just as the malevolence of Philip Charwyck had changed Lizanne overnight from a carefree child to an angry woman, Graeye had also transformed.

Suddenly weary, he closed his eyes. It seemed each time he touched something wonderful, it came apart in his hands. If only—

"Truly, you are not bothered by the mark I bear?" she asked as she turned back to him.

"I am not." He beckoned her forward. "Come hither and I will show you something."

Though suspicion rose in her eyes, she moved to stand before him. "What is it?"

He turned his back to her. "Lift my tunic."

"I will not." She retreated a step.

He peered over his shoulder. "'Tis not seduction I have planned, Graeye."

She put her head to the side. "Then what?"

Doing his best to hold onto patience, he said, "Do you lift my tunic, you shall see."

She hesitated a moment longer, then raised the hem high.

"To the right," he said. Not that she needed to be told, for the mark just below his shoulder blade was palm-sized.

A few moments later, he felt the brush of her fingers as she traced the mark. He had not expected that, and it was all he could do not to react to the sensations roused by her touch—sensations that drew him back to the waterfall and the stars in the night. Knowing that if he did not distance himself, he might once more be the recipient of her indignation, he stepped away from her.

"You see"—he turned to her—"I, too, bear a mark. And that is all it is."

She was tense, movement amid her skirts drawing his gaze to her right hand that gripped and released and gripped again the fabric as if to wipe the feel of his skin from hers.

"Think you I am a spawn of the devil?" he prompted.

She blinked as if surprised to find herself in his presence—as if she had also come back from that other time and place. Then unexpected mischief leapt into her eyes. "Mayhap not a direct descendant, but…" She smiled.

It was nearly Gilbert's undoing. He returned her smile and held out his arm. "Supper awaits, my lady."

She stepped forward and took his arm, and it seemed as if they had both crossed a very shaky bridge and made it to the other side.

Surprisingly, it was not the curiosity of the castle folk that made the meal an ordeal for Graeye, but the stares of Sir William and Sir Michael.

Though unreadable, they exuded a menace that disturbed her to the pit of her stomach.

She was no fool. Not anymore. She understood why each man was angered by her presence. Sir William because of his natural dislike for her, and Sir Michael because thrice she had refused him. The young man's pride must be sorely wounded to see her now seated next to his baron and burgeoning with that man's child. That Gilbert placed trust in either of them, especially Sir William, made her wonder at his wisdom.

In spite of her unease, she held herself erect throughout the meal, conversed with Gilbert when he addressed her, and managed to consume a healthy serving of the wonderfully prepared viands.

When she finally asked Gilbert about the two Charwyck knights he had taken into his service, his face reflected displeasure. However, he told her that Sir Michael had become a member of his household knights, and Sir William had been allowed to remain castellan of Sulle.

Curious as to the reason the latter was at Penforke, Graeye pressed him further, but Gilbert turned tight-lipped and distant.

Contenting herself with what he had revealed, she retired to her chamber shortly thereafter and found peace in the sleep that quickly claimed her.

19

Curses—loud, angry words that wound up the stairs and slipped beneath Graeye's door—awoke her hours later.

Snatching up the robe Mellie had left at the foot of the bed, Graeye ventured out into the corridor. There, the voices were louder, and as she traversed the darkened stairs, she caught the sound of a struggle.

She hurried into the hall and halted at the sight of a dozen knights crowded around something on the floor.

"What has happened?" she asked as she peered between two of them.

Though none answered her, she saw Gilbert wrench Sir Michael from atop Sir William.

"I will fight my own battles," Gilbert snarled as he pushed the young knight behind him so he might himself confront the one amid the rushes.

Graeye winced at the sight Sir William presented as he struggled to his feet, his bloodied mouth having given up several teeth to what must have been Sir Michael's fist.

"Knave!" the man spat, spraying Gilbert with blood. "I will see you dead for this!"

"Then come now and let us put a quick end to it." Gilbert drew his sword and nodded at the one at William's side.

Though William reached for his hilt, something stayed his hand. Smiling darkly, he shook his head. "There will come another time, Baron Balmaine. You and I will meet again."

"Now is as good as any."

William continued to bare his bloody smile. "Soon," he said, then turned his back on Gilbert and raked his gaze over the knights before him. "Step aside!"

The men looked questioningly at their lord. To Graeye's amazement, he nodded for them to allow William to pass.

As Gilbert watched the knight exit the hall, he acknowledged they would, indeed, meet again. And soon.

"Gilbert!"

He whipped his head around.

Seemingly unaware of the startled looks she received from the others who had surely been as unaware of her presence as he had been, Graeye slipped between two knights and stepped toward him.

He was further surprised by her appearance, so much that he momentarily forgot what he had been about to do. Clothed in a robe, her golden hair tousled, she looked as if she had just come from the arms of a lover.

So disturbing was that thought that it shook Gilbert free of her spell. Ignoring the hand she laid on his arm, he searched out the knights he had earlier chosen to follow William Rotwyld and, catching their expectant gazes, nodded.

Immediately, they hurried after their prey.

Graeye had surely caught the signal, for she glanced over her shoulder to watch the men depart. "What transpires, my lord?" she asked.

Gilbert resheathed his sword. "You should be abed," he grumbled and took her arm and led her away from the others.

"I was," she said. "The commotion awoke me."

"You should have stayed in your chamber." He began drawing her up the stairs. "It is unseemly for you to appear before my men in this manner of dress."

At the landing, she pulled free from his grip. "What is wrong with it?" She swept a hand downward to indicate the fullness of the robe.

Gilbert frowned. It was true she was adequately covered, but still it was a robe and the silken hair falling about her shoulders and the flush upon her cheeks was simply too much.

"Graeye," he groaned and rubbed his hands over the back of his neck so he would not be tempted to touch her in a way he should not. "Do you not know how beautiful you are? I would wager every one of my men is wondering what it would be like to hold you in his arms."

Her face momentarily reflected surprise, and then a shade of bitterness, with which he had infected her, tightened her mouth. "Are you also wondering, my lord?"

Staring into her upturned face, Gilbert struggled against the temptation to go beyond wondering and pull her to him.

"Nay." How he hated that his breathing sounded so ragged. "But I am remembering."

Her gaze wavered, mouth softened, and he thought she might be remembering as well. Then she gave a shake of her head and said, "Why has Sir William gone?"

Gilbert was relieved she had abandoned the game, but he was hardly pleased with the means by which she did so. Still, he would have to tell her, for what had taken place this night would soon be common knowledge.

"He has been divested of the lands over which he held vassalage," Gilbert said and headed down the passageway.

Graeye caught up with him as he reached her doorway. "Why?"

He motioned her inside the chamber. "Return to your rest."

She remained unmoving. "You are not going to give me the reason Sir William fell into disfavor?"

Though he would have preferred to delay the telling, he knew she would not be easily put off, and he had no wish to argue with her. "For crimes committed against the people of Sulle and money stolen from its coffers, I have wrested the lordship from him."

Graeye was not surprised, but still she wondered why Gilbert had given the man a chance in the first place. Then she remembered the knights who had been sent to follow him. She narrowed her lids. "He will go to Edward."

Though his expression gave nothing away, his lack of response provided the answer she sought. This was how he meant to uncover Edward's whereabouts.

"'Tis what you planned all along, is it not? You are not such a fool to place trust in a man like William."

He raised his eyebrows. "You disapprove?"

She lowered her gaze to her protruding belly. Why could he not leave well enough alone? What good would come of seeking revenge against a man for past wrongs? It was done.

"Edward is an old man," she said. "The revenge you seek grows old as well. Why not leave him be? He is no threat—"

"You are wrong," Gilbert interrupted. "Edward Charwyck plagues me still. He and the brigands he has gathered about him attack my villages, murder my people, and steal their goods. Had he but disappeared, I would leave him to his mad misery, but he gives me no choice."

Graeye reached to the door frame to steady herself. She had known nothing of the raids against the villages, nothing of the deaths or thievery. How naive she had been to believe Edward would simply go away, he who had sworn vengeance against Gilbert.

"I am sorry," she whispered. "I did not know."

He lifted her chin, delved her gaze. "You could not. But do not let it burden you. There is naught you can do."

She nodded, caught her breath when his head descended.

His kiss was gentle and brief, giving her no time to accept or reject it, then he pulled back.

"I must needs return to the hall," he said. "Good eve."

When he went from sight, Graeye lifted a hand, touched her lips that still felt his, and returned to the loneliness of her room.

The trap was not as easily laid as Gilbert had expected. Though William had, indeed, led his knights to Edward's camp in the eastern reaches of the barony, by the time Gilbert arrived with his army to do battle, there were only traces that anyone had been there.

Frustrated and angry, he returned to Penforke empty-handed and suspicious. For days he brooded and pondered the question uppermost in his mind. Now that William was gone, could there be another among his men who carried word to Edward, keeping the old man just out of reach?

It occurred to him Sir Michael might have maintained loyalty to his old baron, but always he rejected the possibility. Numerous times, and in numerous ways, the young knight had proved himself loyal to his new lord. Had he not attacked Sir William when that man had hurled insults and curses at Gilbert?

Who, then?

20

ONE DAY FELL into another, then spring was fully upon the inhabitants of Penforke.

On her knees in the soil of the flower garden she had prodded back to life after the frigid winter, Graeye attempted to salvage the fragrant woodruff Groan had turned into a bed. It seemed a hopeless cause, for the small white flowers were crushed, but she was determined to save them.

With the return of the young girl sent for a pail of water, Groan also reappeared, his head hanging as he ambled toward his mistress.

Graeye nearly gave in to his sorrowful eyes, but it was too soon to forgive him. This was not the first time he had damaged her flowers.

"Back with you," she said, doing her best to sound firm.

When he halted and stared at her, she waved him away.

Still, he stared.

"Do not think I will not return you to Medland," she warned. Of course, she would not, for she adored the mangy beast whom Gilbert had brought home to Penforke a month past following a visit with his vassal, Sir Lancelyn.

With a low groan, the dog turned and headed toward the donjon.

"I brought the water ye asked for, milady," the girl said as she lowered the pail.

Graeye smiled up at her. "Thank you, Gwen."

"'Twas nothin', milady." She extended a hand that held a small, polished apple. "For the babe."

Reflexively, Graeye laid a hand to her belly that had grown two months larger since her arrival at Penforke. "'Tis kind of you," she said and reached for the fruit.

She had been surprised it had been fairly easy to gain acceptance at her new home—in spite of appearing to be Gilbert's leman. Or perhaps because of it.

The castle folk's curiosity satisfied, they no longer made her uncomfortable with their seeking stares. Rather, they treated her as if she were the lady of the castle. And Gilbert did not dissuade them of the notion, though neither did he speak of wedding her to make it fact, nor to assure his child's legitimacy.

Still, things were better between them since that night he had told her of Edward's undertaking to destroy the Balmaines.

Though attraction was ever present, Gilbert had not broken his vow, and Graeye had not given in to her own emotions. An innocent touch, an accidental brush against one another, an unguarded smile. That was all. And that was enough.

"Milady," Gwen broke into her thoughts. "I was wondering if this evening ye might show me again that fancy stitch ye put around the neck of the baron's red tunic."

It was Graeye's turn to blush. She had not meant to have anything to do with stitching Gilbert's clothes, for it seemed too intimate a task. However, the young girl's clumsiness with the needle had prompted her to assist in the adornment of that one garment. And Gilbert's coming upon them as Graeye bent her head to the task had taken her completely unawares. His discovery would not have been so bad had he not seemed so pleased. Unnerved, she had nearly thrown the tunic at him.

"Aye, Gwen," she said, "I will show you again." But on one of her own garments.

The girl grinned, then hurried back down the path. At the door to the donjon, she turned around. "I nearly forgot!"

The apple halfway to her mouth, Graeye paused. "Aye?"

"The baron was looking for ye a while ago. I told him ye were here in the garden."

"Did he say what he wanted?"

"Nay, but he was smiling, milady."

What good news had been borne him? Had he again discovered Edward's whereabouts?

She frowned in remembrance of his failure to capture the old man two months past. The week that followed had been difficult for all. Once more glimpsing the wrathful man who had come to take possession of Medland, she had been shaken, but not out of fear for her own wellbeing, for none of his anger had been directed at her. It was then she had begun to appreciate the changes wrought in Gilbert during the months of their separation. His disposition toward her had softened, so much that even when she defied or scorned him, he did not retaliate by word or deed. She knew it must be because she bore his child, but her traitorous heart hoped it was more than that.

When the man in her head appeared before her, she startled so violently she nearly upset the pail of water.

"It seems a waste of time," Gilbert said, grimacing over the wilted plant propped against her knees.

"What? Oh!" Hurriedly, she began packing the soil around the base of the woodruff. "I believe it will come back."

He lowered to his haunches beside her. "Methinks you have too much faith."

"Methinks you have too little," she retorted and reached for the pail of water.

Gilbert took it from her. "You may be right."

Surprised by his yielding, she frowned at him, but he only smiled.

"You behave as if you have a secret you wish to tell someone," she ventured. "Do you wish to tell me?"

His smile turned up a bit more and he nodded at the pail. "How much?"

What a peculiar mood he was in. "Pour, and I will say when to stop." A few moments later, she said, "That is enough. Now, what—?"

A jab to the ribs and a punch to the bladder set her back on her rear end.

Gilbert dropped the pail and took hold of her arms. "What is wrong?"

She drew a long, slow breath, eased it out, shook her head. "Naught. Our child is simply making himself comfortable—and me uncomfortable."

The concern eased from his brow and he released her arms. But rather than pull back, he placed his hands on either side of her belly and bent near.

Graeye was too shocked to do more than stare at the top of his dark head.

He did not have long to wait to feel the next movement, though it was less intense than the last. "He is strong," he said, lifting his face to hers. "And impatient."

She knew better than to encourage him further, and yet she said far too softly, "Like his father."

The blue of his eyes darkened as his gaze held hers, then he angled his head and pressed his mouth to hers.

Ignoring the warning voices that were truly not much more than whispers, she took his face between her hands and leaned up into him. Though every day these last months she had fought the longing to be so near him, she wanted his kiss too much to deny either of them.

"Apologies, my lord," a voice intruded. "I had expected you would be alone."

Graeye and Gilbert quickly parted and looked to where Sir Michael stood a short distance away, eyes cast down.

Gilbert straightened and reached to assist Graeye to her feet.

Though ashamed at being caught thus, she viewed the interruption as divine intervention and, as she rose alongside Gilbert, chastised herself for not only allowing the kiss but deepening it. In that direction lay his bed, and never would she be his leman.

"What is it you want?" Gilbert asked as he stepped forward to place Graeye behind him.

Grateful for his consideration that saved her from meeting the young knight's eyes, for even in benign circumstances his presence made her uncomfortable, she began to pick the dirt and leaves from her skirts.

"A man comes—a villager. He says he knows Charwyck's whereabouts."

Graeye stilled her hands, awaited a response.

At last, Gilbert thought, *an interruption I can forgive.*

Eager to know more, he crossed to Sir Michael. "Where is he?"

"The inner bailey, my lord."

"Take him to the kitchens and see him fed. I will be along shortly."

"Aye, my lord." The young knight strode opposite.

When he was out of sight, Gilbert turned to Graeye. Her posture— hands clasped, chin up—evidenced the opportunity to crumble her defenses had passed. Clearly, she regretted what had occurred between them and would not welcome further advances.

"You have not told me your secret," she reminded him.

"Secret?"

"You certainly did not seek me out to assist with saving a doomed plant."

Gilbert smiled in remembrance of the news he had received. He should go to his sister, having promised he would visit when the child was born. But that was before Graeye, before the child growing in her. He could not leave her now, nor could he risk being absent from his lands while Edward Charwyck was still out there.

"My sister, Lizanne, has been delivered of a girl child," he said.

A smile rose on Graeye's face, but then, as if remembering the wrongs she believed his sister had done her brother, her mouth thinned. "I see."

"You are not pleased for her?"

"Should I be?" She stepped to a rose bush and fingered a bud. "She is, after all, responsible for my brother's death."

He sighed. "I have told you, Graeye, the only one responsible for his demise is Philip himself."

She met his gaze. "Until you offer evidence otherwise, I have no choice but to believe what Edward told me."

He wanted to argue that, but he knew it would be futile. "You are not ready to know the truth," he said.

She narrowed her eyes. "When do you think I shall be ready? When I am an old woman?"

"When you trust me enough to know I would not lie to you."

Bitter laughter dropped from her lips. "As you have not seen fit to offer me the same consideration, that could be a very long time." She lifted her skirts and stepped past him.

When she slipped inside the donjon, Gilbert raked a hand through his hair and shook his head. "A long time," he muttered. "'Tis good I am learning patience."

Knowing Gilbert and his men would leave at first light to ride in pursuit of Edward, Graeye arose from a restless night's sleep and hurried about the castle awakening those who still slept despite the clamorous preparations being made for departure. She set the kitchen servants to making the morning meal, though it was still hours before it was normally served, and the others she directed to transforming the hall from sleeping quarters into its favored state—communal dining room.

As was often her habit, she worked alongside those in the kitchen. Normally, bread, cold meat, and ale made up the first meal of the day, but she had decided roasted venison, a variety of cheeses, fruits, and hot bread should be served. The servants did not question her, though they were clearly disconcerted by the effort required to serve a sumptuous morning meal.

While the hot viands were being arranged on platters, Graeye returned to the hall. A good fire burned in the hearth and numerous torches were lit about the room. The mess of sleeping pallets that had covered much of the floor earlier had been cleared away and the benches and tables reassembled. Even the rushes had been turned and respread.

Pleased, she called for ale to be poured, then crossed to the great doors.

On the landing outside, it was nearly as dark as it had been an hour past, and she paused to savor the cool air against her warm skin. She sighed, swept the hair out of her eyes, and looked across the bustling inner bailey. By the light of torches, horses were being outfitted, weapons and armor cleaned and polished, and soldiers spoke excitedly of the raid upon Edward's camp.

When she located Gilbert where he stood alongside his destrier with several of his men, she saw his gaze was upon her. Suddenly aware of her appearance, she lifted a hand to smooth her hair, only to snatch it back to her side at the realization of what the gesture revealed about her. But it was too late, as evidenced by the half smile lightening his face.

Since yesterday's meeting in the garden when she had acted the fool by returning his kiss, been shamed by Sir Michael's witness, and frustrated by the continued refusal to discuss her brother's death, she had hardly spoken to Gilbert. She knew her silence made her appear petty, but she had found it to be her best defense against a weakening resolve when he showed her too much kindness, such as when he had brought Groan to Penforke. Behind the wall of silence that he rarely attempted to breach, she was given time in which to repair the holes he rent in her resolve—holes that, if left untended, might find her in his bed.

Gilbert disengaged himself from his men, crossed the bailey, and mounted the steps. "I had hoped not to awaken you," he said when he stood before her.

"You did not. I intentionally arose early to ensure your men are well fed before departing."

"That is good of you, but not necessary." He moved his gaze over her face, then her hair, much of which had escaped its hastily worked braid. "Ale and a crust of bread would have sufficed."

Fingers once more itching to put her hair in order, she curled them into her palms. "Sufficed, but that is all. It would hardly be fitting for them to ride into battle with hunger gnawing at their bellies."

When his eyes returned to hers, desire shone from them. "Do you also worry about my hunger?" he asked low.

Suppressing the urge to cross her arms over her chest, she said, "Only of that in your belly, Gilbert Balmaine."

He considered her, then took her arm and pulled her to the left of the doors where the shadows were deepest. Gently, he set her back against the wall and pressed his forehead to hers. "How long do you think to punish me, Graeye? How long will you deny what is between us?"

She quivered to be so near him, to know his eyes peered across the dark, brief space just as hers did. "You speak of desire," she whispered.

"I make no secret that I want you."

"And I make no secret that I do not wish to be merely desired." To herself she added, *I wish to be loved and to know the respect that goes with being loved. And that I will not have as your leman.*

"Desire is not a bad thing," he said.

"Desire alone is."

He sighed. "You know I feel more for you than that."

"What, then?" She hated herself for asking, for she knew he would not answer in any way that would give her hope.

He groaned. "How long, Graeye?"

"Forever."

He lifted his head and, with no small sum of bitterness, said, "Unless I marry you."

She drew a deep breath. "That is the bargain we struck. That is the bargain that stands. Should you need to ease your desire, you will have to look elsewhere." That last surprised her, but she knew whence it came, for she was not blind to the serving girls who liked to look upon him.

"How do you know I have not?" he said.

Graeye startled so hard her belly bumped against him. *Had* he looked elsewhere?

He muttered something that might have been a curse. "Forgive me. That was a cruel thing to say."

Cruel, but true? Feeling her throat tighten and tears at the backs of her eyes, she swallowed hard.

He laid a hand upon their babe. "I give you my word, Graeye, I have not been with anyone since you."

She was afraid to believe him, but she allowed it. "I am glad," she breathed.

He turned out of the shadows and, with his back to her, looked out across the bailey.

Graeye watched him some moments, then stepped toward the doors. "Gather your men," she said. "The meal is about to be served."

"Why do you act the lady of the castle when I have denied you the title?" he asked.

She faltered. Would he take this from her—that which was all she had to show she was the mother of his heir?

She changed course and came alongside him. "You do not wish me to?"

He looked down at her. "It seems much work for little reward, especially now that you are so heavy with child."

She sighed. "'Tis not as if I have anything else with which to occupy myself. Besides, 'tis my destiny."

"Destiny?"

She managed a faint smile. "I may never be your wife, Gilbert Balmaine, but I shall always be your child's mother." She turned and crossed to the doors.

21

SOMETHING HAD GONE terribly wrong—and not for the first time, Gilbert reminded himself as anger boiled through him.

Two of the three men he had set to keep watch over the village were dead, and the third had sustained wounds that might see him crippled for life.

Knowing well the long suffering that lay ahead of his loyal retainer, that for a fighting man the loss of a limb could prove worse than death, it took all of Gilbert's control not to rage as he urged his destrier forward and surveyed the devastation through eyes that burned amidst the smoke.

In silence, his men followed him past smoldering ruins and buildings that yet burned. At the center of the deserted village, whose occupants had likely escaped to the wood and were now making for the protection of the castle, Gilbert dismounted with the others. Mantles drawn over the lower halves of their faces to preserve some purity of air, they spread out in search of the wounded and discovered casualties—fortunately, only two.

Still, it was difficult to be grateful for such a small loss of human life. These were his people, and it had been his responsibility to keep them safe. He had failed, and it grieved him deeply. And fanned the flames of vengeance as he watched the village complete its descent to the ground.

Further convinced there was another traitor among his men, he methodically analyzed the events that had led to this atrocity. When word of the discovery of Charwyck's camp had come yestermorn, he had been anxious to get his hands on the old man. But, ever cautious, he had sent men to verify the information. Once confirmed, he had gathered his army, leaving only a handful of men at each village to continue the watch he had set them months earlier.

Somehow, though, Charwyck had been warned of their coming. The remains of his camp had revealed an almost leisurely departure, and the old man had left a message—stringing up the man-at-arms who had remained behind to keep watch over the brigands' camp until Gilbert's arrival.

In a blur, they had progressed through the countryside in pursuit of the brigands, passing villages mercifully untouched by Charwyck's evil hand.

Gilbert had just begun to feel relief that no others had suffered ill when smoke rising to the north had turned them toward this village.

Now, clenching his hands, he looked at the men who awaited his next order from atop their mounts. He considered each. Most had been in his household for years, and never had he been given cause to question their loyalty. He was almost ashamed he did so now, but this tragedy was no happenstance.

As Sir Michael was partially hidden behind another knight, Gilbert almost overlooked him. Though he nearly dismissed the possibility the young man could be a traitor, he recalled Sir Lancelyn's remark of months earlier. On the morning Gilbert had readied to depart Medland, believing he could leave Graeye behind, his vassal had warned of Sir Michael's reaction to the news it was Gilbert's child she carried.

Gilbert had not bothered to learn the specifics, for he had been too annoyed by the idle talk that had led to the conclusion, accurate though it was. Now, he realized, he should have given Lancelyn's warning its due, for Sir Michael had the greatest motive for betrayal. Had he not made clear his desire to have Graeye for himself? And then to discover his new lord had himself claimed her and gotten her with child…

Berating himself, Gilbert swung into the saddle and looked to the young knight. "Sir Michael, come forth!"

The man's gaze skittered away, and he turned his horse aside. But he was not quick enough. The others, surely sensing something was amiss, closed ranks around him. Thus, he had but one path of retreat—that which would carry him near his lord.

"Come forth, man," Gilbert repeated. "I must speak with you on a matter of great import."

The knight looked to the trees beyond the one to whom he had given his oath of fealty.

Gilbert guided his horse nearer, watched for the moment his enemy would attempt to charge past him. "Will you not enlighten us as to how the man you once served knew of our coming?" he pressed.

Sir Michael shifted his gaze back to Gilbert, then to the wood again. "Did he promise you Lady Graeye in return for that information?"

The young knight shouted, drove his heels into his destrier, and set a course to the right.

Gilbert turned his horse in that direction, forcing Sir Michael to veer opposite and take the less desirable course that led through the obstacle-strewn village.

Determined he would not get that far, Gilbert gave chase and shortly drew alongside the other man. Releasing the reins, he launched himself sideways and slammed into the knight, sending them both crashing to the ground.

It seemed they equally took the brunt of the fall, but it was Gilbert who recovered first. Ignoring the pain that shot up his injured leg, he thrust to the side and threw his greater weight atop Sir Michael.

"She should have been mine!" the young man cried as he fumbled for the dagger on his belt. "You ruined her, took your pleasure with her as if she were a common trollop."

"You know naught!" Gilbert seized the weapon the other man sought and pitched it to the side, then pinned Sir Michael's arms to his sides.

"*I* know naught?" the knight growled. "You are mistaken, Baron. I know much. I know Charwyck will see you dead and your misbegotten whelp sliced from his daughter's belly."

The threat against Graeye and their unborn child closed a fierce hand around Gilbert's heart. "How long have you betrayed me?" he demanded. "Since giving your oath of fealty?"

"Nay, I meant those words. But when I discovered you had taken Lady Graeye for yourself, I knew you were not worthy of my allegiance."

"Your attack on William—"

"'Twas convincing, was it not?" He snorted. "You are a fool, Balmaine."

Gilbert surged back and upright, dragging Sir Michael with him. "Will you die a knight?" he snarled as he thrust the man away from him. "Or a coward?"

Sir Michael regained his balance, narrowed his gaze on his opponent.

Gilbert swept his sword from its scabbard. "Draw your weapon, or I shall disembowel you where you stand and save myself the ceremony of chivalry."

The knight's gaze flicked past him to where the others sat astride their mounts, faces hardened against the betrayer. He had to know all was lost, that for a taste of revenge he had forsaken all.

"'Twill not be necessary," he said, then unsheathed his sword and angled it to the ground. He stared down its silvered length some moments before raising its tip heavenward, placing the flat of the blade to his lips, and lifting his eyes as if in prayer. Then, before Gilbert understood his intent, he grasped the honed edges with both hands and plunged the sword into his vitals.

As blood sprang from the mortal wound, he met Gilbert's stare. "All for a woman," he choked. "One you want only so she might warm your bed." He slumped to the ground, convulsed, and drew his last, wheezing breaths.

Gilbert lowered his sword. Grimacing at the ache in his leg, he crossed to the knight and knelt beside him. As he peered into eyes fixed upon the heavens, he murmured, "You are wrong, my poor misguided enemy, I want more from her than that."

Graeye meant to close her eyes for only a moment—to give them rest from the stitching that, with a bit more effort, would see the fine chemise finished before it was time to withdraw to her chamber for the night. Leaning her head back against the chair, she was vaguely aware of her hand losing its grip on the material and hardly noticed when it stole from her fingers and slid off her lap onto the floor.

The warmth of the fire wooed her toward sleep, something she'd had too little of lately. Giving herself over to its comfort, she curved a hand around her belly and went adrift.

It was how Gilbert found her an hour later, that great mangy dog of hers stretched alongside the chair that nearly swallowed her small frame. At his approach, the animal raised its head and gave a rumble of warning.

Gilbert scowled. If not for the possibility an altercation would ensue that would awaken Graeye, he would send the animal from the hall, but it was not worth the chance.

Breaking eye contact with Groan, he turned his attention to the one he had come to see and halted before her chair.

A fierce possessiveness stole over him as he considered Graeye—the bloom of color that enhanced the loveliness of her face, the lustrous sweep of golden hair that fell over her shoulder, the burgeoning evidence of her motherhood, and the way her hand rested thereon. In the sweet innocence of sleep, she was even more beautiful.

Though it had been less than a sennight since he had left her to pursue Charwyck, he felt as if it had been longer.

And still the old man eluded him, he grudgingly acknowledged. As there had been no more raids nor a single sighting since the fire upon the village, the only thing to conclude was that the brigands had left his demesne. For now.

Shaking off anger before it could once more take hold of him, he refocused on the woman whom it was no longer easy to believe was of any relation to the man he burned to put a blade through. He leaned down and lifted a tress of her hair, touched it to his lips, let it slide through his fingers.

As he straightened, Sir Lancelyn, who had three days past joined him in the search for Charwyck, entered the hall. Gilbert waved him away, and immediately he retreated.

With his back to the fire, Gilbert kneaded his pained leg as he continued to watch Graeye. Her lids flickered from time to time as if she might awaken, but she only sighed softly and caressed her abdomen before resuming her deep breathing.

It was the child disturbing her, he realized. Though he was tempted to lay a hand upon her to feel its movements again, he suppressed the urge for fear of awakening her.

He guessed he had been standing there a quarter hour, beneath the glare of Groan, when Graeye narrowly opened her eyes. Frowning, she slid her gaze up him.

"Gilbert?" She blinked as if to test whether he was made of imagination or reality.

"'Tis I." He bent near.

"It is," she murmured thickly. "Your eyes are not quite so blue in my dreams."

She dreamt of him? The admission stirred him, and the thought struck him that at least in this way he was in her bed. Might she not mind that this night he would, in truth, be in that same bed?

"It is late," he said and slid an arm behind her back and one beneath her legs. "I will carry you abovestairs."

Groan sprang to life, thrust his great head between his mistress and the man who meant to take her away, and showed his teeth.

Before Gilbert could bare his own teeth, Graeye said, "'Tis all right, Groan. He will not harm me. Go lie down."

Slowly, the dog backed away and lowered to his haunches.

Gilbert lifted Graeye high against his chest. Though it still took little effort to bear her, he noticed the difference in her weight, for she had not allowed him so near her these past months.

She yawned, nestled her head against his shoulder, and slid a hand up around his neck.

As he carried her toward the stairs, he did so with more of a limp than usual, his leg having yet to fully recover from his encounter with Sir Michael.

He was as surprised as Mellie when the two of them came face-to-face on the landing above.

"Milord!" she squealed. "I-I was not told of your coming."

Gilbert noted her rumpled garments, tousled hair, flushed lips. "That is obvious. What has kept you from tending to your mistress's needs?"

Graeye raised her head, looked around. "Mellie."

"Aye, milady?" There was a note of desperation in the girl's voice.

"Are you feeling better?"

"What?" Mellie said, slow to catch hold of the line her mistress threw her. "Oh! Aye, some."

"Good." Graeye resettled her cheek against Gilbert's shoulder. "See that you get plenty of rest tonight."

Gilbert kept his mouth closed as he edged past Mellie toward Graeye's chamber. There would be time aplenty to reprimand the girl.

To his surprise, the room was in readiness, but only tolerably so. The fire in the brazier was weak, barely keeping the chill from the room. Only a single candle had been lit where there ought to be several. The wash basin on a nearby table was missing a hand towel, and he did not doubt the water had grown cold. As for the bedclothes, they were turned back from a bed that had been poorly made.

Nay, he would not go easy on Mellie. Were he not so bone-weary, he would seek her out as soon as Graeye was settled. He shouldered the door closed against intruders—specifically, that drooling beast—and crossed to the bed and seated Graeye upon the cool mattress.

She rubbed her eyes, dropped her hands in her lap, and drew a deep breath that foretold what she would ask. "Did you find him?"

"I did not." He turned and went to stir the brazier's coal. "He has disappeared again."

Graeye stared at his back, aching for the weariness that sat his shoulders like an iron mantle. As befuddled as she had been coming up out of sleep, she had seen the dark circles beneath reddened eyes, the hollow look of a jaw covered in several days' growth of beard, and when he had carried her from the hall, his gait had told that his leg bothered him more than usual.

"Do you think he will return?" she asked.

"He will."

She lowered her gaze to her hands. Since word had first come of the discovery of Edward's camp, she had lived with a mixture of fear, dread, and relief. Following the burning of the village, Gilbert had returned briefly to gather supplies to pursue the brigands—so briefly she had not had the chance to speak with him before he and his men set off again. This past sennight had been difficult.

She stood, crossed to the washbasin, and dipped her hands in the cool water. Only after splashing it over her face did she discover there was no towel at hand and inwardly sighed. She was not uninformed as to Mellie's trysts with a particular knight. In fact, viewing it as an avenue by which to gain privacy for herself, she encouraged it by feigning ignorance. Though they never spoke of it, they seemed to have come to an understanding.

Settling upon her bliaut to wipe away the moisture, she lifted her skirt.

Gilbert's hand came around and dangled the covering from the small table across the room.

"Thank you," she murmured, stealing a sidelong glance at him as she wiped her hands and face.

When she set the linen aside, he turned her to face him. "I have missed you, Graeye."

She swallowed the ball of nervousness that rose up her throat. "Me?"

"Aye." He slid his hands down her arms, then inward to the laces of her bliaut.

She jumped backward. "You forget yourself, my lord," she said as she fumbled to draw the laces tight again.

"Come." He extended a hand but did not move closer. "I only meant to help you prepare for bed."

"I do not think so."

He drew his hand back. "I will be sleeping here tonight," he said and reached to unfasten his sword.

Graeye gaped, shook her head. "What of your vow? Surely you would not dismiss it with nary a prick of conscience!"

He sat on the edge of the bed and began tugging off his boots. "I would not." He dropped one boot, then the other, to the floor. "I shall abide by my vow not to force unwanted attentions upon you."

"Then what do you think you are doing?"

"Making ready for bed." He crossed to the wash basin.

"Your solar is down the corridor."

"Which I have yielded to Sir Royce."

She caught her breath. Sir Royce, the king's man who had secured Medland for Gilbert so many months past. "I did not know he had arrived," she said as he washed his hands and face. "You have business with him?"

"I do not." He dried himself with the linen he had given her and turned to face her. "He but passes through. We met up with his party this afternoon."

She clenched her hands in her skirts. "He will be staying long?"

"Just this night."

Then she could avoid him. Though she had adjusted to Gilbert's people, she was unsettled by the prospect of meeting the king's man again.

"You could sleep in the hall," she suggested.

He raised an eyebrow. "Aye, but you are here, and the bed is large."

As she searched for a rejoinder, he returned to the bed, laid back, and drew the covers over his lower body. Then, propping a hand behind his head, he stared at her.

She stared back.

After some minutes, he sighed and closed his eyes. "Come to bed, Graeye. You need not fear I will go back on my word."

She knew he would not force his attentions on her, but what if he touched her again as he had done in the garden? What if her desire turned toward his own?

She remained unmoving, and only when his breathing turned deep did she let the tension drain from her. Quietly, she stepped to where the candle burned on the bedside table and looked down at Gilbert. For the first time, she noticed how long his lashes were where they rested on his cheeks. As she lingered over his features, it struck her that she had never observed him during sleep. And yet they had been intimate enough to create a child.

If only things had been different, she silently lamented. If only she had grown up with the love of both parents and been allowed to choose the path her life would take. And how differently would Gilbert have perceived her had his consuming vengeance never been born? Would there have been a chance for them to make a real life together? Could he have grown to love her as she loved him?

Feeling tears, she licked thumb and forefinger, pinched the candle's wick, and turned to make her way toward the chair before the brazier.

Her foot came down on the rough sole of Gilbert's boot, and she gasped. Biting her lip, she made her next step more cautious than her last, but she did not get far before Gilbert turned an arm around her thick waist.

"You are supposed to be asleep," she exclaimed.

"I was," he replied and pulled her toward him.

"Gilbert, do not. I cannot—"

A moment later, what she could not do, he did, tossing the covers aside and easing her down beside him.

"Do you prefer to lie on your side or your back?" he asked.

"I should not be here," she whispered.

Though I long to be.

"I wish to return to sleep, Graeye. Your side or your back?"

I should fight him...

She gulped. "My side."

He turned her toward him where he lay on his back, urged her head down upon his shoulder, and drew the covers over her. "Now sleep," he said. "Just sleep."

As if that were an easy thing to do with him so near.

Minutes passed as she waited for his breathing to deepen so she might extricate herself.

"'Tis like holding a fence post," he muttered. "Pray, relax. I do not bite."

"I am not worried about your teeth," she snapped.

He grunted, beneath the covers caught the hand she clenched atop her belly, and gently pried it open. Then he pressed her palm to his chest and she felt the work of his heart beneath his tunic.

"Sleep," he said again.

With each beat she counted, she relaxed a bit more, and when she finally began to drift with him, she felt his hand move up hers, over her arm, and settle upon the child between them.

22

"How fares Sir Michael?" Sir Royce asked Gilbert between bites, his voice raised to make himself heard above the din of hungry, talkative men. "I notice he is absent from the hall. Is he still in your service?" As he lifted another morsel to his mouth, an expectant silence descended upon the hall.

Meat dagger suspended midair, Gilbert looked from Sir Royce to his men. The abrupt termination of their conversations was something he alone would have to deal with. Grimly, he watched his men flick their gazes from him to the lady at his side who had reluctantly entered the hall with their lord a half hour earlier.

When Gilbert turned his own gaze upon her, it struck him that she appeared to have disassociated herself from any and all. One hand gripping the stem of her chalice, the other turned around the handle of her meat dagger, she stared at the trencher between her and Gilbert.

Not for the first time wishing he had not insisted that she accompany him to the hall, he reflected on the morn that had begun with such promise. He had expected Graeye to awaken in a poor mood upon finding him still in her bed, but her disposition had been pleasantly peaceable. However, when he told her to dress quickly so she might join him in welcoming Sir Royce and others of the king's men, her mood had altered. When pressed, she had said she preferred to break her fast in her chamber. When further pressed, she revealed she was uncomfortable dining with the king's men.

Her aversion had made no sense to Gilbert, for she regularly took her meals in the hall amid the many. Thus, he had insisted she accompany him and, too late, seen his error.

Upon their entrance to the hall, the curious, less than furtive glances bestowed upon her by the king's men had begun to awaken him to her discomfort, and those stares were no less felt throughout the meal. It was one thing for Graeye to adjust to the curiosity of Penforke's castle folk—a necessity, since this was now her home—quite another to be scrutinized by those ranked high among the king's men who were merely passing through.

Not only was she an unwed noblewoman grown heavy with misbegotten child, she was seated beside the man who had fathered the babe—one who had no intention of righting the situation by wedding her.

Gilbert loathed himself for being so insensitive and would have seen her returned abovestairs if he had not feared it would draw more attention. Now, however, with Sir Royce's query about Sir Michael, he wished he had done so.

He looked back at the king's man. "We will speak of it later," he said in a tone he hoped expressed what he did not say.

The meal resumed its previous course, the noise of dozens of conversations once more rising.

"My lord." Graeye lifted her gaze to survey the occupants of the other tables. "Why *is* Sir Michael not among your men?" She turned her lovely pale eyes upon him. "Has he displeased you?"

So she had not been ignorant of all that transpired around her. Resenting the tight corner she backed him into, he looked to the trencher between them. Now was not the time or place to be drawn into talk of the traitorous young knight. Later, in private, he would tell her of Sir Michael's death.

He speared a piece of meat and offered it to her.

She shook her head. "I am not hungry."

"You would have eaten had I allowed Mellie to carry a tray up to you."

The dull emotion in her eyes turned bright, and she hissed. "As I would have preferred."

Gilbert knew anger was her due, just as he knew now was not the time to unleash it. Leaning nearer, he said, "'Tis too late for that. Now eat so our child may grow strong and healthy ere he ventures into this cruel world."

Graeye stared at him, tried to push down that which had writhed in her depths since she had first felt Sir Royce's gaze, but it was all through her now, its tendrils wrapped tightly around her. "Know you what they are thinking?" She jerked her head in the direction of the king's men seated on his other side.

"Graeye—"

"I will tell you. They are thinking they would also like a highborn harlot—a Lady of Eve—to grace their own tables and warm their beds."

Eyes that had been mostly blue deepened to near black as she had not seen them do in a very long time. But though his anger was as tangible as the regard of those who watched them, and inwardly she recoiled, outwardly, she did not flinch.

As if he did not trust himself to speak, he pressed his lips tight and thrust his dagger forward for her to take the meat.

Though tempted to do so with her teeth, she knew she would only be spiting herself by giving the king's men more to muse upon.

Drawing a deep breath, she pinched the morsel and popped it in her mouth.

Expressionless, Gilbert turned back to the trencher to fish out another piece.

Graeye took her time chewing, and when she swallowed, the dagger was there again. "I can feed myself," she said.

"Aye, but our child cannot." He pushed the meat nearer.

She took it, fully expecting him to return with more. However, he pressed her meat dagger in her hand and returned to his own nourishment.

"And do not feed that beast of yours," he muttered with a glance at Groan whose head was on her knee.

Surprised to discover how hungry she was, Graeye applied herself to the trencher. When it was nearly empty, she reintroduced the question Gilbert had yet to answer. "My lord, you did not account for Sir Michael's absence."

Again, his mouth tightened. "I have not forgotten. It will wait."

Certes, he was hiding something, for what harm was there in revealing the man's whereabouts? Resigned to biding her time, she sat back and waited for the meal to end.

"He is dead," Gilbert said.

As if struck with a fist rather than words, Sir Royce recoiled. "How?"

Gilbert met his wide-eyed stare. "By his own sword he took his life. But had he not done so, I would gladly have seen to it myself."

After a long moment, the knight said, "'Tis the same as Sir William, is it not? He betrayed you—to Charwyck."

Tilting back in his chair, Gilbert stared out at the hall that had emptied of all but the two of them. "Aye. His betrayal not only cost the lives of two villagers and three of my men, but the ruination of an entire village."

"But I understood you had set men to watch the villages to ensure against further raiding."

"I had, but when I received confirmation of Charwyck's place of encampment, I left only a token watch at each village and took the greater number of men to ride with me." He drew a hand down his face. "Charwyck was warned of our coming well in advance of our arrival."

"And it was Sir Michael who carried word to him of your intent to raid his camp."

"'Tis assuredly what happened."

"It is because of Lady Graeye he betrayed you?"

Gilbert resettled his chair upon on its four legs. "Aye, he wanted her."

Pressed against the wall near the bottom of the stairway, Graeye squeezed her eyes closed but could not block out the offense laid at her feet. Men had died because of her, villagers left homeless—all in the name of her father's vengeance and Sir Michael's betrayal.

She knew it was wrong to eavesdrop, but she had come upon the conversation unsuspectingly, and Gilbert's pronouncement that Sir Michael was dead had precluded all thoughts of withdrawing or revealing herself. Now she understood his reluctance to speak of the young knight. It was not idle talk, after all.

"Then Edward Charwyck knows of the child she carries," Sir Royce said. "And if not from William Rotwyld, then Sir Michael."

"Aye, and knowing it is my child, he will likely try again to harm her."

Catching the sound of footsteps, Graeye cautiously peered around the wall and saw that Gilbert had risen and begun pacing.

"Sir Michael took great satisfaction in describing exactly what her father intends to do," he said when he had passed Sir Royce a second time.

"Unless Charwyck has gone completely mad," the other man mused, "it is not Lady Graeye's life I would fear for, but the safekeeping of your child—and, of course, your own life."

Gilbert ceased pacing. "What speak you of?"

Sir Royce dropped his elbows to the table, clasped his hands, and leaned forward. "Your heir. The old man wanted an heir for his properties. For that, he brought Lady Graeye from Arlecy. Now he has a grand-child soon to enter this world who will prove more valuable than any made from the union of his daughter with Sir William. If he could lay hands to this child and see to your demise, he would have your properties and those he lost to you."

After some time, Gilbert said, "You are right. That is what he would aspire to—providing he yet has any wits about him."

"What will you do?"

"He will suffer the same fate as Philip. And then I will be free of the accursed Charwycks."

"Do you so soon forget Lady Graeye is a Charwyck?"

Beside Graeye, Mellie tugged her arm. "Milady," she whispered, "we should return to your chamber."

Graeye glanced over her shoulder. Until that moment, she had forgotten the other woman's presence. It was nearly a shock to look into that puckish face.

Mellie shifted her burden of soiled linens to the opposite arm and motioned for Graeye to follow her up the stairs.

Having no desire to hear Gilbert's answer, Graeye hitched up her skirts and accepted the hand Mellie fit beneath her elbow. Together, they stepped lightly up the stairs, neither speaking until they reached the chamber.

"Ye needn't worry I'll be runnin' to the baron with news we overheard his talk, milady," Mellie said as she pushed open the door and stepped aside to allow her mistress to precede her.

Graeye entered and crossed to the window. "I am grateful for that consideration, Mellie." And she truly was, for Gilbert would consider it further deceit should he learn she had eavesdropped.

"Like for like," Mellie answered.

Graeye frowned.

The maid shrugged. "Ye did me a good turn yestereve. I but repay in kind. Of course, now I'm no longer beholden to ye."

Graeye offered a weak smile. "Of course."

To her surprise, Mellie returned the smile. Then, shifting her burden again, she flounced out of the room.

Though the maid still tried hard not to like Graeye, she had lost much of her hostility. Indeed, she was almost friendly at times.

That thought dispelled Graeye's anguish over what she had learned with her eavesdropping, but only for a moment. Holding tight to emotions that threatened to overflow, she turned back to the window.

There was more she needed to know, Graeye decided later that day, and only one person who could tell her. But how was she to convince Gilbert she was ready for the truth about Philip?

As the last of the king's men disappeared from sight over a distant rise, she shifted her gaze to the bailey below and caught sight of Gilbert as he strode toward the donjon. Should she go to him?

Her quandary was resolved minutes later when he entered her chamber.

"I had thought you would be resting," he said as he closed the door.

Her moment at hand, and yet uncertain as to how to broach the subject, Graeye did not turn from the window. "I am not tired," she said, hugging her arms to her and leaning farther out to let the cool breeze snatch at the tendrils of hair about her face.

Gilbert laid his hands to her shoulders, gently pulled her back, and turned her to face him.

She averted her gaze for fear he might read the guilt there, assuming he did not yet know of it. Dare she hope Mellie had kept her word?

Stepping out from beneath his hands, she lifted her loosened hair over her shoulder and began to braid it.

"I prefer it unbound," he said.

She continued plaiting.

"Graeye." He closed a hand over hers to halt the jerky movements that betrayed her anxiety.

She peered up at him from beneath her lashes. "Aye, my lord?"

"You are still angry with me?"

She recalled her resentment at being made to dine at his side as if she were the wife he refused to make her. It all seemed so trivial now that she carried the burden of those men's deaths.

She shook her head. "No more. I behaved poorly, and I repent of any embarrassment I caused you."

Gilbert raised his eyebrows. He had expected her to continue with where they had left off during the meal. Why was she leaving the subject be? "What are you about, Graeye?" he asked as he searched her face and the reddened eyes she tried to conceal beneath spiky lashes. "And why have you been crying?"

"Forgive me," she said. "The pregnancy makes my moods flighty."

He had heard expectant women were ofttimes unpredictable. It was how his father had explained his mother's moodiness when she had carried his sister, Lizanne. Still, instincts told him there was more to Graeye's peculiar behavior than impending motherhood. Her anger was almost preferable to this.

He nodded his grudging acceptance of her explanation and drew her to the bed. "I must needs apologize for insisting that you attend the meal with me." He urged her down beside him. "I did not realize it would cause you such discomfort."

She stared at her hands. "'Tis done, the worst is over and..." She shrugged. "In future, when you entertain guests, I shall keep my dignity about me and not shame you."

Something was amiss. The woman he had lived with these past months would not so easily let go of the quarrel they had begun hours ago. But he would leave it be, for he had yet to answer the question she had earlier put to him. And answer it he must, for she would soon hear it from others.

"I owe you an explanation about Sir Michael—"

"Nay!" She shook her head. "It does not matter."

Her vehemence surprised him. What an enigma she had become. "He is dead," he said quietly.

She threaded her fingers together over her belly. "I had guessed as much."

He lifted her chin. "How came you by that?"

"'Tis obvious ill fortune befell him. Otherwise, you would not have been so reluctant to discuss him."

Gilbert was more inclined to believe she had either overheard his conversation with Sir Royce, or someone had carried the tale to her.

"You are saddened?" he asked.

"Of course." Tears filled her eyes.

Gilbert pulled her against his side and stroked her hair as she spilled silent grief upon his tunic. He did not understand how she could cry over a man whom she had professed to have no feelings for. Unless…

Though the possibility did not sit well with him, when she calmed, he asked, "Mayhap you loved Sir Michael after all?"

She tilted her head back. "Nay, Gilbert, I have told you I did not have feelings for Sir Michael. That has not changed."

His relief was immeasurable, but quickly forgotten when he realized she had not asked the cause of the knight's death. It served to strengthen his belief she had been privy to the information beforehand.

"Graeye—"

"Gilbert," she said urgently, "I wish to know of Philip's crimes. Will you tell me?"

He stiffened. "You tread where you ought not."

"I need to know." She placed an entreating hand on his arm. "'Tis your child I carry, and yet I know little of you—indeed, little of my own family. I would simply hear the truth."

"Would you accept as truth what I reveal?"

"Aye. Methinks I am ready for it."

He dropped his arm from around her and rose from the bed. "Did you know your brother was betrothed to my sister, Lizanne?"

"Edward told me."

"She adored Philip, fancied herself in love with him, though it was only his looks and her youth that led her to believe herself to be in that absurd state. Nearly five years ago, when she was fifteen, at the behest of my father, I took her from Penforke to wed your brother."

When he fell silent and his muscles bunched, Graeye knew the emotions that rose in him were dark.

"Though it was during the time of Stephen's reign when lawlessness abounded," he continued, "I was too self-assured to believe the short ride warranted a sizable escort. You see, I had not counted on the delay caused by such a cumbersome baggage train, and when night fell, we were forced to erect a camp. We had only bedded down when we were set upon. All my men were slaughtered and Lizanne was…"

When he drew a deep breath but no further words were forthcoming, Graeye said delicately, "Violated?"

"Nay," he growled, "though nearly. Still, that accursed brother of yours refused to honor the marriage contract based on grounds she was no longer chaste."

Seeking to distract him from the injustice done his sister, she said, "What of you, Gilbert? Did you manage to escape?"

He swung away from the brazier and advanced on her. "Think you I am a coward?"

She stared at him. His anger was so tangible she felt she would have to physically push it aside to reach the man beyond it—were she strong enough. "Pray, do not put words in my mouth, Gilbert. I did not mean to imply that. I know you are not such a man."

He halted before her. "Did you not accuse me of being a coward before?"

Had she? She had to search backward to discover the encounter to which he referred. It was true that she had accused him of such a failing in the graveyard on the morning he had sent her from Medland.

"I did, and I am sorry for it. But I was angry and only sought to hurt you as you were hurting me."

He did not respond.

"Sit beside me," she urged.

He ignored her invitation. "I fought them…wounded some…killed some. Then they left me for dead. A cripple."

"Not a cripple," she protested.

He caught up her hand and placed it on his thigh. "A cripple," he repeated and drew her hand down the thick ridge of a scar that could be felt through his leggings.

Graeye did not resist as he guided her hand lower and around the side of his calf where the scar melded with the smoother skin below.

"So many promises to keep, and I failed," he said and released her. "I still remember Lizanne's scream. Do you know how it feels to live years with such a reminder of one's failings?"

Graeye sat back, shook her head.

"Would you like to know who ordered the raid upon our camp?" His voice was so raw with pain it grated in her ears.

He seemed like an animal caught in a trap—oddly resigned to its fate, yet ready to hurl itself at the offender if given the chance.

"Not even a guess?' he prodded, his mouth a hard slash across his handsome face.

She knew what he wanted to hear. "Philip?" she whispered.

He raised his eyebrows. "What name was that?"

"It was Philip, was it not?"

Now he smiled, a bitter thing that nearly frightened her. "Perceptive."

"Why would he do such a thing?"

"You have much to learn about the blood that runs through your veins, Graeye Charwyck. 'Twas not simply that Lizanne was not beautiful enough. Her dowry was deemed insufficient when the opportunity arose for him to wed a wealthy widow. Thus, he thought to rid himself of my sister without suffering the consequences of a broken betrothal. He ordered our deaths."

Graeye lowered her eyes. It was not that she did not believe Gilbert, but that she did not want to. Her memories of Philip were alive with the cruelties he had visited upon her, but that of which Gilbert accused her brother was the purest form of evil.

"So you are not ready to accept the truth after all?" he concluded.

"I had not thought the truth would be so terrible." She forced her gaze to his. "It is not easy to accept that such evil resides in a man's soul. It frightens me."

Her reluctant, albeit undeclared, acceptance of the truth seemed to calm him somewhat. "Did you learn nothing from your father's attempt to murder you, Graeye?"

It was not something she would ever forget. But the old man had been half-mad over losing everything dear to him—and all to one he believed responsible for the death of his precious son. What was Philip's excuse for the evil in his heart?

"When did you discover my brother was responsible for the attack?" she asked.

"Last summer, when he decided he would have Lizanne after all, though she was already wed to another." He began to knead his thigh. "He abducted her when she was returning from a village on her husband's demesne. The miscreant beat her, then tried to force himself upon her. He would have had her, too, if her husband and I had not discovered his encampment."

Graeye felt as if he were leaving something out but did not press him.

"Your brother was bested in a fair duel, Graeye, and not one between him and myself, as you think. Though I did long for Philip's blood to dress my blade, I fought and killed another. It was Lizanne's husband who met at swords with your brother, and when Baron Wardieu bested Philip, the coward yielded."

"But then..." She shook her head.

"Unlike Philip," Gilbert continued, "Ranulf Wardieu is an honorable man. It was only when your brother turned on him and attempted to put a knife through Ranulf's heart that Philip earned an arrow through the back."

"Your sister."

"Aye, and it was more than justified."

Now she understood. And believed. "I am sorry. I did not know. 'Tis no wonder you hate me as you do."

He startled, and the anger that had tightened his brow eased. Leaning forward, he cupped her face. "I do not hate you, Graeye. I could never hate you."

Hope bloomed in her. Was it possible he might one day come to care enough for her that they could put aside their differences and raise their child in harmony?

Whatever he saw in her eyes surely disconcerted him, for he drew his hand away, straightened, and said, "But I will not wed you," and strode to the door. Then he was gone.

Graeye lay back on the bed and stared at the ceiling. Now she understood what had driven his anger when he had come to Medland and discovered her identity—why he had believed she had seduced him in hopes of trapping him into marriage. And why he would never wed her, not even to give their child his name.

She had not thought she could entirely forgive him for the wrongs he had done her, but now she had no choice. Her family had given him every cause to distrust and dislike them. His anger was his due, even if she was innocent of much of what he believed of her. If it took her until the end of their time together, she would do all she could to right the wrongs done him and his family and prove she could be trusted. She would fight him no more. If he still wanted her as his leman once she delivered their child—

She clawed up handfuls of the coverlet on either side of her, shook her head. "I will not do that," she said. "I will not!" All else she would give him, playing the lady of the castle in every way but that which landed her in his bed. She had repented of that sin with the promise she would not commit it again, that only marriage would find her as intimate with him as she had been that night at the waterfall, and she would not now turn her vow into a lie.

And if he takes his pleasure with other women? an insistent voice demanded. *If you lose what little you have of him?*

"Then I lose him," she choked. Indeed, it was not *if* but when, for he had a man's needs, did he not? Even if he never married as he had told it was unlikely he would do when he had come for her at Arlecy, eventually he would want a woman in his bed. And that woman might bear him children as well.

Then what will become of your child? the voice asked.

Gilbert had said he would have his heir from her, but what if this babe was not a son? And if it was a son, what guarantee was there he would not be set aside in favor of another?

The possibility nearly had her scrambling backward over her vows and convictions, but she refused to believe Gilbert would turn his back on their child. He did not love her, but he was capable of love, for she felt it when he looked upon her belly and laid a hand to it. With each little awakening throughout the night past, it had been there in his touch that caught the flutterings and kicks of the babe that grew impatient within the confines of her womb. And this morn, as she had stirred awake beneath a kiss upon her lips, Gilbert had moved to her belly and kissed it as well. She had feared he meant to try to seduce her, but he had smiled at her wide-eyed, breath-holding expression and quickly risen from the bed.

That did not mean the next time he would, though. And what if she wavered and, in a moment of weakness, yielded?

"I will have to leave," she whispered. And if their babe was a boy...

With a sob, she released the coverlet and clasped her hands before her face. "Help me stay true. Help me see past this pain and fear so I might know what You would have me do. And give me the strength to do it, no matter how it may hurt."

And, certes, it would be a fierce hurt.

23

FOR TWO DAYS, Graeye tried to repair the breach that had opened between Gilbert and her when she had insisted on knowing the truth about Philip. But Gilbert evaded her, seemingly no longer interested in seeking her out. The only time they were together was at meals, and then he brooded and kept his exchanges with her short and detached. Thus, she had as many days—and yet more reason—in which to ponder her precarious position and her babe's future.

Now as she watched Gilbert leave the smithy where new weapons were being forged for the battle with Edward, she determined it was time they talked. When he entered the stables alone, she squared her shoulders, skirted the corral, and stepped into the building that smelled of horses and fresh-cut hay. Halting, she searched for a sign as to which stall he had entered.

One of the doors on the left-hand side was open, and she crossed to it. And caught her breath. Gilbert had removed his tunic, and his bare back above his chausses glistened with the warmth of the smithy, the muscles rolling beneath his skin as he applied himself to brushing his destrier's coat.

She swallowed hard. "Are there not grooms to do that?"

He must have heard her approach—known it was she—for he showed no surprise. "There are." Keeping his back to her, he drew the brush over the animal's flank.

Graeye stepped into the stall and began to pick her way across the hay-strewn floor.

"Come no nearer," he ordered.

"But—"

"No nearer!" He glanced over his shoulder. "I would not have you trampled beneath this animal's hooves."

She considered the horse and saw what Gilbert knew well. The high-strung destrier was agitated by her presence, its limbs tense, its great eyes rolling. A moment later, it snorted, tossed its head, and stamped a hoof.

"Step away, Graeye!"

She backed out of the stall.

"Now," he said, "what is so important it cannot keep?"

"You have been avoiding me."

"Aye." He did not pause in his labors, now applying himself to the tangled mane. "For good reason."

She was surprised that he acknowledged it. "What reason?"

He kept her waiting, moving about the destrier as if she had not asked a question. Finally, he said, "'Twas I who was not ready to talk of Philip. Though I am ashamed to admit it, speaking aloud the memories made them come alive again."

Longing to ease the torment behind his reserve, she took a step forward. "Gilbert—"

"Stay where you are!" He glared at her. "If you do not have a care for yourself, have a care for our child."

He was right, but his angry words hurt. "Gilbert," she implored, "if I cannot come within, will you not come out? I do not wish to talk to your back."

He ceased with the grooming and leveled his gaze upon her. "There is naught that needs discussing."

She huffed. "You are stubborn, Gilbert Balmaine. I come to make peace and you scorn me. Are we to ever live in turmoil?"

He sighed, set aside the brush, and strode forward. Placing a hand on either side of the stall entrance, he looked down at her. "Is it peace you desire, Graeye, or just another truce?"

With him towering above her, the heat from his half-clothed body breathing across the space between them, it was difficult to think straight. She crossed her arms over her chest. "Peace."

With no small amount of suspicion, he said, "Tell me."

He was right to be wary, for she did not doubt his peace was different from hers—that his would include having her in his bed, making more illegitimate children who would ever be known for their parents' sins, and further earning her the title of 'harlot' such that not even God could dislodge it.

She looked around. "Is there somewhere we can sit? I have much to say."

Still, he did not move.

"Please, Gilbert—"

The sound of lowered voices from one of the stalls farther down the aisle moved his gaze from her. "The grooms are tending the horses," he said, then turned back into the stall, retrieved his tunic, and dragged it on. Shortly, he pulled the stall door closed and held out a hand. "Come. We will find privacy abovestairs."

Graeye looked to the loft overhead. She nodded, reached to him, and tried not to think on how good it felt to have his hand enfold hers as he guided her to the steps and up.

Gilbert led her to a corner radiant with sunlight streaming in through the wide open doors by which bales were winched into the loft. After seeing her seated on one of the smaller bales, he stepped back and crossed his arms over his chest.

"Will you not sit beside me?" she asked.

He slid his gaze down her, and when he returned to her face, a muscle convulsed in his jaw. "I am alone in a loft with a woman I desire above all others, and with beds aplenty to be made amid the hay, so until

I know the terms of your peace, methinks you ought to encourage me to remain standing."

She had not considered that, and thinking on it made her face warm.

"Tell me about this peace of yours," he prompted.

Now that the moment was upon her, it was more heavy than expected, the weight of it causing the words to sink down inside her. Determinedly, she dragged them back to the surface. "These past days, I have given much thought to my place at Penforke and our child's future."

Gilbert had been fairly certain he would not like what she had to say, and this seemed a bad beginning. From what he had come to know about his Graeye, her idea of peace would not likely mesh with his own.

Your Graeye? a snide voice slipped inside his head.

He tensed, then sent the voice scuttling away with the silent affirmation, *Mine.*

"And what have you concluded?" he asked, wishing he had not seated her in sunlight, for it loved her silvery eyes, pert nose, delicately bowed lips, and brilliantly gold hair nearly as much as he did.

Her gaze wavered, throat convulsed.

Nay, he thought, *I will not like this at all.*

"There are things that must needs be decided between us ere our child is born."

"What things?" he asked more sharply than intended.

She momentarily closed her eyes. "When you are done with me—"

"Graeye!"

She threw a hand up. "Let me speak. I know you have said 'tis not likely you will wed, but if you should, and you know the king may order it, or if you decide to take another into your bed for pleasure—"

"I will not."

Something hopeful flickered across her face, and she said softly, "Even if I forever deny you?"

Would she? "Will you, Graeye?"

"'Tis what I aspire to, but..."

That last word set him on edge, and he knew that if she looked near enough upon him, she would see something hopeful on his own face. "What?" he asked, inwardly wincing at how desperate he sounded.

She smiled sadly. "You must know I long for your arms around me, Gilbert, your lips upon mine. For that, I fear I will not be able to forever say 'nay,' that one day I will say 'aye.'"

He nearly quipped that would not be a bad thing, but her eyes filled with tears, and she added, "And the regret I feel now will be tenfold worse. Not only will I have broken the vow I made the Lord to abstain from such sin, but if I swell again with child, all will know I am more of a harlot than already they think me."

How he hated that word! Even as he told himself to keep his distance, reminding himself he needed more time to reconcile that her name and the blood running through her veins did not a Charwyck make—he stepped forward. Dropping to his knees, he gathered her hands between his. "You are not a harlot, and I do not wish to ever again hear you name yourself one."

She gave a sharp laugh. "Tell me, who sought you out that night at the waterfall? Graeye Charwyck, a daughter of Eve who did not care whom she lay with so long as her chastity was undone, who behaved a harlot so she would not be made to take holy vows."

"'Tis in the past," he said.

"Aye, and that is where I wish it to remain, for I do not think I can bear to go through this again."

Her words were so pained that, more than ever, he realized how hard these months had been for her despite her determination to make the best of her circumstances.

"Thus," she continued, "we must needs agree upon what happens when you are done with me."

He nearly argued it again, but forced himself to wait on whatever she was bent on saying.

"When you take another woman into your bed, whether by marriage or merely out of need, it will be time for me to leave."

A growl rumbled up out of him, and she frantically shook her head. "Pray, do not think that is a threat. I vow 'tis not. It is simply what must be. And when—should—that time come, I believe you will see it is for the best."

It would not come. But he once more held his tongue, for he knew there was more that he would like no better. He nodded for her to continue.

Her hands beneath his slid to the crest of her belly that evidenced she was past her seventh month. "This is my child as much as yours, but I know that if it is a boy, and regardless of whether or not he is your heir, he will thrive best with you here at Penforke. Thus, I ask for enough time to wean him ere I return to the abbey so he might ever have that part of me..." A small sob escaped her, but she swallowed and continued. "...and I might ever have memories of him at my breast to sustain me."

Then she thought it possible he might so soon turn from her to another woman...

"However, if it is a girl"—she looked to their hands upon her belly—"when I leave, I ask that you allow me to take her to be raised at the convent where you may visit her if you so wish."

There was such tightness in Gilbert's chest that he thought it must be how one of great age felt when the heart gave up its life's work. That thought nearly made him scowl, for he was reacting like a lovesick fool. He was not going to lose Graeye, most certainly not over another woman.

"Do you agree?" she asked.

He stared at her, the self-serving side of him demanding that he refuse her, the other side, that which he had not known he possessed before Graeye, loath to do so. To his surprise, it was the latter to which he was inclined to defer. What she asked of him was not unreasonable. Indeed, it was wise. God willing, never would he have to act upon her wisdom.

"Gilbert?" she prodded.

"If I do not wed or take another to bed, you will not try to leave me?" He hated that his voice was so low and gruff.

The corners of her mouth twitched as if toward a smile. "I shall stay and we will raise our child together—providing you do not tempt me beyond what I can withstand."

That he could lose her over, for he had spoken true in that there was no woman he wanted more than her. But it was not only the thought of losing Graeye to his desire that once more tested the integrity of his heart. It was what she had said she feared it would to her—that she could not bear to go through this again. It was hard enough to witness her tears, but to see her torn apart...

He looked from her eyes that were yet bright with moisture to her mouth and wondered if she could withstand mere kisses, for he could not imagine never touching her again. But if he was to be denied even that, surely she would allow him one last kiss.

He lifted his hands from atop hers, cradled her face between them, then leaned over her belly and lightly touched his mouth to hers.

She caught her breath, and he thought she would pull back, but she did not.

He deepened the kiss, and still she allowed it. "Graeye," he breathed.

"Gilbert," she answered, and he reveled in the sweet huskiness of the voice he had been denied that night at the waterfall—only to pull back from that place he could not go with her again.

He lifted his head, and when she opened her eyes, said, "Do not give in to me, Graeye."

She frowned. "What?"

He drew his hands from her face and stood. "I shall do my best not to tempt either of us past what we can withstand, but..." He sighed. "Know that I do not wish you to yield."

More tears and a tremulous smile. "You agree?"

"I do."

A tear slid down her cheek. "Then peace we shall have."

He supposed they could call it that, though it was so obviously an understatement it seemed a lie.

He reached to her, and she slid her fingers over his.

"I have agreed to your terms," he said as he drew her to her feet, "now I would have you agree to mine."

She startled.

"Never again refer to yourself as a harlot—of the past, the present, or the future. Agreed?"

She blinked, inclined her head. "Agreed. And?"

"That is all."

This is not supposed to be the outcome, Graeye thought as she stared up at him. *It should be, but it is not supposed to be.* She had asked for all, certain he would not grant everything but hoping for something more than what she had. Instead, the man who possessed her heart had beseeched her not to give in to his desire, as if the possibility of losing her mere presence in his life was more distressing than never having her in his bed. Surely that meant he felt more for her than desire, but what?

She searched his eyes, and in that moment thought she saw there what was also in her heart. Was it possible he loved her but could not bring himself to admit it—just as she, herself, dared not? Or was it something else? Fondness? So deep a love for his child that he would not have it denied its mother? Likely that last, and yet...

He does care for me, she told herself. *And that is enough. It must be enough.*

24

TO SPEND TIME with Graeye had not been his intent when he stepped from his solar, for he had other tasks that needed tending. However, when she halted her advance down the passageway and smiled wanly as if expecting him to pass her by as he had done often since their agreement a sennight past, he heard himself say, "Would you like to go for a ride, my lady?"

Her lips parted on a sharp breath, and the wan of her smile fled. "Truly?"

She sounded so hopeful that he was stung by guilt. Though she tended the garden and was allowed the reach of the inner and outer baileys, she had not been outside the castle's walls since her arrival. It seemed almost cruel, for if there was one thing he ought to know well about this woman, it was that she was drawn to the out of doors, as told by that night at the waterfall when she had arisen from the pool looking every bit an undine. And he must not forget her walks outside the abbey walls that had delivered her into his hands.

Yanking his thoughts back to the present, he said, "Aye, a ride."

She rushed forward and threw her arms around him with such force he was knocked back a step. Gripping her thickened waist to steady them both, he said on a note of laughter that surprised him, "You forget our child, love."

That last word surprised him even more—as it surely did her, causing her eyes to further widen a moment before she dropped her chin.

He was not one to hold his breath, but he found himself doing so as he both awaited her response and searched for an explanation that would satisfy her—and himself.

"Forget our child?" she said in a voice pitched higher than normal. "That would be like forgetting to breathe."

Which he had momentarily done. Relieved she chose not to comment on his slip of the tongue and telling himself it was but a reflection of what he felt for their unborn child, he gently set her back from him. "Fetch your mantle, and I will ask Cook to pack some viands so we might enjoy our midday meal beneath the sky."

Her chin came up. "That sounds lovely," she said and hurried down the passageway.

As he stared after her, he wondered what had possessed him to suggest a ride. She was, after all, past her seventh month of pregnancy. The answer was not as elusive as hoped. He had wanted to please her.

They would not go far, he decided. Just to the stream. And they would take an escort since he still did not trust his lands to be free of Charwyck's brigands.

A half hour later, with the sun edging toward the nooning hour, Gilbert signaled for his men to ease back and guided his destrier into the trees.

"I love the smell of the wood," Graeye said where she sat before him on the saddle.

As did he, though it did not compare to the scent of the woman he held close as was not otherwise permitted. He smiled, shifted his arm around her waist higher, and wondered why he had not thought of this before. A ride was the perfect means to be so near her without falling under the threat of temptation.

Almost as if to prove him wrong, she slid a hand up the arm he curved around her belly, her light touch making him tenfold more aware of how near they were.

"'Tis good you are such a large man, Gilbert Balmaine." She curled her hand around his elbow. "'Twould not be easy to fit your arm around my waist were you not."

He forced a chuckle. "'Tis better you are such a small woman."

"Hmm," she murmured, then stiffened.

"Graeye?"

"I…"

Continuing to guide his destrier toward the sparkling stream in the distance, he waited on her with growing unease.

Finally, she said, "The healer, Lucy, says my labor will be difficult—that I am too narrow."

Gilbert struggled to keep his body fluid so his own reaction would not add to her worry. The effects of birthing on one so small had not occurred to him. Foolish! Had not his mother, a woman not much larger than Graeye, died after birthing Lizanne?

Fighting the longing to hug Graeye tighter, continuing to move with the horse, he momentarily closed his eyes. It would be beyond difficult to lose her to the convent, but if the bright light she brought into his life was forever snuffed…

The mere thought of her gone from his world subjected him to such vicious claws that he could not imagine how it would feel should thought become reality. And he knew then that what he felt for her went well beyond desire, beyond what he had years ago felt for the woman to whom he had been betrothed. And he had fancied himself in love with Atrice—

Graeye peered over her shoulder. "Did you hear me?"

Feigning calm he did not feel, he inclined his head. "Do not worry. Lucy is a skilled healer and has delivered many babes. You will be fine."

She pulled her bottom lip between her teeth. "The baby—"

"Will come into this world hale and bawling for its mother's breast."

She looked unconvinced. "Gilbert, should anything happen to me—"

He lowered his head and covered her mouth with his. It was a brief kiss, but it achieved its objective. Graeye spoke no more of the birthing.

Heart beating wildly, Graeye turned forward again and determinedly set aside Lucy's warning that so troubled—and frightened—her.

Gilbert had chosen a lovely spot, she thought as they neared the stream. Though the water would be deep enough only to dip one's feet in, it ran clean and crisp beneath a sun that had settled at the top of the sky.

Dismounting first, Gilbert held up his arms, and she went into them.

"Still like a feather," he said as he set her to her feet.

She made a face. "You jest, my lord."

"Mayhap a little." He smiled crookedly, then took her hand and led her to a grassy mound beneath a tree whose massive girth could not have been encircled by the spread arms of three large men. There, he laid out his mantle, eased her down to sitting, and lowered beside her. "I am ravenous." He eyed the sack she held.

She settled her back to the tree, picked loose the string that held the sack closed, and peeled the cloth away to reveal a selection of bread, cheese, and fruit. "Perhaps your men should join us." She looked around at where they had taken up positions around the perimeter. "There is much here."

Gilbert paused in carrying a square of cheese to his mouth. "I had hoped you preferred my company to theirs."

She had not intended to imply otherwise. Peering up at him, she glimpsed vulnerability in his face before he masked it with a lift of his eyebrows. "That I do," she allowed. "It just seems a waste—"

"I will eat whatever you cannot. Now feed our son."

"Or daughter," she said, though she remained certain it was a boy.

Gilbert shrugged, popped the cheese in his mouth, and followed it with a swallow of wine from the skin he had removed from his belt.

A comfortable silence fell over them until Graeye asked, "You will be disappointed if 'tis not a son?"

He sliced off a wedge of apple and held it out to her. When she took it, he said, "Though I would like a son, if you gift me with a daughter, I will love her the same."

Gift. Love. His belief that he could feel so deeply for their child warmed Graeye. And she warmed further remembering he had called her "love" not even an hour ago. She knew she should not think too much of it, but that one word had lodged within her.

She leaned her head back against the tree, closed her eyes, and heard his voice speak it again. It was possible that one day—

The more you think it, Graeye, the more it will hurt if you think wrong.

But it was possible, as so many things with God were. After all, was there not peace between them that had seemed unattainable seven months past? Had he not agreed to what he previously would not have consented to?

"Are you well, Graeye?" Concern edged his voice.

She lifted her lids, and her heart fluttered nearly as vigorously as their babe when she saw how near Gilbert leaned. "I am fine. May I ask you something?"

"Ask."

"Have you ever loved a woman?"

His lids narrowed, but before she could too deeply regret asking it, he sighed and sat back. Settling his shoulder against hers, he said, "'Tis a fanciful notion to which I did yield many years ago."

Graeye felt a stab of jealousy. "Who was she?"

He looked sidelong at her. "My betrothed, Lady Atrice—a beautiful woman inside and out."

"What happened?"

"Shortly before we were to wed, she fell from her horse. She lingered a few days before her suffering came to an end."

Graeye's jealousy slipped away as quickly as it had stolen upon her. It was replaced by sorrow, not only for the woman who had died and Gilbert for his loss, but for herself. Here was yet another obstacle between them. To do battle with the hate he harbored against her family was a weighty challenge, to compete with the memory of one he had loved and lost seemed nearly insurmountable.

"And now I would ask something of you," he said.

If ever she had loved? She averted her gaze. *Dear Lord, if only I had not asked him! I cannot admit I have loved and that I still do, and yet I cannot lie. What do I say? How do I—?*

"Are you or are you not going to eat that piece of apple?" Gilbert asked lightly.

Relief flying through her, she blinked at him, then considered the yellowing slice he had cut for her. "I forgot," she breathed and bit into its sweetness.

As she chewed, he hooked a tress that had escaped her braid and pulled it through his fingers. "Surely, only God's angels have hair as lovely as yours."

Disturbed by the gesture, more by his words, she quipped, "Surely not. As well you know, I am no angel." Instantly, she regretted not thinking before speaking, for this time with him was too lovely to cast a shadow over it with reminders of her sin. But then she nearly laughed, for was he not reminded of it each time he looked upon the growing evidence of their one night together?

"I would not have you be," he surprised her, then tucked the tress behind her ear.

Gripped by mischief, Graeye raised her eyebrows. "Pray, tell, who is this man before me? Surely not the mighty Baron Balmaine."

He smiled. "'Tis selfish, I know, but I find I like you here on earth with me."

So much was told in so few words that she thought she might melt, but still she feared assigning too much meaning to what he revealed. And so she embraced the game and said, "Then perhaps I shall deign to stay."

His smile broadened, and the dimple she had suspected would be there if he ever genuinely smiled appeared.

Captivated, she reached up and touched it. His smile faltered, but then he slid an arm around her and pulled her against his side. She did not protest or resist, for no matter the temptation of being so near, the presence of his men would keep them in check.

"It occurs to me," he spoke into the hair atop her head, "that in spite of all, perhaps we were destined for one another, Graeye Charwyck."

"Destined?" She was surprised to hear such a word from him.

"Perhaps it was your God who drew me to the waterfall—"

She jerked her head up. "He is your God, too, Gilbert," she said, though she knew it would be better to turn the conversation in a different direction.

Something struggled across his face, and she sensed the bitterness in him wished to disavow it, but he inclined his head. "You are right. And I am still too angry with Him."

It had to be good that he could admit it—a place to begin.

"Regardless," he continued, "it could have been any of my men who ventured to the pool that night to clean away the sweat and grime. Indeed, I was happily surprised to find I was the only one to avail myself of it. And there you were."

She remembered. And the heat in her face became uncomfortably warm. "I cannot change what I did, Gilbert, but I would have you know it was not an easy thing to do, that I am aware it was wrong and selfish, and I would not have done it had I known who you were and considered that a babe might result—one who will ever be branded by my sin."

"Our sin," he surprised her yet again. "I indulged my desires with as much—nay, more—disregard for the wrong of it and the consequences. And unlike you, I have not the excuse of inexperience and naiveté to explain away my behavior."

Graeye thought she might cry. "I thank you," she whispered.

He kissed her brow, then drew his arm from around her and reached to their barely touched viands. "Enough talk." He broke off a piece of bread and handed it to her. "Now we eat."

An hour later, he lifted her into the saddle.

"Will you bring me tomorrow?" she asked as he mounted behind her.

He drew her back against him. "So soon?"

"Or the day after."

He took up the reins. "I will bring you every day if it pleases you."

She smiled over her shoulder at him. "It would please me immensely."

25

IT WAS NO simple task to enter the great fortress of Chesne, home to Ranulf and Lizanne Wardieu. Though he came with the peasants, the porter at the gate subjected him to much scrutiny before finally allowing him within, and only then after a thorough search to ensure he carried no weapon.

It was a humiliation Edward Charwyck intended to repay on the first unfortunate soul to cross his path.

Toting his basket of bread to be baked in the lord's oven, he followed the others across the outer bailey. Since he appeared to be but an old man outfitted in rags, none paid him any notice when, after leaving his bread at the ovens, he slipped behind the granary to study the comings and goings of the castle folk. There would be a pattern, he knew. He had only to find it.

Sometime later, a large man with pale-blond hair crossed the inner drawbridge, making for the stables with knights in tow. Edward was certain this must be the lord of the castle, Ranulf Wardieu.

It was not easy to contain the impulse his mind urged him to, but the piece of sanity to which he clung reminded him he was without a weapon and would be heavily outnumbered even were the man alone.

Were all spawns of the devil fair of hair? he wondered, thinking of the one carrying Balmaine's misbegotten whelp. Nay, Balmaine and his sister were dark. How could one be certain, then? Not all carried the mark of the devil clear upon their faces as his daughter did.

Slurping the excess spittle from his sagging cheeks, he pressed himself deeper into the shadows and waited to discover whether or not Wardieu would make this easy for him. Within minutes, he had his answer.

"Easy," he muttered when the falcons were brought from the mews. He grinned as the hunting party mounted their horses.

By the time they rode out beneath the portcullis, the old man was trembling with excitement, so much that he feared his heart might burst. Rubbing a hand to his chest, he stepped from the shadows, his empty basket concealed beneath the patch-cloth mantle hanging askew from his shoulders.

He entered the donjon by way of the kitchen. When a serving wench asked him to explain his presence, he knocked her unconscious—might even have killed her—and hid her in the pantry.

"Meddling wench," he grunted, then peered around the corner at the enormous hall that put the one at Medland to shame. There were a few servants about, but none noticed him as he crept along the walls to the stairway.

At the landing above, he heard women's laughter before he came upon the source. He crept down the corridor and paused outside the room whence the voices issued.

The door stood open a hand's width, providing a view of the backs of two women bent over an embroidery frame—one dark-headed, the other fair like the lord of this place. There were others there, but he could only hear them.

"Nay, Daughter, 'tis too large a stitch you make," the pale-headed older woman laughingly admonished.

There came a heavy unladylike sigh. "Give me a sword, a bow, a sling, but pray do not give me a needle!"

Following the heartfelt declaration came youthful laughter from those he could not see.

"And who will teach Gillian the ways of a lady if not you, Lizanne?"

Edward's heart punched his breastbone as he felt again the impulse to slay his enemy. He thought of the knife he had taken from the kitchen, but once more his grasp on sanity prevailed. In good time he would have Lizanne Wardieu's flesh, not this day.

"Ah, Lady Zara, it is a waste of time," Philip's murderer said.

Edward pressed himself back against the wall and darted his gaze along the corridor as he tried to guess behind which door the child lay.

The woman chuckled. "You have already told Ranulf of your gift. What will my son think when you do not deliver it, hmm?"

"Much better of me if he is not obliged to wear it. Look at this! 'Tis more like a pig than a horse!"

"You must needs make its legs longer."

A shriek. "Then it will look like a pig with long legs!" The sound of a stool scraping the floor had Edward gripping the knife handle. Perhaps he would have her flesh this day, after all.

"And where do you think you are going? You promised me an hour—a full hour, Lizanne!"

The feet approaching the door faltered. "It has been at least that long."

"Nay, it has been half that."

A groan. "You would hold me to it?"

"I would."

"But Gillian—"

"Is sleeping. Now sit."

A long silence followed before the woman won her daughter-in-law's grudging capitulation.

Regaining his breath, Edward slipped past the room and headed for the door at the farthest end of the corridor. It would be the lord's solar, and if he guessed correctly, there he would find what he sought.

He eased the door open, pressed his face to the crack, and eyed the room. Though taken aback by the presence of a maid seated alongside the sleeping infant, he was not disappointed.

The girl was humming to herself, holding a small garment close to her face as she pushed a needle through its bodice.

Subduing the half-sighted maid was simple. However, preventing the child from awakening when he lifted its small body and placed it in the basket proved trying.

As he wedged a sheet around the fitful babe, he considered the abundance of flaxen hair covering its head. Though it was a girl child, worthless in his estimation, he did not doubt they would come for it. And when they did, he would exact revenge, gaining for himself the child he really wanted—the Balmaine heir.

He turned to the bound maid who squinted up at him and mumbled something behind the gag he had shoved in her mouth. When he placed the knife against her cheek, her eyes grew round and body shook with fear.

"Tell them this," he rasped, leaning near so she could better see him. "The child's life for Philip's." Then, in one arcing motion, he cut a half circle into her flesh.

She screamed against the gag, but it was too choked for any but Edward to hear. He tossed the bloodied knife on the sheet alongside the child, then concealed the basket beneath his mantle.

Whether or not he made it outside the castle's walls to where his men awaited hardly mattered. The child and the knife with which it shared its bed ensured he would have his revenge, be it this day or a fortnight hence.

Lizanne did not walk from the sewing room. She ran. Eyes feeling crossed, fingers stiff, rear end sore from sitting too long on an accursed stool, she hurried down the corridor.

At that moment there were only two—nay, three—things she wanted. To find a comfortable chair. To place Gillian to her heavy breasts. And to discover a way out of the commitment she had made to take up the needle.

At the door to the solar, she paused, straightened her bliaut, and drew a deep breath. Then, not wishing to disturb her daughter if she still slept, she quietly entered the chamber.

Her smile dropped at the sight of the young maid amid the rushes who struggled to free herself from ropes that bound her hands and feet.

"Gillian!" Lizanne cried and rushed forward to confront what she prayed was not an empty cradle. She pushed aside the covers, searching for the tiny body that was long gone.

Her scream brought all within hearing running.

Lady Zara was the first to reach her. "Dear Lord!" she exclaimed, beginning a search of the empty cradle herself.

Lizanne shook free of the fear paralyzing her and grabbed Zara by the shoulders. "Ranulf! Send for Ranulf!" She pushed her mother-in-law toward the door and caught sight of the steward there.

"Seal all entrances to the castle," she ordered. "Allow none within or without until my husband returns."

The man ran.

Lizanne dropped to her knees beside the maid and pulled the girl's head onto her lap. Wincing at the sight of her poor, ravaged face, she removed the gag with trembling hands. "Marian, where is my baby?"

The girl mouthed words, but no sound exited. She drew a wheezing breath, swallowed hard, and tried again. "H-he took her, milady."

"Who took her?"

Marian shook her head. "Old man. He said…"

"Aye?"

She coughed. "The babe's life for…Philip's?"

Lizanne jerked, then gasped as the implications fell upon her like a violent rain.

"Dear Lord," she breathed, "it cannot be."

She looked again at the cut on Marian's face. Though there was too much blood to be certain, she knew. She lifted her skirt and, as gently as possible, wiped the crimson away.

"Charwyck," she choked as she stared at the crude *C*. With a sob, she covered her face with her hands and began to pray more vehemently than ever before.

It seemed the world would end before Ranulf returned from hunting, though it could not have been much more than a half hour before he sprinted into the hall.

Lizanne flung herself into his arms, loosing the tears she had tried so hard to keep in check.

"Gone," she wept as he held her. "He has taken our baby."

Knowing every second that passed took Gillian farther from them, Ranulf pulled back and lifted her chin. "Who has taken her, Lizanne?"

She muttered something and sobbed louder.

"Strength!" He gave her a shake when she crumpled against him. "Where is your strength, warrior wife?" He shook her again, and this time she met his gaze.

"Charwyck!" she spat and dashed away tears with the back of a hand. "'Tis he who has taken our Gillian."

Only once before, when he had believed Lizanne lost to him, had Ranulf felt such pain and rage. Roaring it, he pulled her to where his mother stood beside the maid who had cared for the babe.

"Everything," he demanded, slamming a fist on the table over which the girl slumped. "Tell me everything, Marian, and be quick about it."

He allowed himself only a moment of regret when the maid lifted her face to reveal the cruelty of Edward Charwyck. He could afford no more.

Since Marian had cried herself out, she was better able to relate to Ranulf the events that had led to the abduction of Gillian.

"A basket," Ranulf said. "And how came he into the donjon?" he asked no one in particular.

"Through the kitchen entrance," Lizanne said.

"And none tried to stop him?" He could not believe the man had slipped inside the walls undetected.

"Aye, but she is dead," Lizanne said and told him they had found the serving woman's body in the pantry.

Ranulf bellowed again. He wanted the blood of the old man as much as he had wanted the blood of the son. And he would have it. Every last drop.

He turned to his friend, Walter, who stood beside Lady Zara. "We ride now!"

The vassal stepped away from his wife and came to stand before his lord. "All is being readied, my lord. The horses are saddled, provisions gathered, and the dogs eager to catch the scent."

Delegating emotion to the confines of his heart so his judgment would not be clouded—truly, an impossible task—Ranulf turned to Lizanne. "We will need a fresh scent," he said, his warrior's logic gaining the upper hand.

"The sheets," she said. "And I must change." She swung toward the stairs.

Ranulf caught hold of her and pulled her back around. "Nay, you will stay. We will find her. I give you my word."

"I will not stay! 'Tis my child! I did not labor to give her life only to abandon her now." She wrenched free. "If you leave without me, Husband," she called over her shoulder, "I will follow. You know I will."

He certainly did. Frowning darkly, Ranulf watched her mount the stairs and disappear from sight. Of course he could set a man—nay, a half-dozen—to ensure she did not follow, but woe to those who found themselves given such duty. And still she would likely escape.

God's eyes! His warrior wife was no tamer than the day she had forced him to take up a sword against her.

Turning to Walter, Ranulf ordered, "See that my wife's horse is saddled as well."

"If she goes, I go too!" Lady Zara declared. Not waiting for the dissent she surely knew would follow, she lifted her skirts and hastened across the hall.

26

Still Gilbert would not attend mass with her.

Would he ever? Graeye wondered as she crossed the bailey with Groan on her heels. In the past month since they had reached their agreement, she had sensed a weakening of his resolve to distance himself from God. In fact, he had hesitated quite a long while before refusing her this morning.

Whether it was tomorrow or when their babe was born—a few weeks hence—she was determined to have Gilbert on his knees beside her in the chapel. Only then, she was convinced, would the wounds of his tragic past heal. Then whatever feelings he had for her might grow, perhaps even into love.

"'Tis the stars you wish for, Graeye Charwyck," she chided herself as she slowly mounted the steps to the donjon. With each passing day, the child grew more heavy, claiming every stretch of space within her until she thought she might burst.

Ah, you will not be small, will you, dear one? she mused. *You will be more of your father than of me.*

Refusing to allow her mind to drift further down the path to the birthing, she stepped into the hall. Instantly, Groan lunged across the rushes and set to growling.

A sharp reprimand from Gilbert sent the big dog skulking beneath a bench where he continued to rumble. Though relations had improved between the two males, it was still far from friendly.

As it took Graeye's eyes several moments to accustom themselves to the indoors, she heard the voices before she saw the men at the far end of the hall. Upon the raised dais sat Gilbert, Sir Lancelyn on his left.

"Lady Graeye," Gilbert called as he rose and started toward her. "We have a guest."

A few moments later, she took the arm he proffered and walked beside him to the dais.

"Sir Lancelyn," she said and made an awkward curtsy.

Having gained his feet, the vassal bent over her hand. "My lady, you grow more beautiful each time I chance to cross your path."

She blinked. Such flowery words? For whose benefit?

She looked up at Gilbert and saw displeasure in his eyes. Jealousy? Regardless, it had not been said for his benefit. For hers, then? But she had thought Sir Lancelyn rather cool toward her…

Courtesy only, she concluded and asked, "You have business at Penforke?"

He glanced at Gilbert. "Aye, business."

"You will be staying long?"

"I fear I cannot. I must needs return to Medland ere night falls."

Then he would have to ride like the winter wind to achieve that end, Graeye mused. "How does Medland fair?"

"All is well, my lady. The people are content, the crops sowed, and soon the donjon will be taken down and a stone tower erected in its place."

"'Tis difficult to comprehend such changes in so short a time," she said. "Obviously, you are, indeed, the laudable man Baron Balmaine claims you to be."

He smiled, once more glanced at his liege. "I am pleased to know I am so highly regarded."

"That you are," Gilbert said, then drew Graeye toward the stairs. There, he halted and said, "As methinks it will be hours ere I finish with Sir Lancelyn, it will not be possible to take our ride today."

"Is something wrong?"

"Naught you must needs concern yourself over."

She did not think she should believe him, but saw nothing in his expression to dissuade her from the sense of security she had enjoyed since arriving at Penforke. "Very well," she said, though disappointed at being unable to take advantage of the lovely day. Since that first time Gilbert had taken her to the stream, they had returned nearly every day that the weather allowed. And the last three had been wet and overcast. Hopefully, the next would dawn as beautifully as this one.

"On the morrow," he promised.

She smiled, then began the trek up the stairs. She got only as far as the second step before he swept her off her feet and settled her against his chest. Quickly, he carried her up and lowered her to the landing.

"Chivalrous, my lord," she teased. "Mayhap I should ask Sir Lancelyn to visit more often."

He grinned. "Such impudence. Your tongue grows more like Lizanne's every day."

It was the first Graeye had heard of it and, considering what she knew of his sister from Mellie, the comparison surprised her. Still, it did not offend, for she had found much to admire in the fearless woman of whom Mellie spoke. The maid had not gone into detail, but she had explained that, a year earlier, while Gilbert was at court, a vengeful baron had ridden on Penforke, demanding satisfaction for some wrong he claimed Lizanne had done him. Rather than risk the safety of the castle's inhabitants, Lizanne had given herself over to the man. Curiously, she later wed the baron.

"I hope you do not think it a bad thing that I should so remind you of your sister," Graeye said.

"I do not, though, certes, it is good I am accustomed to such." He dropped a kiss on her lips, said, "I must leave you now," and started down the stairs.

Inside her chamber, Graeye settled herself in the window embrasure to gain sun upon her face. It felt wonderful, though it could not compare with the excursions to the stream. Resting her hands on her belly, she peered down at the activity in the inner bailey.

Though she paid little heed to the knights and men-at-arms, she missed nothing of the villagers who had come earlier that morning, as they did nearly every day, to perform various duties for their lord. Focusing on a large peasant woman draped in a worn mantle, an idea struck her and she felt a rush of excitement.

An adventure—not unlike those Gilbert's sister had undertaken, though on a far smaller scale. Did she dare?

She nibbled her lip. Since Edward had left the barony, had not Gilbert pronounced the demesne safe? In fact, the last few times they had gone to the stream, he had not brought along an escort.

Her smile faltered as the next obstacle dropped into her path. Where could she obtain peasant's clothes to make herself less conspicuous to the guards? Although each person who came within the castle's walls was thoroughly scrutinized, merely a count was taken when they left to ensure none stayed behind.

One of her mother's old bliauts might do. Providing she left the laces loose to accommodate her girth, it would likely fit. And with a little soil, the coarse black mantle given to her at the abbey would complete the disguise. Both were in her chest.

But how to get past Gilbert? She could not pass unseen through the hall.

It struck her then—she could use the hidden stairway Gilbert had revealed a fortnight past. If she took a torch, she would be able to negotiate it fine and, perhaps, return by it without any knowing of her little jaunt.

Graeye hastened from the window to her chest, propped open the lid, and eased onto her knees. She chose the first old bliaut that came to hand, laid it aside, and dug deeper in search of the mantle. When she came upon the nun's bridal habit she had long ago buried, she pulled it out and ran her hands down the fine material. The last time she had worn it was the day Gilbert had come to Medland. How different he now was from that wrathful man who had cornered her in the chapel. Different, but still cynical.

Wondering if the habit could be used to fashion a baptismal gown for the babe, she laid the garment aside. Next, she drew out the mantle that had been given to her upon her return to the abbey. It was of rough, inferior wool, but though too warm for the day, it was necessary to conceal her shape and face.

She stood and began to loosen her laces.

A tap sounded on the door.

She caught her breath, dropped the chest's lid, and sat down upon it. "Come!" she called.

"You are not feeling well, milady?" Mellie asked as she closed the door behind her.

"I am tired, that is all."

"Ah, the babe," the maid said as she came to stand before her mistress. Her gaze flicked to the garments alongside the chest. Though she frowned, she said nothing.

Nervously, Graeye touched her belly. "It seems he never stops moving."

Mellie fit a hand to Graeye's elbow to assist her to standing. "I'll help ye to bed. Rest will do ye and the babe good."

"I am suddenly quite hungry," Graeye said. "Mayhap you could fetch some bread and cheese?"

Mellie guided her to the bed and peeled back the covers. "Ye'd like a tankard of mead with that?"

Graeye started to decline, then nodded. "That sounds fine—and fruit." She lowered to the mattress.

Shortly, Mellie slipped out into the corridor.

Graeye pulled the mantle around her, slumping within the folds of the hood to hide herself from the castle folk she passed. If any paid her any notice, she did not know, for she kept her head down.

Keeping to the shadows as much as possible, she crossed the bailey without mishap and ensconced herself within the narrow alley that ran the back of the smithy. Only then did she peer out from her hood to spy the gatehouse.

The portcullis was raised, the two guards who stood before the gaping portal exchanging boasts of one kind or another. Still, they were alert.

Deciding she would wait until she saw another pass from the castle unhindered, she settled herself back against the wall and shifted the sack containing the food Mellie had brought her to the opposite hand.

Something cold and wet touched her palm, and she nearly screamed. A hand to her mouth, she stumbled back and stared at the large dog who gazed up at her.

"Groan!" she gasped.

He wagged his tail.

Knowing she could not risk being seen with him, she softly scolded, "Nay, Groan. Go back."

He did not move.

She stomped a foot, pointed toward the donjon. "Go!"

He groaned. Then, blessedly, he squeezed around in that narrow space and ambled away. At the entrance, he turned to look back at her, but when she waved him away again, he went with his tail between his legs.

Shortly, Graeye peeked around the building to assure herself he was not lurking near. She was pleased to find he had disappeared completely.

At the sight of a peasant approaching the gatehouse, she held her breath and waited to see if the man would be allowed to pass without search. He was.

Stirred by excitement, and having assured herself the hood hid her face and the mantle her cumbersome body, she stepped forward. The baby kicked, striking her side with enough force to snatch her breath. She had only just recovered when it threw a limb out to the other side.

She moaned, slipped back into the shadows, and ran a soothing hand over her belly. "A few more weeks," she whispered. The impatient babe calmed moments later.

Clutching her sack, Graeye once more stepped from the building and made her way to the gatehouse. Luck stayed with her, and it was not long before she crossed the drawbridge.

Grinning at having succeeded in her venture, she set her course across the wide, open grassland. Beyond, through the trees, lay the stream.

As she approached the cover of the wood, the thunder of hooves halted her progress. Peering across her shoulder, she shielded her eyes against the sun's glare and picked out a group of riders who approached the castle.

Who were they? She looked back at the fortress and, seeing the portcullis had been lowered, caught her breath. Enemies?

Dear Lord, she beseeched, *have I made a mistake in leaving the safety of the walls?*

She once more turned her attention upon the riders who were fast gaining ground. Realizing she stood in their path, she hurried toward the trees.

Still they came upon her, veering away to avoid trampling her beneath their horses' hooves.

In her haste, Graeye stumbled and landed on her fours, both surprised and terrified when a shout brought the riders to a halt.

The hood having fallen from her head, she gained her feet and turned. Her gaze caught and held that of a man with hair so pale it looked nearly white. And he was nearly as large as Gilbert.

A dark-headed man broke from the group and moved with fluid ease upon his horse toward her.

Graeye realized her mistake moments later when she found herself staring up at a woman clothed as a man, a thick braid hanging over her shoulder. She was lovely, though her face was dark with what seemed fatigue.

"You are well?" the woman asked with seemingly genuine concern, unwavering even when her eyes lit upon the stain marring Graeye's face.

"Aye," she said. "No harm is done."

The woman swept her gaze over her once more, then nodded and urged her horse back around.

Relief swept Graeye when the riders continued on to the castle. Slipping behind a tree, she waited to see how they would be received. It was not long before the portcullis rose and they were allowed within.

All was well, then. Friend, not foe.

"Lizanne." Smiling, Gilbert raised his arms to receive her down from her mount.

She had no smiles nor warm words for the brother she had not seen in over nine months. Mouth grimly set, she allowed him to assist in her dismount.

"What is wrong?" Gilbert asked, looking from her to Ranulf.

"Charwyck!" Lizanne spat.

Gilbert dropped his hands from her waist. "What speak you of?"

"He has stolen our child," she burst, eyes suddenly brimming with tears.

Ranulf stepped forward and gathered her against his side. "We must speak, Gilbert," he said and began to mount the steps to the donjon.

Gilbert struggled against the anger tearing at his insides, knowing that to give in would distress Lizanne more. He exchanged a look with Sir Lancelyn and motioned for the man to follow.

In the hall, serving wenches scurried to laden the tables with refreshments for the weary travelers.

With a single sharp word, Gilbert sent them back to the kitchens. However, almost immediately, Mellie appeared, hands flapping with excitement over Lizanne's return, shrill words tumbling from her mouth. He sent her away, too.

When the hall was clear of prying eyes and ears, Gilbert leaned toward Ranulf. "Tell me."

Ranulf finished his tankard of ale. "Four days past, in the light of day, Gillian was taken from Chesne. It is certain Charwyck is the one who stole her."

"How know you this?"

"'Twas an old man," Lizanne answered. "He told the maid it was Gillian's life for Philip's. Then he cut a C into the girl's face."

Gilbert slammed a fist to the table. "God's teeth, will we never be free of the devil?"

Ranulf stayed Gilbert's temper with a hand upon his arm. "The dogs picked up Gillian's scent. We followed it for two days, but lost it on the third. As Charwyck was heading south, we continued on here. Have you—?"

"Aye. Sir Lancelyn brought news this morn of Charwyck's return. The brigands pillaged a village near Medland yesterday."

Sir Lancelyn confirmed this with a nod.

"Then he is near," Ranulf said. "We will find him."

Lizanne rose to her feet, stumbling slightly as she did so. Clearly, she was exhausted, her shadowed eyes haunted, face drawn with worry.

Forcing himself to think logically, Gilbert shook his head. "It will do no good to rush out without direction. We must plan if we are to succeed in recovering Gillian unharmed. Methinks the babe is but a pawn to lure us, the ones Charwyck believes responsible for Philip's death."

Reluctantly, Ranulf and Lizanne resumed their seats.

"We do have an advantage—an unexpected one," Gilbert said, leaning forward. "The villagers felled one of Charwyck's men during the raid. Though he is wounded, methinks he will talk ere long."

"Where is he?" Ranulf demanded.

"Later," Gilbert said, though he, too, was anxious to discover the man's secrets. "He must be tended to. His wounds are severe."

"How many men can you spare?" Ranulf asked.

"As many as you require."

A short while later, with a plan beginning to take shape, the two men and Lizanne rose from the table. They traversed the hall, only to be brought up short by Mellie before they reached the doors.

"Milord," she called, skidding over the rushes in her haste to reach Gilbert. "'Tis Lady Graeye. I cannot find her."

Gilbert met the girl's anxious gaze. "She is not in her chamber?"

"Nay, milord, though I left her there but an hour past. She said she was tired—needed to rest."

"You have *that* woman under your roof?" Lizanne exclaimed and swung around to glare at her brother. "You wrote that you would keep her at Medland. Why is she here?"

"Circumstances changed," Gilbert growled, then returned his attention to Mellie. "Mayhap she is in the garden?"

The maid blinked. "I do not know, milord."

Gilbert turned to Sir Lancelyn. "Send word to search the castle. She must be somewhere near. None would have allowed her to leave."

"Milord." Mellie tugged on his sleeve. "There is the matter of her habit."

"Habit?"

"Aye, that which she keeps in her chest. This morn she had it and one of her mother's old bliauts laid out. The habit is still there, but the bliaut is missing, as is the mantle she brought with her from the abbey."

"Show me," he said and followed her up the stairs.

In Graeye's chamber, Gilbert angrily swept aside the white garment. Had Graeye left him? Returned to the abbey? Or worse, to her father?

"'Tis as I said, milord, the other garments are gone." Mellie wrung her hands where she stood alongside the bed. "Methinks 'tis what she wore to escape unnoticed."

"Why would she want to escape?" he demanded. "Dear Lord, she will soon give birth to our child."

The maid twitched, averted her gaze.

"What are you not telling me, Mellie?"

"Milord, do you beat me," she ventured, "I will understand and take my punishment as you see fit."

"Tell me!"

"'Tis your conversation with the king's man, Sir Royce. Milady and I chanced to overhear your talk of Sir Michael's death—though we did not purposely set ourselves to eavesdropping. Nay, milord, we did not." She ventured a glance at his face, shuddered. "Lady Graeye was quite disturbed—methinks blamed herself for the knight's death and the loss of the village."

Gilbert swung away. It would certainly explain Graeye's odd behavior that day. Still, he could not believe she had left him. She had seemed content enough and their agreement yet stood.

How his leg pained him, alternately throbbing and burning as he paced the room and sought answers to questions he had not thought he would have to ask.

Abruptly, he abandoned his pacing. Would his men think to look in the chapel? With renewed hope, he left the solar and descended to the hall.

He did not get far before Lizanne took hold of his arm. "Gilbert, there was a peasant woman we passed on the approach to Penforke. Methinks it may have been this Graeye Charwyck in disguise."

He frowned. "Why do you say that?"

"She was alone and—"

"What did she look like?"

"Fair. Pretty."

"How was she clothed?"

"A black mantle, and methinks it was a brown gown beneath. Also, there was a stain upon her face—"

"'Twas her!"

"Then she is taking word to her father," Lizanne concluded. "Likely, she has been doing so for some time. She has betrayed you."

Gilbert could not believe that. All was not as it seemed. "What direction did she take?"

"To the east—into the woods."

Relief radiated through him like summer's first heat, certain as he was that she had gone only for the outing he had promised her. "Nay," he said, "she has not betrayed me."

Lizanne laid a hand on his shoulder. "She is a Charwyck. Do not let her make a fool of you."

"You are wrong," he bit.

She blinked, then her eyes widened. "For pity's sake, you do not love the woman, do you, Gilbert? She is Philip's sister!"

Seeing the anguish in her desperate, imploring eyes, Gilbert's anger eased. As no other possibly could, he understood the suffering that prompted her words. Lightly, he touched her face. "In name only is she a Charwyck," he said, accepting the words even as he spoke them. "And even that will no longer be."

Lizanne's eyebrows gathered. "You cannot mean to wed her?"

"I can," he said, hardly able to believe it himself. "And do." He kissed her cheek. "'Tis much the same as when I learned you had wed Ranulf, little sister. And just as you chose well, so have I."

She shook her head, dropped her hand from his arm.

"Come." Gilbert motioned the men to follow. "We ride to the stream." With the possible danger Graeye had placed herself in, he was taking no chances on going unescorted. If Edward reached her ahead of him, he would be prepared.

27

Partially obscured by the leafy trees, its long journey half completed, the sun shone directly overhead.

Graeye sighed. Though she knew she should be making her way back, she could not bring herself to leave. Not yet. Especially considering the amount of effort required to slip away. And no matter Gilbert's wrath. If he had discovered her missing, it would be worth the freedom she had gained, even for this short time.

Picking at her meal, she listened to the water's song as it flowed past. She missed Gilbert—wished he was with her. It was not quite the same.

The sound of hooves startled her. Then she groaned. It would be Gilbert, and he would be angry. However, in the next instant, she questioned why he would come with so many. Perhaps it was Edward and his brigands.

She pushed to her feet and made for the nearest refuge of heavy foliage. But it was too late. The riders reached the clearing before she was halfway to her destination.

Heart pounding, arm curved around her belly, she swung around to face them. Mercifully, her eyes fell first on Gilbert where he rode before the others.

"Gilbert!" she exclaimed when he reined in. "You frightened me."

He tossed aside the reins, dismounted, and pulled her into his arms. "Merciful God!" he said with such ferocity she startled.

When he finally drew back, she could only stare at him.

"'Twas foolish, Graeye," he said. "Have you nary a care for the safety of yourself or our child?"

It was less than she deserved, she reminded herself as she pushed down an indignant retort. "Aye, 'twas foolish." She smiled apologetically. "And rather pointless without your company. But now that you are here..."

"We must return to the castle." He pulled her toward his destrier.

"Ah, the visitors," she said and was surprised when her eyes lit upon two of those who had nearly trampled her beneath their horses. Though the pale-headed man's face revealed nothing of his emotions, the woman alongside him clearly expressed hers—anger.

As Gilbert lifted her into the saddle, Graeye asked, "Who—?"

"Introductions can wait until we are returned," he said.

Something was wrong, Graeye realized.

When they gathered in the hall a short time later, she was not surprised when he introduced her to his sister. On the ride back, she had guessed as much, not only from the woman's resemblance to her brother, but by the enmity she exuded. It was the same emotion with which Gilbert had subjected Graeye that first day at Medland. To be confronted by such an obstacle after having so recently overcome one of similar proportions greatly burdened her.

"Lady Lizanne." Graeye made a shallow curtsy.

The woman stared at her, then turned on her heel and strode away.

Refusing to suffer the same punishment twice in a lifetime, Graeye left Gilbert's side and followed. Near the stairs, she caught up with Lady Lizanne and stepped in front of her. "I understand your hatred for the Charwycks," she said, "but do not pass judgment on me ere you know me."

The woman blinked, then her green eyes flashed. "I want my child back," she said in a wintry voice.

Frowning, Graeye looked over her shoulder at Gilbert who strode toward them. Someone had taken his sister's baby?

She gasped. It had to be the work of the man who had fathered her. Yet another nightmare. "Ah, nay," she cried and fled up the stairs. Hardly had she slammed the door of her chamber and pushed the bolt into place than Gilbert arrived.

"Open the door, Graeye!"

She pressed her forehead to it. "Pray, leave me be," she pleaded.

A lengthy silence followed, then his voice came through. "Graeye, it is not your fault. No one blames you."

She almost laughed. "Do they not?" she said, bitterness surging through her over this new trial God had set her.

"Lizanne will come around," he said. "She is frightened, that is all."

That was not all, but it was useless to argue. "Please, Gilbert, I need to be alone."

She heard his harsh sigh. "Very well, but if this door is locked against me once night falls, I will break it down."

She did not answer him and, a moment later, she heard his footsteps. Relieved he had yielded so easily, she crossed to the chair before the cold brazier and lowered into it.

Knowing it would be too easy to lose herself in anguish, she determined she would not cry for the lost child, for no help could come of tears. Instead, she would search for a solution.

"How am I to right this wrong, Lord?" she implored some time later when the dilemma loomed as large as ever. As if in answer, she heard again the conversation between Gilbert and Sir Royce. Edward still wanted his heir—the child she carried.

Pained by the answer she sought, Graeye hugged her arms around her babe. "No harm will befall you, little one," she vowed in an attempt to convince herself of the plan forming in her mind. "And Lady Lizanne will have her child back."

The conversation ceased the moment Graeye stepped into the hall. From among the half dozen seated on benches around a trestle table, Gilbert rose and strode toward her.

Taking her hands in his, he searched her face. "You look tired. Did you get no sleep?"

Not through the dinner hour, nor the supper. "I could not," she said, touched by his concern.

He beckoned to the servant who stood at the sideboard. "Prepare a platter of viands for Lady Graeye."

The man bobbed his head and hurried from the hall.

"You are making plans to go after Edward, are you not?" Graeye asked as she looked beyond Gilbert to the others. Among them were Lady Lizanne, her husband, Ranulf Wardieu, and Sir Lancelyn. The other two—an older man and woman—she did not recognize, though she was fairly certain the latter must be a relation of Baron Wardieu's, for her hair was nearly as fair as his.

"We must," Gilbert answered, and she heard regret in his words.

She looked back at him. "I know. May I join you?"

His hesitation set her further on edge. "We are nearly finished."

She narrowed her lids. "Do you not trust me?"

"I do," he said gruffly, "but I do not think it necessary for you—"

"Please, Gilbert."

"Very well," he said and led her to the table where he seated her beside him.

She was unwelcome, Graeye knew, but she braved the air of discontent that rose around her and the glares Gilbert received from all but Sir Lancelyn and Baron Wardieu.

After she was introduced to the older woman who was Baron Wardieu's mother and her husband beside her, the conversation resumed. As Graeye picked at the food delivered by the servant, she listened. There was much she did not understand, having come too late upon their meeting, but when talk turned to the course their search would likely take, she knew this was information of which she might make use.

"As 'twould seem he is headed north," Gilbert said, unrolling a map of the barony and weighting it with half-empty tankards, "it is the direction we must go." He paused to study the map, then jabbed a finger to a wooded area. "According to Charwyck's man, the encampments have been here, here, and here. Do you see the pattern?"

Charwyck's man? Graeye frowned. "Who speak you of?"

Annoyance flitted across Gilbert's face. "One of Edward's brigands. During a recent raid upon a village, the man was wounded and captured."

Guessing this was the reason behind Sir Lancelyn's visit—to deliver the miscreant to Gilbert—Graeye nodded. She would have liked to ask more, but knew further questions would not be welcome. Returning her gaze to the map, she pondered where her father's man was being held at Penforke.

"Aye, a pattern," Baron Wardieu agreed, "providing this man speaks the truth."

"Which is the reason we must split into two parties," Gilbert said. "You will lead your men in this direction"—he pointed to the northwest portion of the map—"and I will lead mine northeast. If we do not discover Charwyck's whereabouts, we meet here, at Cressing Bridge."

"And from there?" Lady Lizanne asked.

He rolled the map into a tight coil. "From there, we move south."

Baron Wardieu stood from the bench. "Then we ride at dawn."

There was a murmur of agreement as the others moved toward the stairs.

"Come," Gilbert said, taking Graeye's elbow to assist her upright.

"You will be gone long?" she asked as they mounted the stairs.

"A few days, perhaps more. It depends on the chase Charwyck leads us." Upon entering her chamber, he turned her to face him. "This time, I will not return empty-handed, Graeye. Do you understand what that means?"

"I do. Edward must be stopped."

His relief was visible in the easing of his shoulders. "Will you wish me well?"

His question surprised her, for she had not thought him still suspicious of her. Had she misinterpreted these past weeks they had spent together? "Do you not know me yet?" she asked. "Have you not guessed my feelings for you?"

He went very still. "Tell me of these feelings."

She opened her mouth to voice them, then shook her head. A confession of love would only leave her vulnerable. And what if he did not believe her? "It does not matter," she said and turned from beneath his hands.

He recaptured her shoulders, drew her back against him, and lowered his head alongside hers. "I plan to wed you, Graeye Charwyck," he said low and deep.

She caught her breath, spun around. "What?" Certain she could not have heard right—or if she had, that he teased—she searched his face.

He smiled. "When I return, I will make you my wife."

Feeling suddenly weak, she gripped his arms. "Why? You said—"

"I know, and I believed it to be true. But it is not." He sighed. "You are the mother of my child, and it would be unseemly that my son—or daughter—should be named misbegotten."

Legitimacy. Though it was certainly what she wanted for their child, a ripple of disappointment ran through her. Did he feel nothing akin to what she had hoped she had glimpsed in his eyes? "Is there more?" she asked.

"What else would you have me say?"

She pulled her bottom lip between her teeth. "I thought you might have feelings for me."

"Those same ones you profess to have for me?"

"Aye."

"But you have not yet told me what they are."

It could not hurt, could it? Loved or not, she was to be Gilbert's wife and, as such, there had to be a greater chance he would grow to feel deeply for her. "Would you believe me," she said, holding his gaze, "were I to tell you 'tis love I feel for you, Gilbert Balmaine?"

"Should I?" he asked, huskily.

The most difficult part done with, her pride laid out before him, she nodded. "I know no other name for it."

Mouth curving, he murmured, "I believe you." And that was all.

Then he would make no such declaration himself. Whatever it was he felt for her, be it love or simple affection, he would not make himself vulnerable as she had done.

Telling herself it was enough, for it was far more than she had ever truly believed she might have of him, she said, "I shall never love anyone but you."

He swept her up into his arms and carried her to the bed where he gently laid her on the mattress. Then he lowered his head toward hers.

Did he mean to—?

"Gilbert!" she gasped. "We should not."

"Shh." He brushed his mouth across hers. "We shall wait until our wedding night. And we will have one, Graeye. I promise you."

He reached across to the other side of the bed, caught hold of the coverlet, and drew it over and around her. "Sleep well, my lady."

And then he was gone.

28

THE DAWN CAME too soon and took Gilbert with it.

From her chamber, Graeye watched the riders dissolve into the landscape. Though they went as one group, soon they would split in two and move in different directions.

Earlier, when she had looked out upon the bailey, she had been surprised to see Lady Lizanne among those preparing to leave. She should not have been, considering the notoriety surrounding the woman. She was strong and unafraid of what awaited her.

The acknowledgment had deepened Graeye's conviction to recover the child Edward had stolen from its mother. It was not that she did not trust Gilbert to bring Edward to justice, but that she feared for the safety of the babe caught in the battle that would ensue.

If all went as she planned, Edward, thinking to have gained the Balmaine heir, would let down his guard. And when he did, she would have the chance to steal away with Lizanne's child.

She dressed quickly and went in search of Lucy, certain the healer would have access to the prisoner whom Gilbert had spoken of on the night past. In a small room off the cavernous cellar, she found the woman preparing one of the many unguents she used in her healing.

"Good morn, Lucy," Graeye greeted as she drew alongside the table at which the woman worked.

Lucy paused. "What are ye doing here, child?"

"With Lord Balmaine gone, there will be naught for me to do these next days," she said, hoping the woman did not notice how nervous she was. "I thought I would use the time well and learn of your herbs and medicines."

Frowning, Lucy returned her attention to the preparation. "Lord Balmaine said naught to me of it," she mumbled as she picked up a pestle and began to mash the contents of the mortar.

Graeye placed her elbows on the table and leaned forward to see better. "He does not know of my interest." She wrinkled her nose at the unpleasant odor produced by the combination of strong herbs.

The woman finished with her preparation before responding. "If ye like, you may assist me. However, if the babe starts troubling you, I want yer promise you will tell me."

"Of course."

The next hours were filled with treating all manner of ailments from which the castle folk suffered, and it was not until after the noon meal that Lucy paid a visit to the prisoner locked in the lower room of a tower.

"Ye needn't worry about this one," Lucy reassured Graeye as she fit the key in the lock and pushed the door open. "Angry he may be, but never again will he carry a sword for that devil, Char—" She cleared her throat. "I am sorry, milady. I forgot."

"I am grateful you did." Graeye smiled. It was good the castle folk no longer drew parallels between Edward and herself. And soon, if all went as planned, none would be able to ever again.

As soon as they entered the room, she understood the reason for Lucy's nonchalance toward the prisoner. The man lay on a pallet in the center of the room, the rough blanket covering him unable to hide that one of his legs had been removed to preserve his life.

It was nearly enough to send Graeye from that place, but with firm resolve, she followed Lucy to the pallet.

With his long, dirty hair and heavily bearded jaw, the man seemed as unfamiliar to her as any stranger, but when he lifted his lids and peered at her, she recognized him. Though she could not recall his name, she knew he was one of Edward's senior knights, a man second only to William.

"Is it you, Lady Graeye?" he asked, delirium evident in the slur of his words.

"Aye."

He turned his head and stared at the far wall.

On her knees beside him, Lucy asked, "Ye know him, milady?"

"He looks familiar," Graeye said evasively as she bent down beside the woman.

Clearly, Lucy felt misgivings over bringing Graeye with her, but she said nothing more. Returning her attention to the man, she turned the blanket aside and examined the bandaged stump that remained of his leg.

How am I to gain a few minutes alone with him? Graeye wondered. She could not ask questions with Lucy present. However, when her gaze fell to the sack containing the woman's medicines, she found the answer.

While Lucy removed the bandages, Graeye withdrew the pot the healer used on open wounds and pushed it beneath the straw pallet.

"Hand me the brown pot," Lucy directed, holding the wad of bandages to the wound as blood began to flow again.

Graeye made a pretense of searching the sack. "'Tis gone."

"Nonsense," Lucy said. "Here, hold this and I will look."

Fighting down the anxiety that rose at the prospect of drawing so near the man's horrible wound, Graeye came around the pallet and relieved Lucy of the task.

"Ah, where could I have left it?" Lucy cried a short while later.

"Mayhap at the armorer's," Graeye suggested. "It was last used on that man."

Lucy sprang to her feet and hurried to the door. "Do not get too near him," she called over her shoulder, then disappeared.

Knowing she did not have much time before the woman returned, Graeye bent over Edward's man. "Sir Knight, I must speak with you ere the healer returns."

Slowly, he turned his head toward her. "I am going to die," he said. "Soon."

"Nay." She shook her head. "Lucy is a great healer. You will not end your days here."

He closed his eyes. "You forget. A man must also want to live in order to be healed."

And he did not. Having been a man of the sword, the prospect of life as a cripple could have no appeal. "I will pray for you," she said, hoping to offer some solace.

"Save your prayers, lady."

Graeye touched his shoulder. "Sir Knight, is it true Edward is headed north?"

His eyes opened to fine slits. "That is what I told your lover."

She ignored the gibe. "Was it true?"

"Why do you wish to know?"

The lie. She had to make it convincing. "I would go to my father. He wants the Balmaine heir, does he not?"

The man nodded.

"'Tis revenge I seek against Baron Balmaine," she continued. "As he has mistreated me, I would deliver the child into my father's hands. Then all that Balmaine has taken from us will be ours again—and more."

The knight mumbled something and once more lowered his lids.

Graeye sank back on her heels. She had not convinced him. How was she to find Edward if—

"Long I served your father," he said, "and well I know how his mind works, even as mad as he is. 'Tis true he headed north, but he will not go there now."

Graeye leaned near him again. "Why? Where will he go?"

"Though he knows not whether I lived or died, he will not chance my knowledge of his plans. He will turn south now."

"Toward Penforke?"

"Aye, but not too near. Not yet."

"Where?" She was growing impatient. Any moment, Lucy could return, and then she would never know this man's secrets.

"Dewhercy," he breathed. "That is where he will do battle with Balmaine."

Dewhercy. Where had she heard the name before? Was it not Gilbert who had spoken of it? She hit upon it a moment later. It was the lake into which the rivers around Penforke emptied. He had promised to take her there after the babe was born.

Hearing footsteps, Graeye retrieved the medicine pot and rolled it across the floor. When the woman entered, wringing her hands, Graeye pointed to it.

"There," she said, continuing to press the bandages to the wound. "I spotted it a moment ago. It must have fallen from the sack."

Mumbling prayers of thanks, the woman retrieved it and returned to the pallet. She shooed Graeye aside and made quick work of applying the unguent.

"I must needs return to my chamber and rest," Graeye said, moving to the door. "Mayhap I can assist again on the morrow?"

"If you feel well enough," Lucy tossed over her shoulder.

29

As the sun fell beyond its zenith the following day, Graeye reflected on the events of the previous night.

If not for Mellie's help, which had been gained at the cost of much pleading and reasoning, she might not have found a way out of the castle. Fortunately, the servant's loyalty still lay with her former mistress, Lady Lizanne.

Although Graeye had given few details of her plan to rescue the child Edward had abducted, she had convinced Mellie of the worthiness of her scheme. In fact, the woman had added to it, which was the reason Graeye traveled by horse, rather than on foot.

The greatest obstacle encountered thus far was Mellie's attempt to distract the guard at the postern gate long enough for Graeye to slip through. Though the maid was attractive, the man had been resistant to her wiles, and it had taken much ale to bring him around.

As promised, the horse had been tethered at the edge of the wood, a gentle old nag that looked to pose no threat. The difficulty had come in mounting the animal, for Graeye had not reckoned with the encumbrance of her pregnancy. Always Gilbert lifted her astride. But she had made it and now found herself many leagues distant from Penforke as she followed the river's course south.

It could not be much farther to Dewhercy, she assured herself. Mellie had said a swift horse could deliver one to that place in a few hours. However, the nag was hardly swift, and Graeye's pregnancy made her averse to pushing the animal. Thus, she had guessed it would take several times the maid's estimation.

Though she was aware of the struggle that faced her to remount the nag, Graeye finally yielded to her thirst and drew to a halt. She had taken only her first handful of water from the river when a noise drew her attention. Straightening, she looked around but was unable to locate the source. Even as she resolved that it must be of her imagination, it came again.

She raised a hand to shield her eyes from the sun's glare and searched out the wooded area. It would be one of Edward's brigands. It had to be.

A moment later, she was proved correct, though she would have wished it to be any man other than the one who led his horse toward her.

Show no fear, she told herself.

"'Tis good you came alone, Lady Graeye." William gave a twisted grin.

"I have come to see Edward," she said as his shadow fell over her. She hated the way his eyes sparkled, hated the rough hands that grasped her and pulled her toward him.

"Release me," she demanded.

He hauled her closer and pressed a hand to her belly.

She stilled. When he began an exploration of her firm roundness, she thrust his hand away and jumped back.

To her surprise, he did not attempt to catch hold of her again. "What business have you with the old man?" he asked.

Pulling her mantle closed over the evidence of her pregnancy, she held William's hateful gaze. "I bring him the Balmaine heir that will gain him all he seeks."

His eyes narrowed. "What is it *you* seek?"

Summoning the word she had used to learn Edward's whereabouts, she raised her chin higher. "Revenge." Would he believe her?

It did not appear so, but then he laughed. "'Tis not very godly of you." He shook his head in mock disappointment. "What did those nuns teach you at the abbey?"

"It is not what the nuns taught me," she retorted, "it is what Balmaine taught me. I would see him suffer for the wrongs he has done my father and me."

"That he will." William turned to his horse and beckoned to her. "Come, you will ride with me."

"Nay, I will ride my own horse." She moved to gather the nag's reins.

William quickly returned to her and gripped her arm. "Think you I am fool enough to trust you, Graeye Charwyck? You will ride with me."

She tried to dig in her heels, but to no avail. A sharp jerk and she was stumbling after William.

"I warn you," he growled as he lifted her onto his horse, "if you defy me, 'twill be your misbegotten whelp that suffers."

She glared at him. "You would not dare harm me or my child."

He fit his foot into the stirrup. "It is Edward who would not take such a risk," he said as he swung up behind her. "And he does not yet know he is to be delivered the prize he seeks. So if harm befalls you, he will be none the wiser."

He fit an arm around her stiffly erect body and put his mouth to her ear. "It matters not to me what becomes of your ill gotten child. Do you understand?"

Too much. "You are a cruel man, William Rotwyld."

"I am. And you would do well to remember it, Lady Graeye."

The followers of Edward Charwyck cleared a path for them, their voices lowering as they gazed at the woman come among them.

Some Graeye recognized as being Edward's former retainers, but most were unknown faces belonging to men, women, and even dirty, ill-fed children—villeins turned outlaw to satisfy the whims of a deranged old man. What had he promised them?

Cold swept her as William guided his horse to the center of the camp where Edward stood beside the fire.

Hands on hips, he watched their approach. Had there been a breeze to move his long silver hair, it would have been the only movement about him.

All the courage Graeye had gathered during her long journey seemed for naught when she met his feral eyes. Thought it was certain William felt her tremor, she was grateful it did not manifest itself outwardly. She could not allow that, for Edward would use her fear against her.

William broke the silence. "See what I have chanced upon, my lord!"

Edward turned his gaze upon his man. "She came alone?"

"Aye, my lord. I followed her some time to be certain. She says she brings Balmaine's heir to you that she might take revenge upon the man."

Edward looked back at her. "Is that right, Daughter? You seek revenge against your lover?"

More than anyone, she had to convince Edward of the lie. "It was a mistake I made," she said with great bitterness. "Balmaine treated me cruelly and refused to wed me to grant his child legitimacy. I would see him dead and all that is his become ours."

His jaw shifted as he continued to stare at her. Then he said, "Come down from there," and raised his arms to her.

Though she longed to vault over the opposite side rather than go into that evil embrace, she muffled the desire. Forcing her expression to remain impassive, she leaned toward him.

At the touch of his hands, she stopped her breath, releasing it only when he set her upon her feet and stepped back to look at her.

Throughout his scrutiny, she held her head high, unflinching even when his gaze settled upon the stain.

"You should have died," he said. "Was it the devil who snatched you from the flames?"

Always it came back to the devil. So be it. Knowing Edward would do her no harm as long as she carried Gilbert's child, she said, "It must have been."

Around her, anxious whisperings rose like a swarm of bees. Before her, Edward reacted as if slapped. "You...you..." He took a step back. "Where is your head covering?"

"I no longer wear one."

His eyes widened. "You will in my presence!"

"I will not." She brushed the hair back from her face and tucked it behind her ears.

Edward's eyes flew to the stain.

"You fear me," she stated matter-of-factly.

Her words were enough to wipe much of that fear from his face. "Fear you?" he spat.

Now that she had gained the advantage, she could not back down. "Think you a piece of linen will take the devil from me, Father?"

Hands clenched at his sides, he stared into the face of a woman who was not the same as the one he had known nine months past.

"Come," he finally said, "I have something to show you."

Gathering her mantle against the cooling of afternoon, she followed, passing shadowy figures and faces, curious and fearful alike.

Outside a crudely constructed tent, an older woman was seated cross-legged on the ground, a babe suckling at her breast. Beside her was a basket that held another infant.

Graeye knew the latter had to be Lizanne's child, but formed a frown upon her face. Since she had first formulated her plan, she had determined it would be best to feign ignorance of the abduction.

A smile cracked Edward's face when she looked to him, and he went down on his haunches and lifted the sleeping baby from the basket.

Instantly, the child awoke and began to fuss, its whimperings growing louder as Edward clumsily turned it around to show Graeye.

"Know you whose child this is?"

It was not easy to contain the impulse to snatch away the distressed infant. She stared at the baby, noting its thatch of pale hair and chubby face. "Is it not the woman's?"

"Nay, she cares for this babe when she is not caring for her own." His mouth twisted as the infant began to wail.

"May I hold him?" Graeye asked, suddenly fearful Edward might do the child harm.

"Her," he corrected but did not relinquish the baby. "You may call her Gillian Wardieu."

"Wardieu?" Graeye widened her eyes. "Surely not."

He laughed. "Took her from the cradle myself. You did not know?"

"I heard naught of it. But why would you take this child?"

He fingered the infant's pale locks as it began to cry in earnest. "It will deliver Philip's murderers to me."

Hands itching to wrest Gilbert's niece from him, Graeye said, "Methinks she is hungry."

"I have no more to give her," the woman snapped and rose to her feet. "Me own child grows weak for all I give that one." She swept past Edward.

Graeye watched her go. "Perhaps you should give the child into my care," she suggested.

"Who would nurse her?" Edward asked. "You?"

Could she? In recent weeks, her breasts had begun to provide evidence of her body's preparation for birth such that it had become necessary to pad her bodice lest she dampened it. Lucy had said it was normal, that it was the first of her babe's milk.

She inclined her head. "I believe 'tis possible."

Edward regarded her with suspicion. "If it is true you seek revenge against Balmaine, why do you care what happens to this brat?"

Knowing it had been unwise to insist so soon, she frantically searched for an answer that would appease him. It was a weak argument she came up with, but it was the only one at hand. "Of what use is this child if she dies from lack of sustenance?"

He sneered. "It will still bring me Balmaine and Wardieu."

"Perhaps." She glanced at the babe who had calmed somewhat, "but should something go awry, you could strike a powerful bargain providing she yet lives."

Edward's anger surfaced in the crimson color that suffused his face. "Naught will go awry. My vengeance is assured."

Where she found her next argument, she could not have said. "Aye, providing William does not turn on you."

He startled. "What mean you?"

"He thinks you quite mad," she planted the seed and prayed it would take hold. "On the ride here, he boasted it was he whom the people followed, not you."

Edward shook his head. "I do not believe you."

She stepped near him and placed a hand on his arm. "Do not let him fool you, Father. He deserted you once before when he gave his oath of fealty to Baron Balmaine. He will do so again."

A hunted look entered Edward's eyes. Without another word, he pushed the infant into her arms and hurried away, one hand worrying his long hair.

Graeye drew a long breath. She had won this battle, but there would be more. Somehow, she must get Gillian away from here.

The babe continued to fuss, her fists and stiff legs punching at the air until, at last, she found uneasy comfort in her protector's arms. Whimpering, she turned her face to Graeye's breast and began to search for the milk that would fill her rumbling belly.

Uncertain as to what she should do, Graeye looked around for privacy in which to explore the rituals of motherhood to which she had not expected to be introduced for a fortnight or more. The woman's tent would do, she decided.

Crouching low, she entered the cramped interior. She was pulling the flap down over the opening when William pushed it aside.

"You may frighten the old man, but you do not frighten me, Graeye Charwyck," he said, squatting to view her where she sat.

"Do I not?" she tossed back. "Certes, you would do well to be frightened of me, William Rotwyld."

He gave a harsh laugh and retreated.

Wondering at the depth of the well from which she had drawn the courage to face the two men she feared most, Graeye looked down upon the shadowed, angelic face nestled against her. "Ah, little one," she cooed, "all will be well."

30

WHILE EDWARD'S BRIGANDS prepared for the coming battle, Graeye plotted, finding that pitting Edward against William was easier than anticipated. And it did not take long to understand the reason. She had thought she had lied in warning Edward to be wary of William. She had not.

She could come to no other conclusion after two days of observing the happenings around her, which, prior to her arrival, Edward must have been too blinded by madness to see. The old man was a figurehead, and one for which William had very little tolerance. Nearly every directive given by Edward was countermanded by William, and it became apparent that the brigands did, indeed, follow the latter.

Now, it seemed, Edward also saw this, and Graeye knew it was only a matter of time before the confrontation that would provide her the opportunity to escape with Gillian.

That evening, not until her belly began to gnaw with hunger, did she emerge from the tent to the smell of cooked venison. With a slumbering Gillian propped on her belly and clasped to her breast, she ignored the man who had been set to shadow her and crossed to where the food was laid out. As usual, she found the leavings of the others modest, for she had not come soon enough to choose the best of the meal. Still, it would suffice.

As she settled on a fallen log, the child in her belly kicked, reminding her that soon it would enter the world.

Disturbed by the sharp movement, Gillian whimpered and wiggled.

Graeye held her breath, hoped the babe would not awaken hungry and ready to feed again. Having been unable to satisfy her appetite with the small amount of milk produced for a newborn, Graeye had been forced to seek the help of the one into whose care Edward had first given Gillian. Fortunately, the wet nurse had been needed only twice this day, but if Gillian awakened now before Graeye's body replenished itself, it might be necessary to once more call upon the woman.

Blessedly, Gillian nuzzled back against the pillow of Graeye's breasts and resumed her soft breathing.

The bread was hard, the cheese moldy, but the venison tender. As Graeye had done with each meal, she hid a portion in the small sack beneath her mantle. It would sustain her on her journey back to Penforke.

When she had eaten her fill, she rose and started back to her tent.

Edward stepped into her path. "I would see the child."

She eased the cloth back from Gillian's head and stepped sideways to show him.

Edward reached to take her.

"Nay!" Graeye backed away. What did he intend? He had not attempted such before.

"Give me the child," he ordered.

"What do you want with her?"

"I must send a message to Balmaine and Wardieu." He smiled—a twisted, ugly thing.

"Then send your message. It does not require the babe."

"You are wrong. If my threat is to be taken seriously, I need something of the child."

"Something?" How Graeye feared the meaning behind those words! "Nay, send your message and leave her be."

He reached again and nearly succeeded in snatching away Gillian.

Graeye stumbled back, jolting the babe and rousing another whimper.

"Give me the child!" Edward demanded.

Surprisingly, it was William who stepped between Edward and Graeye. "The message has already been sent," he said.

All of Edward jerked. "By whose order?"

William crossed his arms over his chest. "Mine."

Hoping this was the confrontation she had awaited and praying Gillian would not awaken with cries that drew attention to them, Graeye stepped out of harm's way—and just in time. Edward charged the younger man, threw his great bulk into him, and sent them both sprawling in the dirt.

As the two regained their feet, their followers rushed forward and surrounded them.

"You think to usurp my place?" Edward roared. "I will cut you in two." He reached for his sword and, finding it missing, drew his dagger.

Though William had his own sword at his belt, he also took up a dagger. "Come, you crazy old man!" He sliced the air with his blade. "Let us see if you can still wield a weapon."

As Graeye cautiously retreated, she searched out the one who had followed her earlier and was relieved to see that he, too, was caught up in the excitement of the brawl.

Edward lunged and laughed triumphantly when his blade sliced William's ear. William bellowed and countered with a swipe that narrowly missed the other's chest.

"Your blood is mine!" Edward shouted, but his dagger made no further contact.

Graeye continued her backward trek and glanced around to be certain she was not followed. In that fleeting space of time, she heard Edward's cry of pain. When she looked back, she saw William had drawn blood from the old man's upper arm.

"If you have prayers to say," William jeered, "you had best get to them quick as your death will not be long in coming."

The knight could not have known how true he spoke, for moments later, Edward clutched his chest and plummeted to his knees.

But William had not struck him in the chest. Had he? A moment later, she understood what had taken Edward down, for she had once witnessed the same thing with an elderly nun.

Fighting a surge of compassion, telling herself she cared not that his heart was giving out, she looked to the refuge of the trees. If she could make it—

"Lady Graeye," William called, "will you not see to your father's last rites?"

Her heart sank. The opportunity was lost. Would there be another before Gilbert arrived and Gillian and she were caught in the midst of a battle?

Certain William had seen through her plans for escape, she stepped forward and, clutching Gillian tighter, knelt beside Edward who was flat on his back.

Eyes wide, he held to his chest. "Knave!" he rasped, tilting his head back to stare at William. "I would have given you all."

William grunted. "All would have belonged to the whelp growing in that harlot's body. There would be naught for me."

Another pain gripped Edward, and he cried out, shut his eyes, and rolled his head side to side.

"At least have some dignity in death," William scorned and walked away.

The others disbanded, leaving Graeye alone with Edward.

Gently, she placed Gillian on the ground beside her and touched the old man's shoulder. "Do you accept the cross?" she asked, then drew forth the one hung around her neck.

His eyes opened and fixed on her. "Alienor? Is it you?"

Surprised to hear him speak her mother's name, she stared. It was true she resembled her mother, though she was slighter of build and fairer of hair, but she had never expected to be mistaken for her. The depth of the old man's pain had surely brought on delirium.

"Ah, 'tis!" He lifted a hand toward her face, but it fell back to his side.

Graeye shook her head. "Nay, Ed—"

His weak, coughed laughter cut across her words. "See what I have done to your precious daughter? You thought to close me out and punish me, but 'tis I who won." Pain spasmed across his face. "Why could you not have loved me as I loved you? I gave everything to have you. I sent Hermana away so I could wed you. And you hated me for it."

Graeye gasped, dropped back onto her heels. "Hermana," she whispered, the face of the woman who had plagued her days at Arlecy Abbey rising before her.

"Never did Philip forgive me for sending his mother away and taking you to wife," he continued. "Ever he hated me for it."

Graeye sank her teeth into her lower lip. That Hermana had been Edward's first wife and Philip's mother explained much. Philip's taunting, Hermana's ill will...

"I tried to make amends to him." Edward squeezed his eyes tight as he was shook by another pain. "I sent your daughter to live alongside that bitter old woman. And for a time, it pleased Philip. But he always wanted more."

Graeye did not care to bear further witness to his ramblings, but he was not finished. As his life ebbed, his body began to slacken. This time when he reached for her, he found the curve of her face.

"You should not have scorned me, untouchable Alienor—righteous Alienor whose silence condemned me for everything." His rough fingers caressed Graeye's cheek. "Had you but shown me some of the kindness you extended to others, I might have accepted the devil's child you bore me, but you loved only her."

Pity that Graeye would not have expected after all he had done, rose within her. That this man had once been capable of love, even if manifested to the detriment of others, tugged at her.

"Father," she breathed and leaned down to kiss his aged cheek, "accept the cross and be delivered from this torture."

"Never!" He pushed her away. A short while later, he expelled a final, shuddering breath.

Throat constricted, Graeye crossed herself and began her prayers.

When she finally lifted Gillian and started to stand, her eyes caught the glint of the dagger that had dropped from Edward's hand. With her back to the man who stood watch over her, she secreted the weapon within Gillian's blanket and stood. What use it would be she did not know, but it might gain her an advantage.

The advantage came sooner than expected.

As night moved toward the day to come, Graeye tried to sink into sleep. However, each time she happened upon it, it was short-lived, for the child in her womb was more restless than usual, making much ado over being unable to find a comfortable position.

At long last, she fell into sleep marked by fitful stirrings and dark dreams that warned of danger. She saw Gilbert and blood, heard Gillian's cries, felt a hand close over her mouth and steal her breath—

She opened her eyes wide and focused on the shadowy form above her. Was this part of her dream? It was not.

She started to struggle, but remembered that Gillian lay asleep in the crook of her arm. Heart thundering, she brought to mind the dagger hidden beneath the blanket she lay upon.

"Ah, Graeye," a familiar voice slurred, William's breath so soured with alcohol she nearly retched against his hand. "Know you what I have come for?" He drew a hand over her belly.

Shuddering, she slowly extended her arm and lifted the edge of the blanket.

"I have waited long to have you," he continued. "Now that the old man is gone, I shall take that which you denied me and gave Balmaine."

It was the cutting edge of the dagger's blade she first found. Suppressing a cry of pain, she inched her hand to the hilt and wrapped her throbbing fingers around it.

"I have warned you before," William said, "fight me, and the child will suffer. Do you understand?"

She nodded and was relieved to be freed of the pressure of his hand upon her mouth.

He reached to Gillian.

Knowing it was best to have the babe out of the way, Graeye eased her hold on Gillian and allowed William to set her aside.

He quickly returned to Graeye and thrust aside the rough blankets.

Ignoring the pain in her fingers, she gripped the dagger tighter, but not until she felt the loathsome man's hand upon her leg did she force herself to action. Unable to bring herself to set the blade to his flesh, she swept her arm above her head and brought the hilt down upon his skull.

He sucked air and dropped to the side.

"Heavenly Father," she breathed, unable to believe she had bettered him. But then, William was beyond drunk from all the celebrating in which he had indulged following Edward's demise.

Graeye scrambled onto her hands and knees, lifted Gillian, and crept to the tent opening. It seemed too much good fortune to find her guard absent, and she assumed William had sent him away.

She gathered the few items she would need for the return journey—the sack of food, mantle, blanket, dagger.

Though a horse would speed her flight, she knew it was too much of a risk to acquire one.

Holding Gillian close, Graeye crept from the tent toward the trees. It seemed a long way as she stepped lightly around the other tents and sleeping forms, but she made it without mishap. Unfortunately, it would not be as easy to get past the sentries set around the camp.

She advanced slowly, all the while praying William did not soon recover from the blow.

31

THRUSTING HIS BLOODIED sword into its sheath, Gilbert remounted, though not his own destrier. The great white stallion had fallen in the short-lived skirmish of early morn when Gilbert had led the attack against Edward's brigands. It was a terrible loss, but the horse had likely saved his life, taking the arrow aimed at its rider. Shot from a crossbow, it would easily have pierced a coat of mail.

"There is no sign of either one," Ranulf said of Graeye and Gillian as he urged his destrier alongside Gilbert's. "Nor of William."

Gilbert swept his gaze over the destruction left by the clash between Charwyck's men and his. It was a pity how much blood had needed to be shed before the brigands were defeated, but he was grateful to have lost so few of his own and that none of the women and children of the camp had been harmed. But still he did not have that which he sought!

As they had trailed Charwyck's progress south, word of Graeye's disappearance had come from Penforke. It had nearly driven Gilbert mad as old beliefs about her resurfaced, but he had not held to them long. Now, however, testimony had been given of her presence in the camp by those of Charwyck's men who had survived. Too, they told of the old man's demise on the night past. There was some relief in that, though not enough.

Why, he wondered again, had Graeye sought her father? It was not answer enough to learn she had cared for Lizanne and Ranulf's child while among Edward's followers, for he could not believe she would endanger their child to protect another's.

Perhaps she had simply been biding her time to escape him, had lied in declaring her love—

Nay! He could not—would not—believe it.

There was Mellie's confession to consider. Believing Edward wanted the Balmaine heir, Graeye might not have considered herself, or their child, to be in immediate danger. It was possible she had left Penforke to seek Gillian's release. But what had driven her to such desperate measures?

A moment later, Gilbert had the answer, and it pained him to know he was responsible for the guilt thrust upon her for the wrongs her family had done the Balmaines.

I will make it up to you, love, he silently vowed then asked Ranulf, "Do you think William has Gillian and Graeye?"

The other man ran a weary hand along the back of his neck as he stared up at the sky the sun had penetrated a few short hours ago. "Likely."

Lizanne, face drawn, urged her horse alongside her husband's. "I do not believe it," she said. "Methinks Graeye must have escaped with Gillian during the night and William set off after her."

"How come you by this?" Gilbert asked.

"If all you tell about this woman is true, 'twas her intent to take Gillian from here. Mayhap she succeeded. It would certainly explain why William was not here when we rode upon the camp. As the new leader of these brigands, he would have no reason to flee."

"Yet he told no one of her escape?" Gilbert asked.

"None that survived," Lizanne pointed out. "Also, he may not have expected it to be a difficult undertaking to find her and bring her back."

"Then we must find her first." Gilbert motioned for his men to regroup.

As tempting as it had been to follow the river so she would not become lost, Graeye had known it would be to her detriment, especially once the sun rose. It was what William would expect, and she would not aid in her recapture. Instead, she paralleled the river as best she could, occasionally turning in to catch sight of it to assure herself she had not gone off course.

How long and how far had she walked? she wondered, her legs and back aching. A dozen hours or more, she guessed, and throughout, Gillian had been mostly patient.

Graeye could not thank the Lord enough that she had been able to satisfy the little one's hunger, for if the babe set to wailing, they would likely be intercepted before they reached Penforke. And Graeye sensed they were not far from that place. Most evident of this was the land's sudden incline. Until recently, it had been gradual, but now it pointed the way toward the great fortress upon the hill.

Not allowing herself to feel too much relief until she was safely within the castle's walls, she hurried her awkward legs beneath her. "Soon," she whispered when her body's protests became more insistent. Hearing the faint sound of running water, she veered away, still careful not to venture too near the river.

The first cramp that caught her midsection was not bad, though it took her breath away. Pausing, she drew a hand down her belly.

It is nothing, she told herself. *It is not yet my time.*

Continuing on, she was soon taken by another cramp. Again, she denied its cause and resumed her journey.

Over the next hour, the pains grew more intense and frequent, but still she did not pause except when absolutely necessary. If the child was readying for birth, it was that much more important she reach Penforke quickly.

Gillian's hungry cries finally forced Graeye to stop. Grateful for the reprieve, she chose a place among the low-lying bushes that offered adequate cover.

The babe was not long into the feeding when a crashing sound brought Graeye's head around. Scooting farther back into the bushes, she searched the wooded area for the cause of the commotion.

Dear Lord, she prayed, *let it be a wild beast ere it be William.*

The latter appeared a moment later on a heavily lathered horse whose hindquarters shook with exertion.

Slowly, Graeye drew up the hood of her mantle to conceal her pale hair and, holding Gillian close, peered at the man through the leaves before her.

Wild-eyed, color high, William pulled hard on the reins, forcing the animal to step a circle as its rider searched the area.

"I know you are out here!" he roared. "I can smell you." He threw back his head and sniffed the air.

Graeye shuddered. He was nearly as mad as Edward had been. And that likely meant he had not come to take her back but to put an end to her.

He guided his horse nearer her refuge and narrowed his eyes to scrutinize the undergrowth and surrounding trees.

Though she longed to withdraw more deeply into the bushes, she forced herself to remain still, barely breathing for fear William might hear her. It would be miracle enough if his ears did not prick to the sound of Gillian's feeding.

A bird took to flight, drawing William's regard. After that, a hare skittered out into the open and also quickly went from sight. The quiet of the wood warmed by the afternoon sun followed.

Graeye's fortitude was rewarded when, with a savage growl, William jabbed his heels into his horse's sides and rode off in the direction of Penforke.

Still unmoving, she wondered what she was to do now that William had overtaken her. To gain the sanctuary of Penforke, she would have to get past him, which might prove impossible since he would surely set himself to watching the castle. If he caught her out in the wide expanse of land surrounding the fortress, he would have little difficulty capturing her. Perhaps night would provide cover—

Another pain tore through her. Sealing her mouth with a fist, she waited for the cramp to pass. It did, but left her more drained than before.

My child is coming, she acknowledged and allowed herself a moment of wonder before resolving to reach Penforke without further delay. Be it by the postern gate or over the drawbridge, she would find a way in.

When Gillian was more content, Graeye emerged from the bushes and cautiously made her way forward. Though she believed William presented no immediate threat, she took no chances and veered farther from the river.

Every unexpected sound made her skin crawl, but she stopped only when the birthing pains were too great and she was forced to wait them out.

With the thinning of vegetation, she saw she was nearly clear of the woods. Though she did not have the energy to run, she pushed herself to a faster pace, drawing herself up short only when, through the sparse trees, Penforke rose before her.

"Merciful Father," she breathed and wiped the perspiration from her brow. Moving nearer, she scrutinized the fortification and saw it was in a state of preparedness. Though it was still day, the drawbridge was raised, and atop the walls soldiers crossed back and forth.

Could they protect her? Perhaps, but first they would have to know who she was. She searched out the fringes of the wood for signs of William and was not surprised when she found none, for the man was not fool enough to reveal himself before he had her.

Knowing it would be safer to approach the rear of the castle and the postern gate there, Graeye decided to use the cover of the surrounding wood to reach it. Keeping the castle within sight, she began the last leg of her journey with the same caution she had exercised throughout. However, with each pain came the desire to strike out across the open ground.

As she plodded onward, she made all sorts of promises to herself— a hot, scented bath, a long day and night's sleep, fresh fruit and warm bread, the comfort of Gilbert's arms...

Noise thrust upon her musings—not the clamor of a single rider, but of many. She hastened to the edge of the wood and pressed herself against a tree. Peering around its girth, she spied the riders emerging from the left, near where she had first caught sight of the castle.

The vivid colors the knights wore and the banners they carried revealed they were of Penforke. Relief shot through her as she settled her gaze upon the large figure riding before the others. Gilbert.

Though a voice warned that she was not yet out of danger, she pushed it aside in favor of the safety offered by Gilbert's arrival. She could not risk being left outside the castle's walls with William still hunting her, especially now that her child was demanding entrance into the world.

Drawing from deep within herself, she found the strength to carry her forward. Though she could not be said to run, neither did she walk.

Awakened by the jarring movements, Gillian began to whimper.

"'Twill be over soon," Graeye soothed as she pushed back her hood to reveal her hair and waved a hand to draw attention to herself. She was about to lend her voice as well when the riders turned toward her.

Though tempted to drop to her knees in thanks, she hurried forward.

Gilbert was but a dozen lengths from her when another pain tore through Graeye, but it was not like those other pains. This one burned, so much that it, not God, dropped her to her knees.

A howl of fury rose above the pounding of hooves.

Gilbert? Wondering at the depth of rage that produced such a horrendous sound, Graeye peered over her shoulder and saw that a shaft protruded from her upper back. The pain intensified, and she was flushed with remorse at the hazy realization it had to have been William who had put her through.

"Ah, nay," she breathed as she looked back at Gilbert who was nearing in a measure of time that seemed not of the real world. He moved much too slowly.

As pain took her all the way to the ground and she fell heavily onto her side, Gillian began wailing.

Graeye squeezed her eyes closed, and when she opened them, Gilbert was bent over her, his face distorted with anger, concern, and fear.

"Our baby," she croaked as he lifted Gillian from her and handed the infant into waiting arms. "He comes, Gilbert."

Disbelief furrowed his face. "Dear Lord, not now!"

She lifted a hand and touched his unshaven jaw. "Soon," she breathed, then her hand fell to the ground and she lost sight of him as her lids lowered.

Gilbert stared at her, all the promises he had ever made to not allow her into his heart dissolving as if they had never been. He could no longer deny it—he loved her as he had never loved another.

"Do not leave me, Graeye." He hardly recognized his strangled voice. "You cannot. I will not let you."

"Gilbert!" Lizanne shouted. "We must hurry else she will lose too much blood."

Carefully, he lifted Graeye into his arms. As he strode to where Ranulf sat astride his mount, he pressed his lips to her forehead. "I love you, Graeye," he said.

Her lashes fluttered. "And I you," she murmured.

Gilbert savored those words, then handed her up to Ranulf. To leave her now seemed almost a sin, but he must. "I am going after William," he said. "This day, there will be an end to this."

"Likely he has already been taken," Ranulf said.

It was possible, the knights having set off after him when Graeye was struck. "Perhaps," he said and turned to his destrier, "but it is not over 'til I have been satisfied."

"I should go with you."

One foot in the stirrup, Gilbert looked over his shoulder at his brother-in-law. "I yielded Philip to you," he reminded Ranulf of that day a year past when he had been given a choice of two men to fight. Though it was Philip he had wanted, to ensure justice was done, he had chosen the other man— Ranulf's twin brother. "Now," he said, "it is my turn to set things right."

Grudgingly, Ranulf nodded.

Gilbert ordered those of his men still with him to return to the castle, then rode alone toward the wood.

One by one, Gilbert turned back the men who had gone after William. Now, as darkness hovered on the horizon, he alone sought the miscreant who had taken refuge in his woods, and who surely awaited the opportunity to slay him.

Refusing to allow anger and impatience to interfere with his judgment, he rode weapon-ready through the trees. Always, though, he found his thoughts turning to Graeye and their child.

Was she well? Would she survive both the wound and the birthing? Had their babe arrived?

Each time he forced the worries aside with a reminder of the capable hands into which he had entrusted her—Lizanne's and Lucy's.

It was instinct that told Gilbert he was no longer alone. Readying himself for the attack, he searched for a glimpse of William's clothing but found none. Thus, he was surprised when the assault came from above. Reacting quickly to the shout of anger as the man descended from the tree, Gilbert twisted around in time to throw up his sword and deflect the blade that aimed to sever the great vein in his neck.

The sudden force of William's weight propelled them both from the horse and they crashed to the ground.

Gilbert quickly gained his feet. Though his impaired leg protested at the weight placed upon it, he swung his sword in a wide arc that had William stumbling back.

"Now it ends," Gilbert said, standing his ground as the other man raised his sword. "Say your prayers, for death is nigh."

William laughed and stirred the air with the side-to-side movement of his sword. "I need no prayer to spill your blood, Balmaine. Soon you will join that harlot and your misbegotten whelp in death."

That Graeye might even now be forever gone from him—and their child—fueled Gilbert's fury. Snarling, he leapt forward and took aim to end the man's life. But William was endowed with quick responses, the suddenness of his retreat leaving his assailant with only air upon which to exact his revenge.

Gilbert countered the attack that came at him a moment later with a thrust that sent William back several steps. Secure in the knowledge that what he lacked in speed he made up for in strength, Gilbert followed.

Steel met steel, and William retreated again to maintain his balance. Then, suddenly, he was to the left, his swing catching Gilbert across the ribs. The blade pierced the protective chain mail, but only just.

William waved his blade before his opponent to show the blood that trickled its length. "That is one, Balmaine," he taunted. "Two will take a piece of your flesh, and three will end your life."

Further angered at having lost the first contact to the miscreant, Gilbert spat between his teeth, "That is the last of me you will have, Rotwyld."

"You think so?" William moved opposite, but he gained no advantage as Gilbert anticipated the move. "Were you not so lame, Balmaine, I might believe you, but it takes more than strength to down one's opponent."

Aye, it takes observation, Gilbert reminded himself, refusing to rise to the same taunt with which others had attempted to best him in the past. He nearly smiled, for he had discovered the key to predicting William's movements. As was most often the case, it was in the eyes that fell to his next place of attack a moment before his legs followed. As simple as it was, it gave Gilbert the advantage when William next attacked, and earned his blade a taste of the man's upper thigh.

William shouted, having nothing to protect his flesh from the blade's bite. A moment later, he countered with a blow that missed Gilbert's neck by the width of a sword.

"Now we are more fairly matched," Gilbert jeered as he pushed William's blade off his. "Both lame."

"A slow death you shall suffer!" William raged and lunged again to catch Gilbert's sword arm. As the man's blade skittered over the links of armor, Gilbert took the opportunity to flay open the vulnerable shoulder presented to him, causing his opponent to lurch backward.

"Are you prepared to die, Rotwyld?" Gilbert demanded.

William's pale visage brightened, and he clasped his free hand over the other, taking a two-handed grip on his sword.

Gilbert lunged.

Time and again, William parried and sidestepped. Time and again, his attempts to land a blow went mostly unrewarded, hindered as he was by the loss of blood and the pain that showed in his twisted mouth and the deepening lines of his face.

Gilbert did not relent. Though several times he stood a good chance of landing the final blow, he did not push it that far. Not yet. First, he wanted fear. He wanted this man to experience the terrible emotion that had choked Gilbert when Graeye had fallen before him with William's arrow protruding from her back. And he would have it.

Beneath a slowly darkening sky, they traded blows until, weapons crossed above their heads, Gilbert found what he sought in his opponent's desperate eyes. Using his greater strength, he thrust his weight into his sword, sent the man careening backward, and arced his blade downward.

William screamed with the opening of his belly, lost hold of his sword, and landed hard upon his back. Wrapping an arm around his bloody innards, drawing strident breaths through clenched teeth, he stared up at Gilbert. Then he laughed. "So, 'tis me. It should be you, but...it is me."

Gilbert leveled his sword at the man's heart. "Soon you will join your earthly lord, Charwyck, and never again will you do Lady Graeye harm."

"She was to have been mine!"

"A pity you did not deserve her, Rotwyld."

He bared his teeth. "You think you do?"

Gilbert knew he did not deserve Graeye, but he was determined to spend the remainder of his life aspiring to be worthy of her. "She is to be my wife, and whatever wrongs I have done her, I will make right."

"Wife? A harlot?"

Though Gilbert ached to give the final thrust, he managed to stay his arm, the effort required to do so making it shake.

William eyed the steel. "Ah, poor Baron Balmaine. You have a..." He moaned, coughed up a froth of blood. "You have a care for that devil-kissed wench. I could not be happier."

Still, Gilbert held back.

"It does me good to know you shall not have her for long, for if my..." More bloody froth. "...bolt did not strike her heart, it came near enough that she is lost to you. And your misbegotten pup as well."

Gilbert refused to believe it. The arrow had pierced her shoulder. It could prove deadly, but it was not as certain as William believed.

The man made a sound not unlike a mewl, then dragged open the neck of his tunic to expose his throat. "Finish me."

Gilbert longed to. How he ached for the satisfaction of—

Revenge soaked in crimson.

He shifted his gaze to the man's torn abdomen. Undoubtedly, death would be the end of him, and though the final blow could be excused as an act of mercy, he knew himself—knew mercy would have nothing to do with it, that it would only satisfy him in a way of which his gentle Graeye would not approve.

He drew a deep breath. "You are finished, William. As you do not need me to speed your journey, I leave you to God."

A stunned silence followed him all the way to his horse, then the man set to cursing and spewing vile names against the woman Gilbert loved.

"It is done," Gilbert called and spurred his destrier toward Graeye.

32

Pray to God? Ask for a miracle for which he would shortly find himself mocked? Gilbert shook his head, but his feet carried him toward the chapel.

He had waved away those who thought to provide him with details of Graeye's condition beyond word that she yet lived, for he was not ready to face the possibility of losing her. Good or bad, he had first to do what he had long denied himself—and Graeye.

Entering the chapel he had spurned years ago, he went to the altar, knelt, bowed his head, and prayed.

It was where Lizanne found him an hour later. She laid a hand on his shoulder. "You prayed well, Brother."

So fervent had been his prayers that he had not known of her presence until that moment. He surged to his feet and gripped her shoulders. "Graeye? She is well?"

She looked down at her hands. "Your son is healthy."

Struggling against the temptation to shake her, he demanded, "What of Graeye?"

She lifted her chin. "The labor was hard, Gilbert, but your lady did a fine job. She is a strong woman. Providing there are no complications, she stands a good chance of fully recovering."

"Providing...chance..." he rasped. "Then the arrow—"

"It struck nothing vital, but she lost a lot of blood."

Gilbert tightened his hands at his sides. "I will not lose her."

She inclined her head, smiled lightly. "I believe you, Brother."

"I wish to see her."

"She is resting."

"Now, Lizanne." He turned and she hurried after him.

To his surprise and vast approval, it was the solar to which Graeye had been carried to birth their child. By the light of a single candle beside the bed, Gilbert crossed the chamber and sank down on the mattress. He leaned over Graeye and was heartened by the bit of color in her cheeks. Still, she was quite pale.

He feathered a finger across her cool brow, flinching when a soft moan parted her lips.

"I have prayed, Graeye," he murmured.

Her lids slowly rose. "Have you?" she breathed.

"I have, and I shall continue to." He bent nearer, brushed his mouth across hers. "What else can I do to prove my love? What more to earn God's favor?"

"'Tis enough," she whispered, and when he drew back, her lips curved gently.

"Can you ever forgive me for not trusting you?" he asked. "For the things of which I wrongly accused you?"

"Naught to forgive. You could not have known."

"But I should have—"

"All is healed, Gilbert."

Sending up another prayer that she would be healed as well, he pressed his forehead to hers. "Soon we will wed and naught will ever come between us."

She touched his face. "What of William?"

Gilbert raised his head. "We fought, he fell to a mortal wound, and I left him to God. Certes, he lies dead."

"Then it is over."

"Not for us, Graeye."

More light moved into her eyes and color into her cheeks. "Have you seen our son?"

"Not yet. First, I had to come to you."

"Then go now so you may sooner return with our child."

Gilbert fleetingly kissed her. "I will not be long."

Their son was, indeed, healthy. As he peered up at his father out of eyes like Graeye's, the babe gurgled and waved a tiny fist.

"So small," Gilbert murmured.

"Not at all," Lizanne said. "He is a good size, the same as Gillian was."

He shook his head. "Still small. May I hold him?"

"Of course." She passed him into his arms.

The babe fidgeted a bit, then yawned wide and closed his eyes.

"Methinks he is bored with me already," Gilbert mused, very much liking the feel of the small, warm body.

Lizanne stroked his son's cheek. "Nay, he is simply content."

"You think so?"

She looked up. "You will make a wonderful father—and husband—Gilbert."

As he beheld the certainty shining from her eyes, he was nearly overwhelmed by the realization that the tormented past with which they had both been afflicted was truly in the past. In its place was a future neither had dared hope for, one Philip Charwyck could not have foreseen. More, one that would not have been possible without him.

"What is it?" Lizanne asked.

He shook his head in wonder. "'Tis strange the way God works—that He leaves some evil be and takes other evil in hand and turns it into good."

"And in His own good time," she said knowingly. "I do not understand it either, Gilbert. I know only that you and I have been blessed and we ought to hold our blessings close."

He looked to his son, murmured, "I intend to," then leaned down and kissed his sister's cheek.

"Thus, a new beginning for both of us," she said as he drew back.

He smiled. "A new beginning." Then he returned to Graeye whose arms awaited her son and the man with whom she would go through life.

Epilogue

HENRI BALMAINE, FIRSTBORN and heir of Gilbert Balmaine, was not one to let events of great import pass him by—at least, not without a valiant struggle to keep his gray-blue eyes out from behind his lids.

During the final act of the wedding ceremony that would also legitimize his birth, the babe shifted where he lay huddled between his parents who were prostrated in prayer beneath the pall stretched over them.

As he continued to test his swaddling cloths, Graeye lifted her face from the floor to peer at the child with whom she and Gilbert had been blessed a fortnight past.

Henri blinked at her and made a sweet sound somewhere between a squeak and a coo.

His father raised his head, grinned at his son, smiled at his wife, and slid a hand up over the arm Graeye turned around their babe. "I love you," he whispered and stroked the backs of his fingers across her cheek.

She momentarily closed her eyes to savor this moment when all was made right, not only in God's eyes but the eyes of men. "As I love you," she breathed and brushed her lips across his fingers.

"My Graeye."

She smiled. "My Gilbert."

The babe squeaked again, wriggled his upper body, and thrust his little legs beneath the bindings.

"Our Henri," Gilbert murmured, "he who is as restless as a man whose wedding night seems too far off."

Graeye barely contained a laugh. "Ah, but in his case, 'tis his belly that hungers."

Above the pall, the four corners of which were held by Lady Lizanne, Baron Wardieu, Lady Zara, and Sir Walter, the priest paused in intoning the mass and loudly cleared his throat. Beneath the pall, husband and wife exchanged looks of chagrin and returned to their prayers.

By the time Gilbert and Graeye Balmaine were raised to their feet, Henri's sweet little sounds were less so and of a more urgent nature.

Quickly, the flustered priest bestowed the kiss of peace upon Gilbert, then stood aside and nodded at Graeye. It was time to kiss the bride.

As Gilbert turned to her, his sister said, "It must be done proper," passed Gillian to her husband, and reached for the little one who bore the name of her and her brother's father.

Graeye relinquished Henri, and Gilbert gently drew her into his arms, exercising care in consideration of her injury. Though the wound healed well and, of late, caused little discomfort, he continued to handle her as if she were exceedingly fragile.

She was not. Thus, it was she who pressed her body nearer his, who drew herself up to her toes to more fully give her mouth to him, who chased his lips back to hers when he started to lift his head, who whispered into him, "Night, come soon."

He drew back, searched her eyes, and said low, "Then I can be assured this time you will stay with me?"

Remembering that long ago night when he had beseeched her to remain and she had agreed only so she might flee him, she drew a hand up and pressed it between their two hearts. "All through the night, all through the day, all through our lives, Husband. May God take note."

Excerpt

DREAMSPELL

A Medieval Time Travel Romance

A TIME TO LIVE. A TIME TO DIE. A TIME TO DREAM.

SLEEP DISORDERS SPECIALIST Kennedy Plain has been diagnosed with a fatal brain tumor. When her research subject dies after trying to convince her he has achieved dream-induced time travel and her study is shelved, she enlists herself as a subject to complete her research. But when she dreams herself into 14th-century England and falls into the hands of Fulke Wynland, a man history has condemned as a murderer, she must not only stay alive long enough to find a way to return to her own time, but prevent Fulke from murdering his young nephews. And yet, the more time she spends with the medieval warrior, the more difficult it is to believe he is capable of committing the heinous crime for which he has been reviled for 600 years.

Baron Fulke Wynland has been granted guardianship of his brother's heirs despite suspicions that he seeks to steal their inheritance. When the king sends a mysterious woman to care for the boys, Fulke is surprised by the lady's hostility toward him—and more surprised to learn she is to be his wife. But when his nephews are abducted, the two must overcome their mutual dislike to discover the boys' fate. What Fulke never expects is to feel for this woman whose peculiar speech, behavior, and talk of dream travel could see her burned as a witch.

Prologue

London, 1376

EVEN I WOULD have killed for thee.

Dawn lit the words etched in stone, bade him draw near. Aye, he would have killed for her, though not as it was told he had done. Still, this day he would die. For three years, he had languished in this wretched cell awaiting a trial that was only a formality, and yesterday he had been brought before his peers. Now, with the newborn day, the Lieutenant would take him through the city to Smithfield where a noose awaited him.

He rose from his pallet and crossed his cell to where he had carved the words by which he would soon die. Head and shoulders blocking the light that shone through the small window, he traced each letter through to *thee.*

"Nedy," he whispered, remembering everything about her, from the gentle curve of her lips to her long legs to mannerisms not of this world. More, he remembered the last time they had kissed and the promise she had made him—a promise not kept. But at least he had loved.

The door opened, but it was not the Lieutenant who came for him. Though the years had cruelly aged the man who stepped inside, rounding shoulders that had once been broad, there was no mistaking the third King Edward.

"Wynland." The king inclined his head.

It was three years since Fulke had been granted such an audience, but he remembered himself and bowed. "Your majesty."

Edward peered into his prisoner's face. "You are prepared to die?"

"I am."

"Yet still you say it was not you?"

Fulke stared at him, those few moments all the confirmation needed of the idle talk of guards. Edward's mind was on the wane. Was the recent death of his son, the Black Prince, responsible? Though not since the queen's passing seven years ago could he be said to be right in the head, this was worse, as evidenced by his neglect of affairs of state. The great King Edward was no longer worthy of the crown, the power he had once wielded now in the hands of his greedy mistress, Alice Perrers.

"I trusted you," Edward said, his jaw quivering in his fleshy face. "When all opposed your wardship of your nephews, I granted it. When my fair Lark was attacked, I would not believe 'twas you."

It was an opening for Fulke to defend himself, but he was done with that.

"Have you naught to say?" Edward demanded.

"I have had my say, my liege. There is no more."

Edward cursed, turned to leave, and came back around. "Beg my forgiveness and mayhap I shall allow you an easier death."

"There is naught for which I require your forgiveness." This did not mean he did not seek the forgiveness of others. But it was too late for that.

Anger staining the king's face, he looked around the cell and lingered on the words that covered the walls. "I was told of this. The troubadours pay well for the guards to bring them these words by which they compose songs of love."

Fulke considered all he had carved into the stone these past years—words never spoken.

"Why do you do it?"

Feeling a pang at his center, Fulke said, "That she might know."

Edward shook his head. "You loved wrong in choosing a woman such as that when you could have had—" His voice broke. "I would have forgiven you anything, except my Lark." He stepped from the cell.

As the door swung closed, Fulke stood motionless, each moment that passed drawing him nearer his last. Finally, he crossed to his pallet and retrieved the worn spoon that was only one of many to have lent itself to his writings. Thumbing the rough edge of all that remained of its handle, he eyed the last words he had inscribed: *Even I would have killed for thee.* They said much, but there was more.

When they came for him an hour later, the final line read: *And now I shall die for thee.* As he stood to be shackled, he considered his words carved around the walls. They were for Nedy, wherever she was.

1

University Sleep Disorders Clinic
Los Angeles, California

"I was there," Mac said amid the tick and hum of instruments. "Really there."

Kennedy waited for his eyes to brighten and a grin to surface his weary face. Nothing. Not even a flicker of humor. Dropping the smile that was as false as the hair sweeping her brow, she said, "Sorry, Mac, I'm not buying it." She turned to the bedside table and peered at the machine that would monitor his sleep cycles.

"You think I'm joking?"

Of course he was. For all the horror MacArthur Crosley had endured during the Gulf War, he was an incorrigible joker, but this time he had gone too far. She unbundled the electrodes.

"I'm serious, Ken."

Her other subjects called her Dr. Plain, but she and Mac went back to when she had been a doctoral student and he was her first subject in a study of the effects of sleep deprivation on dreams. That was four years ago and, at this rate, it might be another four before she was able to present her latest findings. If she had that long…

Feeling the snugness of the knit cap covering her head, she said, "Serious, huh? I've heard that one before."

The familiar squeak of wheels announced his approach. "It happened."

Meanwhile, the clock kept ticking, the minute hand climbing toward midnight.

"Listen to me, Ken. What I have to tell you is important—"

"Time travel through dreams, Mac?" She uncapped a tube of fixative and squeezed a dab onto the electrodes' disks. "How on earth did you hatch that one?" Though she might concede some dreams prophesied the future, time travel was too far out there. "Let's get you hooked up."

"That's not what I'm here for."

She turned and found herself sandwiched between the table and the wheelchair that served as his legs.

"I've been holding out on you, Ken. I would have told you sooner, but I couldn't—not until I was certain it wasn't just an incredibly real dream."

"Come on, Mac. It's midnight, I haven't had dinner yet, and I'm tired."

He clamped a hand around her arm. "I'm dead serious."

Though she knew she had nothing to fear from him, alarm leapt through her when a tremor passed from him to her. Never had she seen Mac like this, and certainly he had never taken his jokes this far. Was it possible that what he said was true—rather, he *believed* it was true? If so, he was hallucinating, a side-effect not uncommon among her subjects, especially beyond sixty hours of sleep deprivation. But she had never known Mac to succumb to hallucinations, not even during an episode four months back when his consecutive waking hours broke the two hundred mark. That had complications all its own.

He released her and pushed back. "Sorry."

Kennedy stared at him. The whites of his eyes blazed red, the circles beneath shone like bruises, the lines canyoning his face went deeper. Forty-five years old, yet he looked sixty, just as he had when his two hundred and two waking hours had put him into a sleep so deep he had gone comatose. But he had reported eighty-seven waking hours when he called an hour ago.

He had lied. Kennedy nearly cursed. She knew what extreme sleep deprivation looked like, especially on Mac. True, he had cried wolf before, convinced her of the unimaginable to the point she would have bet her life he was telling the truth, but this came down to negligence. And she was guilty as charged.

She consulted her clipboard and scanned the previous entry. Five weeks since his last episode, a stretch considering he rarely made it three weeks without going a round with his souvenir from the war. But why would he under-report his waking hours? Because of the safeguard that was put in place following his coma, one that stipulated all subjects who exceeded one hundred fifty waking hours were to be monitored by a medical doctor?

Knowing her own sleep would have to wait—not necessarily that she would have slept since she was also intimate with insomnia—she said, "How many hours, Mac?"

He pushed a hand through his silvered red hair. "Eighty...nine."

"Not *one hundred* eighty nine?"

"Why would I lie?"

"You tell me."

"I would if you'd listen."

Realizing she was picking an argument when she should be collecting data, she rolled a stool beneath her. "Okay, talk."

He dragged a tattooed hand down his face. "The dreams aren't dreams. Not anymore. When I went comatose, I truly crossed over, and that's when I realized it was more than a dream. And I could have stayed." He slammed his fists on the arms of his wheelchair. "If not for the doctors and their machines, I *would* have stayed!"

Pain stirred at the back of Kennedy's head. "You would have died."

"In this time. There I would have lived."

Then he truly believed he had been transported to the Middle Ages of his serial dream. Interesting. "I see."

"Do you?"

Was this more than sleep deprivation? Had Mac snapped? "I know it seems real—"

"Cut with the psychobabble! Sleep deprivation is the key to the past. It's a bridge. A way back. A way out."

She took a deep breath. "Out of what?"

"This." He looked to the stumps of his legs, wheeled forward, and tapped her forehead. "And this."

Stunned by his trespass, Kennedy caught her breath.

He sank back in his wheelchair. "In my dreams, I have legs again. Have I told you that?"

She gave herself a mental shake. "Many times."

"I walk. I run. I feel my legs down to my toes. It's as if the war never happened."

She laid a hand on his shoulder. "It did happen."

"Not six hundred years ago."

She lowered her hand. "What makes you believe this isn't just an incredibly real dream?"

"I don't know the places in this dream, and I've never seen any of the people."

That was his proof? Though dreams were often forged of acquaintances and familiar landscapes, it wasn't unusual to encounter seemingly unfamiliar ones.

He reached behind his wheelchair, pulled a book from his knapsack, and pushed it into her hands. "I found this in an antique book shop a while back."

It was old, its black cover worn white along the edges, all that remained of its title a barely legible stamped impression. She put her glasses on. "The Sins of the Earl of...?"

"Sinwell," Mac supplied.

Kennedy forced a laugh. "Catchy title." She ran her fingers across the numbers beneath. "1373 to 1399. History...never my best subject."

"He's the one."

"Who?"

"Fulke Wynland, the man who murdered his nephews so he could claim Sinwell for himself."

Mac's dream adversary. Though he had told her the dream arose from a historical account, he hadn't named the infamous earl or the British earldom for which Wynland had committed murder.

"I'm in there." Mac nodded at the book.

Kennedy raised an eyebrow.

"Look at the pages I marked."

A half dozen slips protruded from the book. She opened to the first and skimmed the text. There it was: Sir Arthur Crosley. Okay, so someone in the past had first claim to a semblance of MacArthur Crosley's name. What proof was that? She read on. With the King of England's blessing, the errant knight pledged himself to the safekeeping of orphaned brothers John and Harold Wynland. She read the remaining passages, the last a single sentence that told of Sir Arthur's disappearance prior to the boys' fiery deaths.

Kennedy set the book on the bedside table. "You're telling me you're Sir Arthur?"

"I am."

"Mac, just because your name—"

"When I first read it, there was no mention of Crosley. His name—my name—appeared only after the dreams began. And when the book says I disappeared, guess where I went."

Pound, went her headache.

"That's when I came out of the coma, Ken."

Worse and worse. "But you've reported having these dreams since then. If what you say is true, where are *those* experiences documented?"

"They're not. Though I've returned four times since the coma, the present keeps pulling me back before I can save the boys from that murderer." Fury brightened his eyes a moment before his gaze emptied.

"Mac?"

"Fifty waking hours isn't enough, not even a hundred. It takes more."

This explained the man before her whose years came nowhere near the age grooving his face. "Two hundred?"

"It's a start."

She held up a hand. "The truth. How many hours?"

"Two hundred seventeen."

She came off the stool as if slung from it. "You know how dangerous—"

"Better than anyone."

He didn't look like a madman, but he had to be. "You're forcing it, aren't you? You could have slept days ago, but you won't let yourself."

"Dead on."

Kennedy reached to rake fingers through her hair, but stopped mid-air. There was too little left beneath the cap, stragglers that served as painful reminders of her former self. She laid a hand to Mac's arm. "You're going to kill yourself."

His smile was almost genuine. "That's the idea."

Over-the-edge crazy. Deciding her efforts were better spent admitting him to the university hospital, she straightened.

"I'm not going," Mac said.

For all his delusions, he could still read her like a book. "Please, Mac, you have to."

"It's my way out."

Pound. Pound. "You think I'm just going to stand by and let you die?"

"You don't have a say in it."

"But you're my patient. I can't—"

"You think I like living in this thing?" He gripped the arms of his wheelchair. "When I lost my legs, I lost everything—my wife, my boys, my career. All I do is take up space, and I'm tired of it. You have no idea what it's like."

Didn't she? Her world was crumbling, and though she had no choice as to whether tomorrow came, he did.

His gaze swept to her cap, and he muttered a curse. "I'm sorry, Ken."

She crossed the observation room and stared through the window at the monitoring equipment.

"How's the chemo going?"

She tossed her head and achingly acknowledged how much she missed the weight of her hair. "It's going well." A lie. There had been progress early on, but the tumor was gaining ground.

"The truth, Ken," he turned her own words against her.

She swung around. "This isn't about me."

"You're wrong." He wheeled toward her. "My dream is a way out of the hell I'm living. And it could be yours."

Nuts. Positively nuts.

He rolled to a halt. "Not my dream, of course. Something of your own choosing."

Pound. Pound. Pound. She stepped around him. "I need to take something for this headache."

"You think I'm crazy."

She looked over her shoulder. "I'll be back in a few minutes, and we'll discuss this some more."

After a long moment, he said, "Sure. Can I borrow your pen?"

She tossed it to him and steered a course to the washroom where she gulped down the pills prescribed for just such reminders of her tumor.

Though she rarely did more than glance in the mirror, she searched her features: sunken eyes, ashen skin, pinched mouth, the hollows beneath her cheeks evidence of her twenty-pound weight loss. As for the hair sweeping her brow, it and the knit cap to which the strands were attached was a gift from her well-meaning mother. She looked almost as bad as Mac, far from the green-eyed "looker" she had been called before...

Almost wishing she was as crazy as Mac, she hurried to her office. After being reassured two orderlies were on their way, she returned to the sleep room. It was empty. "No." She groaned. "Don't do this, Mac."

She ran down the corridor, through the reception area, and out the glass doors into the balm of a Los Angeles summer night, but there was no sign of Mac or the cab that had delivered him to the clinic. Where had he gone? It would be a place where no one knew him, where he wouldn't be bothered if he didn't show his face for days. Unfortunately, the possibilities could run into the thousands.

What about the cab? If she could find the company he had used, perhaps she could discover where they had taken him.

She went back inside and, in the sleep room, saw the pen Mac had borrowed on the bedside table, beneath it his book. He had forgotten it. Or had he?

She opened *The Sins of the Earl of Sinwell*. If not that she recognized Mac's handwriting, she would have flipped past the inscription on the inside cover. She slid her glasses on. *Ken*, it read, *think of this as a postcard. Your friend, Mac*

"Oh, Mac." Try though she might, she knew that if she found him it would be too late. But knowing it and accepting it were two different things. Keeping an eye closed against the pain hammering at her head, she tucked the book under an arm and hurried to her office.

2

A WAY OUT.

Mac's words of a month ago whispered to Kennedy as she stared at the reflection of a woman she recognized less each day. Radiation and chemotherapy had taken the last of her hair. And for what? The hope she could beat unbeatable odds. Four weeks, eight at the outside, Kennedy Plain, twenty-eight years young, would go out with a whimper.

"A way out," she muttered. "Crazy Mac."

She tightened the belt of her robe and crossed her living room to the glass doors of her condo. A quarter mile out, waves battered the rocky beach, swept sand in and dragged it out again. Stepping onto the balcony, she sighed as cool morning air caressed her bare scalp. It was just what she needed to get through another waking hour. How many was she up to? She glanced at her watch. Seventy-two, meaning it was Monday.

Since forced to take medical leave two weeks ago, she had found it increasingly difficult to track her days—until this past Friday when she began marking time by the hour.

She turned back inside. The journal lay on her desk on a pile of paperwork that represented eighteen months of research. Research that would molder in some forgotten closet if the clinic director had his way. But she wouldn't let that happen. If it killed her—ha!—she would conclude her study with data culled from her own dream experiences.

She dropped into the desk chair and reached for the journal. It would be her fourth entry, likely the last before her self-imposed sleep deprivation compelled her to sleep. With a quaking hand, she wrote:

8:25 a.m. Seventy-two waking hours. Not sure I can make it to ninety-six. Hands trembling, eyes burning, headache worsening, nauseated. No hallucinations, some memory lapses. Can't stop thinking about Mac.

She lifted the pen and recalled the night he had borrowed it. For four days she had clung to the hope he lived, but on the fifth day, his lifeless body was found in an abandoned warehouse.

Kennedy swallowed hard. "Wherever you are, I pray you've finally found peace." She rested her forehead in her hand and squeezed her eyes closed. Like a thief, sleep reached for her.

She jumped up and steadied herself with a hand on the chair. "Twenty-four hours," she murmured. Could she do it? Her chronic insomnia having never exceeded sixty, she was ahead by twelve, but another twenty-four?

What she needed was a good book. Unfortunately, as her library consisted mostly of textbooks and periodicals, the best she could do was *The Sins of the Earl of Sinwell.* She eyed it where it lay on the sofa table. It had to be less dry than her other choices.

Sliding on her glasses, she retrieved the book and fingered the ridges and recesses of the worn title, then opened past Mac's inscription to the first chapter. "1373," she read aloud as she began to walk the room.

An hour later, she gave up. Not because the reading was dry, but her comprehension was nearly nil. One thing was clear from the little she had learned about Fulke Wynland, the Earl of Sinwell: he had no conscience. Not only was he suspected of having a hand in the accident that killed his brother, the Earl of Sinwell, but as a military advisor during the Hundred Years War, he had been party to the atrocious massacre of men, women, and children following a siege on the city of Limoges. So what chance had two little boys, aged four and six?

She trudged into the kitchen, opened the freezer, and stuck her face into it. Frigid air returning her to wakefulness, she congratulated herself on that bit of genius and closed the door. "And caffeine will do it one better," she murmured.

After the coffee maker sputtered its last, putting an exclamation mark on the smell of freshly brewed coffee, Kennedy carried the pot to her cup with a hand that shook so violently that nearly as much made it on the counter as in the cup. When the caffeine kicked in on her third serving, she reached for Mac's book.

The seventh chapter, marked by a slip of paper, held a scant introduction to Sir Arthur Crosley. Then came the mysterious Lady Lark and a color illustration of the type of clothing a fourteenth-century lady might wear—a pale yellow gown with fitted bodice and long flowing sleeves, a hair veil secured by a tiara set with red and blue jewels, and flat-soled shoes with ridiculously long toes.

Kennedy returned to the text. According to the author, Lady Lark made her first appearance at King Edward III's court in 1372. No one knew where she came from, her surname, age, or whether she was of the nobility. The only thing for certain was that the king wasted no time numbering her among his mistresses.

During the summer of 1373, two months after appointing Sir Arthur Crosley to watch over the Wynland boys, King Edward dispatched Lady Lark to Sinwell to care for the motherless children. Though it was suggested his other mistress, the ambitious Alice Perrers, had worked her influence over Edward in order to rid herself of a rival, the author was more given to the belief that the king had simply tired of Lady Lark.

Kennedy trudged past the sofa, pushed her glasses up, and rubbed her eyes. She resettled the glasses.

On the approach to the castle of Brynwood Spire where the boys resided, Lady Lark's baggage train was attacked and her entourage murdered. Of the lady herself, no trace was ever found. The one responsible for the carnage: Fulke Wynland, the author suggested. Sir Arthur Crosley, fearing for the boys' lives, spirited them away that very day...

Kennedy didn't recall reading this particular passage at the clinic, and there was no slip of paper to mark its reference to Sir Arthur. Likely,

Mac had lost the marker without realizing it. However, when she dug further into the book, she found three other unmarked references. Odd, especially as they were more significant than the ones Mac had asked her to read. But nothing compared to the final reference near the end of the book. She read it twice. Hadn't Sir Arthur disappeared at book's end? Not according to this passage that stated that, following two weeks of pursuit, Wynland overtook him. Swords were drawn and the knight's life severed by the man who would be earl.

Of course, it *was* a month since she had read the passages. Was that it? Or was she delusional? She shrugged off the niggling at the back of her mind and, a short while later, slammed the book on Wynland's ascension to "earl" following the deaths of his nephews in a fire of unknown origin.

"Murderer," she muttered. And caught her toe on the sofa table. The book flew from her hand and landed on the floor at about the same time she did. It should have hurt, but she was too numb to feel anything but relief at gaining a prone position.

Get up, walk it off. Only ten hours to go. She forced her head up. Seeing the book had fallen open to Mac's inscription, she pulled it toward her, read his scrawled inscription, and pressed her forehead to the carpet. "A postcard, Mac?"

Don't close your eyes. But she was too busy melting into the carpet to give more than a glancing thought to hooking herself up to the EEG she had borrowed from the clinic. Sleep descended, scattering her thoughts here, there, everywhere—until they met the enigmatic Lady Lark.

What would it have been like to live in an era of knights and castles? To have been of the privileged class? To dress in gowns with beautiful bodices and long flowing sleeves? To be the mistress of a mighty king? To travel across country in a baggage train with an entourage? Imagine that...

The sweet smell of earth, the breath of a breeze, a gentle tapping against her cheek. Wondering who disturbed her, Kennedy opened her eyes.

Not who, but what. She stared through the hair fluttering across her face—thick, dark, sprung with wave, the likes of which she hadn't seen in a long time. A tremor of expectation swept her, but she let it go no further.

This was a dream. When she awakened, not a single strand would remain. She fingered the darkness and lingeringly pushed it out of her eyes. There was something silken at her forehead and, above that, a metal band encircled her head. She drew the former forward and stared at what appeared to be a veil.

A moan sounded from somewhere nearby, and she pushed the veil aside. Only then, with a forest spread before her, did she realize she was prostrate. Where had her dreaming taken her to this time? And what was the vibration beneath her cheek?

She rolled onto her back and stared up at a canopy of trees. It was beautiful the way the sunlight pierced the leaves, thrusting shafts of light into a place that might otherwise appear sinister. There was the twitter of birds and, somewhere, the babble of a brook. It was vibrant, as if—

A mordant scent struck her, causing the dream to veer in a direction she preferred it didn't go. She sat up and caught her breath. Twenty or more feet out, the bodies of a dozen men were gored and grotesquely bent, most conspicuously two draped across an overturned wagon. And there was more. She felt it, feared it, tried to ignore it, but looked around. Behind her lay a horse, its teeth bared in death, its rider pinned beneath, the man's chest sliced open and his arm nearly severed.

Kennedy clenched her teeth and lowered her gaze to where the blood of beast and man pooled on the ground. It spread outward, running in rivulets toward her. Nausea rose as she followed its path to the skirt of her dress. Knee to ankle, crimson saturated the pale yellow fabric, causing it to adhere to her skin.

Not a dream. A nightmare.

She scrambled to her feet.

"My lady?" someone croaked.

Kennedy forced herself to look among the bodies. Had she ever before had such a vivid dream? Swallowing hard, she settled her gaze on the man beneath the horse who stared at her through half-hooded eyes.

"My lady…are you…?" He reached with his uninjured arm.

She knew she ought to flee before her imagination transformed him into something more heinous, but she couldn't turn her back on him. Too, this was only a dream. Though it might cause her to awaken in a cold sweat, that was the worst she would suffer.

When she dropped to her knees beside the man, she saw that, though he had closed his eyes, his wheezing chest told he still lived.

"What can I do?" she asked.

"I saw the miscreant's…device." His thick accent sounded almost British.

"Device?"

"Had his medallion…in my hand." He spread his empty fingers. "Upon it a wyvern…two-headed…above a shield…bend sinister."

"I'm sorry, I don't understand."

He lifted his lids. His eyes, pinpoints of pain, traced her face. "You are not my lady."

"No, I—"

He caught hold of her arm. "What have you done with her?"

For a man about to die, he exhibited incredible strength. "I don't know what you're talking about."

He dragged her toward him, affording her a close-up of his death mask. "You come to steal from the dead," he spat, flecking her with saliva.

A more morbid dream Kennedy could not recall. She wrenched backward and broke free, but not before he tore the veil from her hair.

She shot to her feet and nearly tripped over her hem. Why was the dress so long? And why was she wearing something like this in the middle of a forest?

Once more, she felt the vibration through the ground. It was stronger. Nearer. Horses? From which direction?

She whipped her head to the side and the breeze caught her hair, sifting it across her face and into her eyes. Though she longed to pause and relish the feel of it, something bad was coming.

It's only a dream. Stay put and get it over with, and you'll be awake in no time. But she couldn't. Heart pounding, she gathered her hair high at the back of her head, knotted it, and hiked up her skirt.

As in the days before her illness, she sped across the ground, vaulted over debris and fallen trees, and nearly forgot the reason she ran. She thrilled to the rush of blood and tightening of her lungs, the strength in her calves and thighs. The only thing missing was a decent pair of running shoes.

When a shout resounded through the trees, she glanced over her shoulder. A horse and rider bore down on her. She pumped her legs harder, but she was no match for the four-legged beast that drew so near she could hear its breath.

Wake up! she silently called to where she lay sleeping. *Open your eyes!* Though a thread of consciousness often allowed her to talk her way out of disturbing dreams, her pleas went unanswered. Thus, she veered right, seized a branch from the ground, and whirled around.

Her pursuer reined in his horse, scattering leaves and dirt, and guided the animal sideways to look down at her. Clad in metal neck to toe—a jangling, clanking get-up that sounded with each quiver of his horse—he stared at her out of eyes so blue she knew her imagination was in overdrive. Though her dream had neglected to place a helmet on his head, it had made sure there was a sword at his side.

Only a dream. He can cut you in two and you'll awaken whole. At least, as whole as a person with a death sentence hanging over her head...

"You do not need that." His voice was deep and accented, though of a more precise nature than the dying man who had mistaken her for his lady. "You have naught to fear from me."

Of course she didn't. He was only a figment, though from where he had originated she had no idea. But with those cheekbones, shoulder-length blond hair, and closely clipped beard and moustache, he was likely a belly-button-bearing model from a billboard she passed on her way to the university.

"Lady Lark?"

She blinked, then nearly laughed at the realization she had dreamed herself into the mysterious lady of Mac's book. What was the year? 1373? As for this behemoth, was he Fulke Wynland? He had to be. Forget that he was blonde rather than darkly sinister as she had imagined, that his eyes were blue, rather than bottomless black. He was surely the one responsible for the carnage to which she had awakened, not to mention the death of his nephews and the disappearance of the king's mistress—the same woman he mistook her for.

She jabbed the branch at him in hopes it would send horse and rider back to wherever they had come from.

The animal rolled its huge eyes, reminding her of the one time she had ridden a horse, a mistake that culminated in her missing a barbed wire fence by inches.

"I am Lord Wynland of Brynwood Spire."

And beneath his armor he probably wore a medallion with a two-headed—what was it? Wyvern? "Stay back!"

"I am King Edward's man. Be assured, no harm will befall you."

She swung the branch. "I'll brain you!"

He frowned deeply, as if her words were foreign, as if her subconscious had not formed him from the pages of an old book. "After what you have seen, my lady, 'tis natural you would suffer hysterics."

"Oh, puh-lease!"

He lowered his gaze over her. "You are injured?"

No sooner did she follow his gaze to her bloodied skirt than he lunged, seized hold of the branch, and used it to haul her toward him.

Kennedy let go, but not before he caught her arm. Handling her as if she were a child rather than a woman who topped out at five foot eight, Wynland lifted her off her feet and deposited her on his saddle between his thighs.

She reached for his face. Unlike her hair, she hadn't dreamed herself a set of long nails, and she fell short by the split second it took him to capture her wrist and grip it with the other.

"Calm yourself!"

She strained, kicked, bit—and got a mouthful of metal links that made her teeth peal with pain.

"Cease, else I shall bind you hand and foot!"

Before or after he killed her? She threw her head back and got a closer look at her version of Fulke Wynland. Not model material after all. As blue as his eyes were, his face was flawed. A scar split his left eyebrow, nose had a slight bend, and the jaw visible beneath his beard was mildly pocked as if from adolescent acne or a childhood illness. Handsome? Definitely not. Rugged? Beyond. Deadly? Ever so.

Realizing her best hope was to catch him off guard, she forced herself to relax.

Wynland gave a grunt of satisfaction, reached down, and yanked up her skirt.

Horrified that her dream was taking a more lurid turn, she renewed her struggle.

The horse snorted and danced around, but neither Kennedy nor the skittish animal turned Wynland from his intent. His large hand slid from her ankle to her calf to her knee.

It was then she felt the draft and realized that, somewhere between reality and dream, she had lost her underwear.

When his hand spanned her thigh, she opened her mouth to scream, but just as quickly as the assault began, it ended. He thrust her skirt down and smiled—if that wicked twist of his lips could be called a smile. "Worry not, my lady, I place too high a value on my health to risk it with you."

What, exactly, did he mean? That she was promiscuous? Diseased? Of course, she did portray a king's mistress...

"Whose blood if not yours?" Wynland asked.

That was why he had touched her? She didn't know the man's name, only that he had rejected her as being his lady. She frowned. How was that? If she was Lady Lark, why had one of the players in this dream not recognized her?

"Whose?" he growled.

She shifted around to fully face Wynland. "What does it matter?"

His lids narrowed. "A soldier—nay, a dozen—bled their last to defend you. What does it matter who they were? Who their wives and children are?"

When he put it that way...But she wasn't the villain, *he* was. Those men were dead because he had ordered it. Or done it himself. "Put me down."

"What befell your escort?"

Why the pretense when he meant to kill her? Or did he? According to Mac's book, no trace of Lady Lark was ever found. Had Wynland allowed her to live—for a while, at least?

It's a dream!

Though she knew he was only smoke floating about her mind, she detested him for the sins of the man after whom she had fashioned him. "Why don't *you* tell *me* what happened to my escort?" She was bold, and it felt good, so like her old self before this thing in her head pulled the life out from under her.

Wynland's face darkened. "You think I am responsible?"

"If the shoe fits..."

Confusion slipped through his anger. "What shoe?"

One would think she had truly hopped back in time. If this was anything like what Mac experienced, no wonder he thought it was real. She only hoped that when she awakened she would remember the outlandish dream long enough to record it. "You don't want me at Burnwood."

"*Brynwood,* and, nay, I do not. But I assure you, had I wished you dead, we would not be having this conversation."

Nothing came between him and what he wanted, including his nephews. The deaths those little boys had suffered incited Kennedy further. "Just goes to show that if you want something done right, do it yourself."

He puller her closer. "If you have anything else to say to me, my lady, you would do well to choose your words carefully."

His hands on her, thighs on either side of her, and breath on her face, were almost enough to make her believe he was real. *Only a figment. He holds no more power over you than the next dream.*

"Do you understand?"

"What is there not to understand?"

He stared at her, then released her arms and turned her forward. Before she could gulp down the view from atop the horse, he gripped an arm around her waist and spurred the animal through the trees.

She was riding sidesaddle. How much worse could it get? Though she tried to shut out memories of her last horse ride, she remembered exactly how bad it could get. She squeezed her eyes closed. Where was Wynland taking her? And if murder was on his mind, why the stay of execution? No one would hear if she cried out—

He wasn't alone. The thundering of hooves had surely been of many riders, meaning others could have seen her flight. Fortunate for her, unfortunate for Wynland.

She opened her eyes. Trees sped by at breakneck blur, the forest floor rose and fell, shafts of sunlight blinded.

She retreated behind her lids again and was all the more aware of the hard body at her back and the muscled arm against her abdomen, the sensation so real she felt the beat of Wynland's heart through his armor. She chalked it up to it being a long time since she had been in a man's arms, which was more her fault than her ex-husband's. Graham would have held her if she had let him, but the marriage had coughed its last long before the onset of her illness. Kennedy Huntworth was no more— not that she had gone by her married name. At the urging of Graham's mother, she had retained her maiden name for "professional purposes." In the end, it had worked out for the best. Or was it the worst?

Wynland dragged his horse to a halt, and a grateful Kennedy opened her eyes, only to wish she hadn't.

About The Author

TAMARA LEIGH HOLDS a Master's Degree in Speech and Language Pathology. In 1993, she signed a 4-book contract with Bantam Books. Her first medieval romance, *Warrior Bride*, was released in 1994. Continuing to write for the general market, three more novels were published with HarperCollins and Dorchester and earned awards and spots on national bestseller lists.

In 2006, Tamara's first inspirational contemporary romance, *Stealing Adda*, was released. In 2008, *Perfecting Kate* was optioned for a movie and *Splitting Harriet* won an ACFW "Book of the Year" award. The following year, *Faking Grace* was nominated for a RITA award. In 2011, Tamara wrapped up her "Southern Discomfort" series with the release of *Restless in Carolina*.

When not in the middle of being a wife, mother, and cookbook fiend, Tamara buries her nose in a good book—and her writer's pen in ink. In 2012, she returned to the historical romance genre with *Dreamspell,* a medieval time travel romance. Shortly thereafter, she once more invited readers to join her in the middle ages with the *Age of Faith* series: *The Unveiling, The Yielding, The Redeeming, The Kindling,* and *The Longing.* Tamara's #1 Bestsellers—*Lady at Arms, Lady Of Eve, Lady Of Fire,* and *Lady Of Conquest*—are the first of her medieval romances to be rewritten as "clean reads." Look for *Baron Of Blackwood,* the third book in *The Feud* series, in 2016.

Tamara lives near Nashville with her husband, sons, a Doberman that bares its teeth not only to threaten the UPS man but to smile, and a feisty Morkie that keeps her company during long writing stints.

Connect with Tamara at her website www.tamaraleigh.com, her blog The Kitchen Novelist, her email tamaraleightenn@gmail.com, Facebook, and Twitter.

For new releases and special promotions, subscribe to Tamara Leigh's mailing list: www.tamaraleigh.com